Praise f

Nora Roberts Land
"Ava's story is witty and charming."
—Barbara Freethy #1 *NYT* bestselling author

Selected by *USA Today* as one of the Best Books of
the year alongside Nora Roberts' *Dark Witch* and
Julia Quinn's *Sum of all Kisses*.

"If you like Nora Roberts type books, this is a must-
read." —Readers' Favorite

Country Heaven
"If ever there was a contemporary romance that
rated a 10 on a scale of 1 to 5 for me, this one is it!"
—The Romance Reviews

"*Country Heaven* made me laugh and cry...I could
not stop flipping the pages. I can't wait to read the
next book in this series." —Fresh Fiction

Country Heaven Cookbook
"Delicious, simple recipes... Comfort food, at its
best."   —Fire Up The Oven Blog

The Bridge to a Better Life
Selected by *USA Today* as one of the Best Books of
the Summer.

"Miles offers a story of grief, healing and
rediscovered love." —USA Today

"I've read Susan Mallery and Debbie Macomber...but
never have I been so moved by the books Ava Miles
writes." —Booktalk with Eileen Reviews

The Gate to Everything
"The constant love...bring a sensual, dynamic tension
to this appealing story." —Publisher's Weekly

More Praise For Ava

The Chocolate Garden
"On par with Nicholas Sparks' love stories."
—Jennifer's Corner Blog

"A must-read...a bit of fairy magic...a shelf full of happiness." —Fab Fantasy Fiction

The Promise of Rainbows
"This is a story about grace, faith and the power of both..."
—The Book Nympho

French Roast
"Ms. Miles draws from her experience as an apprentice chef...and it shows...I loved {the} authenticity of the food references, and the recipes...looked divine." —BlogCritics

The Holiday Serenade
"This story is all romance, steam, and humor with a touch of the holiday spirit..." —The Book Nympho

The Town Square
"Ms. Miles' words melted into each page until the world receded around me..." —Tome Tender

The Park of Sunset Dreams
"Ava has done it again. I love the whole community of Dare Valley..." —Travel Through The Pages Blog

The Goddess Guides Series
"Miles' series is an **exquisite exploration** of internal discomfort and courage, allowing you to reclaim your divine soul and fully express your womanhood."
—Dr. Shawne Duperon, Project Forgive Founder, Nobel Peace Prize Nominee

"The Goddess Guides are a **world changer**. Well done, Ava." —International Bestseller Kate Perry aka Kathia Zolfaghari, Artist & Activist

Also by Ava Miles

Fiction
The Love Letter Series
Letters Across An Open Sea
Along Waters of Sunshine and Shadow

The Dare Valley Series
Nora Roberts Land
French Roast
The Grand Opening
The Holiday Serenade
The Town Square
The Park of Sunset Dreams
The Perfect Ingredient
The Bridge to a Better Life
The Calendar of New Beginnings
Home Sweet Love
The Moonlight Serenade
Daring Brides

The Dare River Series
Country Heaven
Country Heaven Song Book
Country Heaven Cookbook
The Chocolate Garden
The Chocolate Garden:
A Magical Tale (Children's Book)

Fireflies and Magnolias
The Promise of Rainbows
The Fountain of Infinite Wishes
The Patchwork Quilt of Happiness

Dare Valley Meets Paris Billionaire Mini-Series

The Billionaire's Gamble
The Billionaire's Courtship
The Billionaire's Secret
The Billionaire's Return

The Goddess Guides to Being a Woman

Goddesses Decide
Goddesses Deserve The G's
Goddesses Love Cock
Goddesses Cry and Say Motherfucker
Goddesses Don't Do Drama
Goddesses Are Sexy
Goddesses Eat
Goddesses Are Happy
Goddesses Face Fear

Other Non-Fiction

The Happiness Corner: Reflections So Far
Home Baked Happiness

Along Waters of Sunshine and Shadow

~ The Love Letter Series ~

Ava Miles

ISBN-13: 978-1-949092-03-5
www.avamiles.com
Ava Miles

Dedication

To everyone who's stood up for what's right—be it for love or freedom—in a city, community, or playground. We need more of you.

And to my divine entourage, who continues to help me grow and flourish.

"Without their efforts and sacrifices our world would be a far different place today. When the war was over, men and women who had been involved, in uniform and in civilian capacities, joined in joyous and short-lived celebrations, then immediately began the task of rebuilding their lives and the world they wanted. They were mature beyond their years, tempered by what they had been through, disciplined by their military training and sacrifices. They married in record numbers and gave birth to another distinctive generation, the Baby Boomers. They stayed true to their values of personal responsibility, duty, honor, and faith."

—Tom Brokaw, *The Greatest Generation*

Chapter 1

July 1945

Chicago

ANNA SIMS' HOUSE WAS EXACTLY AS HE'D PICTURED IT.
Endless days and weeks and months and years spent fighting Germany and its allies, slogging through mud, and eating dust had given Noah Weatherby more than a few opportunities to dream about his wartime pen pal. The woman he knew only through her letters.

He'd guessed, correctly, the house would be built of brick like most of Chicago's houses were after the Great Fire, and she'd mentioned an upstairs in her letters to him. Those lifelines were tucked inside the single leather satchel he'd brought, holding all his earthly possessions. Before enlisting in the war after Pearl Harbor, he'd sold or given most of his meager belongings away, not knowing when he'd return.

Or if he'd return.

But somehow he'd made it through. Anna's words came to him as he approached the porch of the brick house.

When you finally come home from the war and we

meet, it's going to be one of the best days of my life... Every day I leave our house I stop at the end of the porch and let the sun warm my face. I imagine you coming up the path in your uniform, home from the war. Then you take my hand, and we take a nice stroll in my neighborhood together.

The day they'd both dreamed about was finally here, and he was as eager as a boyfriend on a first date—and as scared as the small abandoned child he'd been.

He was finally going to see Anna for real.

The Sims' small yard was freshly mowed, the grass blades looking wilted under the hot July sun. He wondered what neighbor boy had cut it for them. With no man around the house, Anna and her mother had received various kindnesses from boys in the neighborhood too young to fight but eager to do their part on the home front. Noah hoped those boys would never be called into action.

There was a white flag with the words *Serving Our Country* hanging in the window, the same one he'd seen displayed in other homes in the neighborhood. Some of the flags had blue stars, some gold, and the significance finally dawned on him. The gold star on that gold-trimmed white flag was for Martin, Anna's brother and the best friend Noah had ever had. They'd met at Fort Meade in advanced infantry training and been assigned to the 3rd Infantry Division together.

Grief rolled over him. Damn but he wished his friend were here, returning to his home and family. Somehow it didn't feel completely right without him. He shouldn't have been taken. Out of all the men Noah had fought with, no one had been Martin's equal in terms of pure marksmanship or gut instinct. But war didn't care for fairness. Nor did it care that the guys in the unit had *needed* Martin. Known for his Irish wit, he'd always been so quick with a joke, and his levity had defused more than one tense situation. His faith had stuck with him too, somehow, and he'd always muttered an Our Father before a battle.

Martin had asked Noah to look out for his mother and sister, and he had given his word. He'd written them both letters, and Anna had written him back—and then again and again for over a year and a half.

Noah made himself open the gate and continue down the path to their door, his heart hammering. The acrid smell of gunpowder filled Noah's nose, a smell he knew was an illusion. He shook himself and took a deep inhale of the summer air to settle himself. Funny how the gentle splendor of the Sims' front yard, what with the roses and flowers, couldn't push back his greasy memories.

He was lucky they were just memories. The war was still ongoing in the Pacific. The Japs hadn't given up yet, but his commanding officer had sent him home anyway.

Had he made the right choice, coming here so soon? In her last letters, Anna had urged him to come at once. Heck, he'd thought he'd be home in June, but things had taken a little longer than expected. He'd had to wrap up some duties around the surrender of the Germans—or the Jerries as most of the guys called them—and then there had been the crossing of the Atlantic back to his hometown of Washington, D.C. He'd settled his affairs there as quickly as he could and taken a train to Chicago, eager to see Anna. Surely she was impatient as well, what with it being the second week in July.

But should he have waited a touch longer? He wasn't sleeping well, and when he did, he awoke from violent nightmares, sweat dripping down his face.

The fact was he wanted to see her. Wanted it badly enough to take the risk.

Their front door beckoned, and he took the remaining steps toward it and knocked. His foot started to tap nervously, but he couldn't seem to stop himself. What if she wasn't everything he imagined? What if he wasn't?

What if she ended up not liking the man from the letters?

Oh, for God's sake, buck up.

An older woman outfitted completely in black opened the door, and he knew at once it was her mother. Martin's mother. If Anna hadn't told him about how hard she'd taken the death of her son, he would have seen it in the sunken eyes and harsh lines around her mouth. He made himself smile.

"Mrs. Sims," he said, "I'm—"

"Noah Weatherby," she replied, her tone as worn as the black shoes on her feet. "Anna said you'd be arriving any day based on your last telegram. I imagine I should say something like 'welcome home.'"

He searched the dark entryway over her shoulder, watching for Anna to appear. "You can say anything you like. I know I already said so in my letter, but I'm so sorry about Martin, Mrs. Sims. He was one of the best men I've ever met. I was lucky to know him and serve with him."

Her dark eyes narrowed, pinched at the corners like a folded handkerchief, which reminded him of what he'd brought for her. He dug into his bag.

"I wish it were my son standing here."

His gut burned as he located the object he'd brought. "I do too, Mrs. Sims. More than you know. Here, I have something—"

"I used to think I understood God, but I don't anymore," she said, her eyes glassy.

She wasn't listening to him, so he dipped at the knees to meet her gaze. "Mrs. Sims, I...ah...kept the handkerchief you gave to Martin before he left for the war with the hopes of delivering it in person. I...wasn't sure it would make it back to you along with his personal...items." Plus, there had been blood on it, Martin's blood, and Noah hadn't believed the Army would launder the handkerchief of a dead solider before giving it to his grieving mother.

He held out the folded white cloth with her initials

embroidered in blue thread, and her hands shook as she took it from him.

"I thought it would keep him safe," she said, her voice thin and reedy. "I prayed it would. Oh, God, my boy. My precious boy."

When she pressed the handkerchief to her mouth and hunched over, Noah felt his eyes water in response. He'd never known a mother's love. His had left him on the steps of the orphanage shortly after he was born, likely because he'd been born out of wedlock. Martin had hoped his mother would "adopt" Noah, and after hearing countless tales of the Sims' happy family, Noah had started to hope so too. He'd always longed to have a family, and now, with Anna, his hope was stronger than ever.

"Mrs. Sims, Martin kept your handkerchief in his pocket everywhere he went. Said it helped him feel you were always with him." Noah had cried when he'd uncurled that same handkerchief from Martin's limp hands.

Mrs. Sims' blue eyes flashed toward his, and then she started to rise out of the stooped stance she'd fallen into. The hand holding the handkerchief fell to her rounded stomach.

"Thank you," she whispered. "You can wait for Anna. She went to the market."

He thought of sitting in the parlor with Mrs. Sims and passing the time in tense silence. He didn't think he could handle it right now.

"I'll come back in a bit," he said. "Don't tell her I'm here. I'd...ah...like to surprise her."

Her chin seemed to lift, almost like she'd taken his words as a challenge. "Surprise her? Young man, I know you were Martin's friend, and it's probably none of my affair, but I'm going to say right up front that you'd better be careful with my daughter."

That drew him up short. He hadn't meant anything untoward. "Mrs. Sims?"

She pointed her hand at him, the one holding the handkerchief. "You boys are streaming back home after V-E Day and filling our girls' heads with all sorts of nonsense about the future, now that the war in Europe is over. You and Anna *barely* know each other. I know you *think* you do, but it takes more than words to make something work. Letters don't a relationship make, Mr. Weatherby."

He'd had some of the same thoughts, which was why he'd told Anna they wouldn't rush things. Her views on the subject had been both practical and poetic, and he'd valued her all the more for them.

When we do meet, we can see where this connection of words and souls takes us. The main thing is that we have the chance. The war won't steal that from us like it has for so many people.

"Mrs. Sims, please call me Noah," he told her, clearing his throat. "Like I told Anna—"

"Then there's Martin," she said, managing to look down her nose at him even though she barely came to his chest. "I wasn't going to say anything, but seeing you standing here alive and well in your uniform, I feel I must. You do realize that your very presence reminds us that Martin is gone forever."

He couldn't think of a proper reply.

"You might have been Martin's best friend, but my son is dead. Nothing is going to bring him back. Do you really want to be a daily reminder of that to me and Anna? Even with this so-called 'affection' between the two of you?"

Noah knew Anna didn't feel he was an unpleasant reminder. Even though she'd told him about her mother's struggle with grief, it was a shock to hear her say such a thing. "I don't want to cause you or Anna any more pain, Mrs. Sims. I figure this war has caused enough for all of us."

"Yes, it has," she said, "and it doesn't seem to be over yet. Thank you for bringing back my son's handkerchief."

She stuffed it in her dress pocket, her mouth pinched.

He tipped his hat. "I think it would be best if I came back another time to see Anna." Before she could reply, he made a crisp turn and walked back down the sidewalk.

His hands were clammy as he fumbled with the gate, but he didn't wipe them on his pants until he was out of view from the house. His mind was spinning. The last thing he wanted to do was cause Mrs. Sims more pain, but he couldn't step away from Anna before he even got to know her.

"Noah!" he heard someone shout.

He swung his head in the direction of the voice and stopped short. Everything slowed down, even the car that went by. Anna Sims stood across the street in a patch of sunlight. He recognized her from Martin's photo—he'd recognize her anywhere—but the still image hadn't captured the essence of her. God, she was pretty. Prettier than he'd ever dreamed up, standing there in a light blue dress and white heels. Her auburn hair was done up in that hairnet she'd mentioned in her letters, the one a pigeon had gotten caught in. The two grocery sacks she was holding dropped onto the sidewalk, and she put a hand to her mouth.

A deep peace settled over him as he looked at her. "Anna!" he heard himself call back finally.

Then he was running into the now empty street, and she was running too. His arms caught her to him, and hers wrapped around him.

"You're here!" She squeezed him tightly, and he buried his face against that soft hair, soaking in her warmth and the sweet perfume on her bare neck. "Oh, Noah, you're home. I can't believe it! I've been waiting and waiting."

The way she said *home* made him squeeze his eyes shut. He'd never had a home, and in her arms, he was feeling like he might have found it. *Oh, Martin, I wish you could have been here, seen this.*

"I'm here," he said in a hoarse voice clogged with emotion. "Oh, Anna, I can't believe I'm finally here with you."

"When did you get in?" she asked.

He did an internal calculation. "Over an hour ago, I imagine, shortly after three." He'd washed up as best as he could in the Capitol Limited train's bathroom and found a taxi the moment he left the station.

"You must be exhausted," she said. "The train ride is close to a full day, isn't it?"

"I didn't mind," he replied. "I wanted to get here as soon as I could." He'd given her a range of possible arrival dates in his telegrams, not wanting to disappoint her if the train was delayed or cancelled.

She gave him one more squeeze and then edged back. He could immediately see the resemblance to Martin, from the way her well-lashed blue eyes crinkled at the corners to the shape of her nose. Her hair was a fiery auburn whereas Martin's had been more brown than red. Those details made him miss his friend, but somehow it was comforting too.

"Oh, look at you!" she cried. "You're *so* much more handsome than your picture. And you're safe. That's what matters most. Oh, I'm going to start crying."

He didn't point out that tears were already streaming down her face. "I might join you. Oh, Anna. You're so beautiful. I mean I knew, but..."

Her smile tipped up at the corners. "I'm so glad you think so, Noah," she said softly. "I...wanted to please you."

He fought the urge to touch her face with his fingers, trace the high cheekbones and the graceful brows framing her light blue eyes. He reminded himself this was their first real meeting, and it was best not to be presumptuous.

"You're more than beautiful. I mean, didn't I compare you to Maureen O'Hara in one of my letters?"

"Because I'm an Irish girl with red hair and moxie?" she teased. "Like I haven't heard that before."

She'd told him about the soldiers getting fresh with

her sometimes at the USO, and no wonder. She was a magnet, a firefly, a flame.

"Oh, Anna, it doesn't feel real. Being here with you. Just a short while ago I was..."

He trailed off. The things he'd witnessed in the German concentration camp he'd liberated with his unit didn't bear repeating. Ever. He'd pledged to be honest with her, but some things were so vile, a man had to take them to his grave.

There was a flicker of something dark in her eyes before she hugged him again. "None of that matters now. We should get out of the street probably."

"We're safe," he said. "I've been watching for cars."

Of course, there were people watching them from windows, but it wasn't like they were snipers or spies. Only curious neighbors. Still, he led her back to where she'd dropped the groceries, and when he made a move toward them, she put her hand on his chest and stopped him.

Those blue eyes were aglow. "You're here, and I'm going to see to it that you're taken care of for a while. Is it impolite to mention you're a trifle thin?"

He'd gotten so used to being this lean, he'd forgotten how it might look to her. "I'll put some weight back on, don't worry. The steak I had last night helped." And yet, he'd found he couldn't eat but half of it, unused to regular meals.

She brushed his shoulder like she was ironing out wrinkles in the cloth. He'd done his best to be presentable in his uniform, but it had been a long train ride.

"I'll have to get over worrying about you. It's been a full-time job for some time."

He caught the womanly speculation in her gaze as she surveyed him and felt his muscles tighten in response. Though he hadn't told her so, he'd thought about her romantically even before they began their correspondence. Martin had shown him her picture, and he used to read her letters out loud at night. Something about her words had captured Noah. Had made him want to know her. Even so, he'd tried not to think about the future, not wanting to make promises to her when he didn't know where he'd be sleeping at night. She deserved better than to fall for someone who might not make it out.

Her mother's words came back to him. No, they might not know each other like a normal couple might over nights out to a movie or having a soda at a drugstore, but that didn't change the truth.

He knew her, and she knew him.

In the orphanage library, he'd learned the power of words. A book's words could teach you. They could take you on a grand adventure to a place you've never visited in person.

With Anna, he'd learned that the words in a letter could fill a man's heart with love and give him the strength to do his duty. He didn't know where his feelings for Anna would take them, but he was determined to learn what his words had done to her. Had they changed her as much as hers had changed him?

They were about to find out.

Chapter 2

"ANNA SIMS, IS THAT YOUR YOUNG SOLDIER?" ANNA HEARD Mrs. Fitzsimmons call out. She turned and spotted the elderly woman out on her porch.

Of course, they would be attracting attention. Heavens, she'd even dropped the groceries! But seeing him...with that thick sandy hair and adorable dent in his chin, well, they were lucky her mouth hadn't dropped to the floor as well.

"Yes, Mrs. Fitzsimmons, this is Noah Weatherby." She gave Noah a smile. "When you grow up in a neighborhood, everybody knows you."

The woman lifted a hand in greeting from the shade of her front porch. "I've been praying for you, young man. It's good to finally see you. Anna here has been waiting for weeks. Thank you for doing your duty, and welcome home."

Noah's face seemed to ripple in shock before he tipped his hat with his hand. "Thank you, ma'am, for your prayers. And for the greetings."

Oh, he was embarrassed. His face was turning the color of a ripe tomato like the ones they had in their neighborhood victory garden. Wasn't that adorable?

"I expect you're going to have a lot of people thanking you around here," Mrs. Fitzsimmons said. "We're all devastated by the boys we've lost in the neighborhood like Martin and Paddy O'Shea, but we keep moving on, don't we?"

They had lost so many boys, and Anna feared they would lose even more if the Japanese continued to hold out.

"Yes, ma'am," Noah said, clearing his throat.

"You come around for some tea and pound cake," she said. "I've been saving up my rations. I make the best pound cake in the neighborhood if I do say so myself."

Anna squeezed Noah's arm when his mouth parted for a brief moment. Dear Mrs. Fitzsimmons. She'd always been a sweetheart, giving out her famous pound cake and cookies to the kids in the neighborhood for decades.

"That's a mighty fine invitation, Mrs. Fitzsimmons. Thank you."

"Anna, you're welcome to come too, of course," she said. "I'm going to get back inside. It's a warm day out. Nice to meet you, Noah."

"You too, ma'am," he said.

And so it went as they walked back to her house. Some of the neighbors called out greetings from their porches, and others hustled out and met them on the sidewalk. Old Mr. Dunne pumped Noah's hand vigorously and offered to buy him a pint down at Dougherty's bar. Mrs. Walsh introduced her three young boys, praising Anna's teaching, which had made her give her former pupil, Davey, a wink. Katherine Kenna gave Noah a hug after he shared his heartfelt condolences for the loss of her fiancé, who'd died in the Pacific.

Anna knew everyone wanted to get a better look at the soldier she'd been writing, the one who'd been Martin's best friend. But it seemed Noah didn't know how to respond when people mentioned Martin or asked him about his service. And no wonder. He'd told her more than once how guilty he felt to have survived when so many had not.

She kept moving down the street, Noah in tow, promising to hold a welcome home party soon so everyone could properly meet him. Otherwise, they would have been caught on the street greeting everyone for hours. Of course, they all meant well, but she wanted him solely to herself after all this time, and she didn't think there was anything wrong with that. No, not at all.

She found herself smoothing her hair more than once as they moved along. Was her make-up still fresh? She imagined she could use a dab of powder and a touch of lipstick. When a girl waited this long to meet a boy, she couldn't help but be a little self-conscious. At least she was wearing her white shoes. They were worn out, but with the war on, people were only allowed two new pairs of shoes a year. She'd chosen more practical ones, and boy, wasn't she glad she wasn't wearing them. She and her friend Alice joked they looked like elderly aunts in them.

When they finally reached her house, she said, "Let's get inside before anyone else stops us. Goodness, what a welcoming committee. You look tuckered out."

"I didn't expect that," he said, her grocery sacks still in his hands. "Anna, were all those people truly praying for me?"

Her hand stilled on the doorknob and she turned to look at him. His green eyes were searching hers for answers, his incredulity obvious.

"Of course. You mean a lot to me, and you meant a lot to Martin. Everyone knows about you. I told you that I added your name to the soldiers our church prays for. That was all right, wasn't it?"

She'd told him as much in one of her letters, and he also knew she went to Father Shaughnessy's Friday night rosary to end the war when she wasn't volunteering at the USO.

He nodded briskly. "I know you wrote me about the whole praying thing, but I never imagined other people..."

"When you're...ah...friends with a Sims, you become friends with everyone we know."

His brow wrinkled and he looked up. The wonder in his eyes took her aback, but then again, Noah had grown up without a family or a home, hadn't he? That was why Martin had told him that he'd become part of *their* family.

Her throat clogged. Oh, how she missed her brother. She wanted to hug him and squeeze him tight for bringing Noah to them. In some ways, she knew it was his way of taking care of her, and she liked thinking about him smiling down from heaven, filled with the knowledge of how right he'd been to do so. But maybe he'd been taking care of Noah too. Yes, that sounded just like Martin.

She opened the door to their house and gestured inside. "You have people who care about you, Noah Weatherby. More than just in this house. It might take some time to adjust to that, but you'll manage. I know you will."

She watched as his Adam's apple moved, but he didn't step forward.

"It's a heck of a thing to adjust to, but you're right. I want to."

"That settles it then," she said with a firm shake of her head. "Now, I want to make you some coffee. Then I plan to simply gaze at your wonderful face and soak up you being here."

"The coffee sounds good," he said, "but the whole gazing thing you might save for the stars."

It took her a moment to process what he meant, and then she smiled. "We'll start with coffee." She'd talk him into staying for dinner, at the very least. Pot roast and blueberry pie, just like she'd promised in her letters.

"All right, if it's not an imposition," he said.

His hesitance took her aback, but perhaps this was a little overwhelming for him. He'd just gotten back, after all, and she'd met enough soldiers through her volunteer work at the hospital and the USO to have a good sense of the struggle most of them faced on a daily basis.

Leading him into the kitchen, she took the bags and set them on the table they used for everyday eating. "Let me just call my mother. I'm sure she'll be so happy to see you."

His hand curled around her arm, stopping her. "We met earlier."

This time it was she who blinked in shock. "What? You were here?" How could her mother have let him leave? She knew how excited Anna was to see him.

He cleared his throat. "You were out, and I...told her I'd come back."

This didn't make any sense. "But why?"

He shifted on his feet. "It wouldn't be easy for any mother to see her son's best friend standing on her doorstep when he's...not with him."

Had her mother given in to her grief? "Did she make you uncomfortable?"

His brief hesitation told her all she needed to know. "Of course not," he said after a moment, but he wouldn't meet her eyes. "She's simply grieving, and I'm a reminder of that. It didn't help that I returned the handkerchief she'd given Martin."

She felt her heart tear. "Oh, we wondered what had happened to it." When his things had come in a small box, she'd barely mustered the will to open it. Her mother certainly hadn't embraced the task.

They both fell silent, and Noah reached up and rubbed her shoulder, his fingers strong and warm. She leaned into him like a cat bathing in sunshine.

"It was a shock, seeing me and that memento," Noah said. "Let her be for the moment. If she wants to join us, she will."

Her mother *was* grieving, but that was no excuse to lock herself away in her room all the time. Goodness, if she wasn't at Malloy's Insurance, working as a secretary, or at her Victory Knitting group, she barely left the house.

Loss had affected them so differently. Anna was more determined than ever to live life fully while her mother cloaked herself in grief. Death shrouds were supposed to be for the dead. Not the living. Her mother didn't seem to understand that.

"I can't imagine how that must have made you feel," she said.

"Don't give it another thought," he said, the corners of his mouth lifting weakly. "She's entitled after losing a son."

He might say that, but she knew better. How could her mother's grief not have affected him? Anna was affected by it every day, and she loved her mother. Plus, he'd told her more than once in his letters how guilty he felt that he was alive and Martin wasn't.

"Is this why you were so surprised by how welcoming everyone was in the neighborhood?" she made herself ask.

"Partly," he said. "Now, can I help you put away the groceries? I haven't been around them in so long I might not recognize staples like butter or...oatmeal, but I still remember how to use a refrigerator"—his eyes darted to theirs and he whistled—"even if this *is* the newest model I've laid eyes on."

"Martin insisted we buy it before he went off to the war." She knew he was trying to reassure her. It was so kind of him to do so, but she wasn't ready to let it go. "I'll only say one more thing about my mother."

"Your brother used to tell me that you liked to have the last word," he said, a spark of something flashing in his eyes. Whatever he saw in her own eyes doused it. He took a step toward her. "Oh, Anna, I'm so sorry. Being with you reminds me of everything he told me, about you and him, and how happy your mother used to be. Should I...not mention him or any of that?"

Sorrow shot out of her heart like an unstoppable geyser, and tears tracked down her cheeks. "Noah Weatherby, don't you dare pretend you didn't know

Martin just because he's gone! I miss him too, but I'm not going to stop talking about him. In fact, I want to hear more stories about your time in the war...and how he...died."

He flinched. "You don't want to hear that. Suffice it to say he died a hero."

She swiped at her tears. "I know it will be hard for you to tell me, but I want to hear it. Noah, sometimes I dream about it, and I...need to know what happened."

He reached for her face, and then he was rubbing her tears away, his touch so tender and loving she was sure she was going to cry buckets if she didn't get a hold of herself.

"I'm sorry you dream about it. I know how bad dreams can be. Let's see how it goes. It...won't be easy to tell you the details, but I'll do it if you want."

She did want, and she didn't want. She only knew she had to know. "I wouldn't put away Martin's pictures when Mom asked me to after V-E Day. It would be like having...him die all over again. I can't do that, Noah. He doesn't deserve to be stuffed in some stupid shoebox. He was my twin. We...shared everything since birth—except this stupid war that took him. Oh, I'm being a ninny. Please forgive me."

He took out a handkerchief and handed it to her, and it made her think about the handkerchief he'd carried for over a year and a half with the hopes of one day returning it to her mother. He'd never mentioned it in their letters, and she wondered why. She would have to ask him later. Right now, everything was too intense.

"You're a brave woman, Anna Sims, and missing Martin doesn't make you a ninny. It makes you a good sister."

"I don't know about that. I'm only a sister who loved her brother." She wiped her cheeks. "How about that coffee?" she asked. "Then I'm going to make you a blueberry pie like I promised."

"You certainly wrote me a lot about your pie," he

said, smiling. "Sometimes I even dreamed about it. I savored those dreams."

She was glad not all of his dreams were bad, but had that added to the physical hunger he'd written her about or had it been a comfort? She hoped the latter. "I made sure I had everything I needed the minute I read your telegram. Oh, and I have a pot roast I've been marinating too. You're staying for dinner, right? I mean, we have so much to talk about."

Taking both her hands, he gazed deeply into her eyes. Her chest felt tighter suddenly, and she felt short of breath. He was so tall and those green eyes of his were arresting under his dark brows.

"Anna, let's start with coffee and sit a spell," he said. "We have plenty of time to talk about pies and the like. I thought I'd take you to dinner tonight, if you'd be willing to go with me. You don't need to make a fuss."

She squeezed his hands. "I'd love to have dinner out with you sometime, Mr. Weatherby, but tonight I want to make a fuss. Good heavens, I've prepared for this for days! Noah...you're here. I...want to celebrate you being home safe and with me. I want..."

His eyes lowered to her lips, and she found herself at a loss for words. His hands suddenly felt hot in her own. She inhaled sharply and watched his eyes darken. Yes, he wanted her. She'd seen the signs often enough to know, but she hadn't felt this kind of want for any man before, even though she'd just turned twenty-two years old. Oh, how nice it was to have him here in the flesh after subsisting so long on the simple words of his letters.

"Noah," she whispered, tilting her head up. "I'm so glad you're here with me. I've...wanted this. You." It made her blush to be so bold, but she'd waited a year and a half, hadn't she?

He looked away for a moment, his jaw clenching. "I thought we'd agreed to take it slow. Your mother seemed to think it was a good idea."

Of course she did, Anna thought, but the war had

made everything seem urgent somehow. "I know I said that, but I can't seem to remember why just now, what with you standing in front of me, all tall and handsome in your uniform."

A smile flickered across his face, and it made him look years younger. "Well, I do. I'm not one of those fresh guys at the USO who make you want to tug your earring."

She'd told him about the signal she and Alice had come up with to save each other from over-eager soldiers. "I'd never tug my earring where you're concerned."

That wonderful smile stretched until it filled his whole face, and she wanted to cheer. Oh, how she'd wondered what he looked like when he smiled.

"Anna Sims, are you flirting with me?"

"Yes, Noah Weatherby, I most certainly am," she said, "and trust me when I tell you that it's a rare thing."

So rare, in fact, she couldn't remember doing so with a single man since she'd started writing him. Sure, she'd met some handsome soldiers at the USO, but none of them had turned her head. They didn't "talk" like Noah, and even though they'd only corresponded through letters, she felt like she knew his soul, everything from how *Robinson Crusoe* was one of his favorite books to how he'd given chocolate to a starving boy in Italy. The boy had offered to shine his shoes even though he had no polish and only a tattered rag.

"Oh, I have something for you," she said. "Be right back."

She ran up the stairs and dashed into her room. She'd bought him a copy of his favorite book as a welcome home present. He was going to be so happy she'd remembered. She clutched the brightly wrapped edition to her chest, her heart so happy from the wonder of having him here in her house. Inside the front cover, she'd tucked the Valentine's Day card she'd made for him the day after V-E Day. Harold Tiller, one of her students, had suggested they make cards for all their returning friends and relatives, an idea she'd loved. She'd daydreamed a little as she cut a red heart out of paper and glued it on the white card.

Her eyes tracked to the only picture she had of Noah so far—taken with Martin and Henry, both of whom were dead. She kept it on her bedside table and looked at it after she said her prayers every night.

She dropped the book on the bed and rushed to the mirror over her bureau. Oh, she looked a fright. Her eyes were red, and her mascara running. Well, she didn't have time for a complete overhaul. Part of her thought the War Department and the USO had gone a little too far telling American women to wear make-up *all the darn time* to hide their sadness and worry about the war.

She grabbed her Max Factor pancake make-up and dashed at her face in quick swipes. If it was good enough for Lorraine Day in *The Story of Dr. Wassell*, then it was good enough for her. The movie made her think about Gary Cooper, the leading man in the picture. How had Marty thought Noah looked like the actor? His jaw was so much squarer, his eyes brighter. Why, if her brother were here, she'd...

Her hand fell from her face. She could never tease Martin about that or even call him Marty, which he'd hated. Sadness filled her up like an overflowing washbasin, but she shook herself. This was a time for celebration. She grabbed a tube of red lipstick and smoothed it on. She'd finally found a shade that worked with her red hair, thank the Lord.

"I see you're making yourself up into quite a ninny with all those cosmetics," her mother said from behind her.

She jumped and smeared her lipstick. The edge in her mother's voice signaled a fight brewing. "I'm only trying to look pretty for our guest, Mom."

Her use of the word *guest* seemed to charge the room, like Christmas lights flickering from a power surge before some of the colored bulbs exploded.

"Anna, I don't think I can bear to have that man stay

here. Seeing him brought it all back like a flood. My beautiful boy is gone."

Her mom's muffled cries stirred her compassion, but they'd had this conversation over and over again since Martin's death. Her mother knew how important Noah was to her. To give herself a moment to calm down, she reached for a handkerchief and fixed her lipstick before turning around.

"I'm sorry you're hurting, but we discussed this, Mom," she said, trying to sound reasonable. "Martin would want Noah to stay in his old room for a spell. We have the space, and he's respectful. He needs time to figure out how to start over. Besides, I want some time to get to know him better."

"I can't bear it, Anna," her mother whispered. "When I saw him at the door in his uniform...it was foolish, but for a second I thought it was your brother. Then I remembered Martin is never, ever coming home."

Her mother left the doorway, and she heard her door slam moments later.

Anna sat down with Noah's book cradled against her chest and took a moment to grieve for all of them.

What was she supposed to do now?

Chapter 3

THE SOUND OF A SLAMMING DOOR PUT NOAH ON FULL ALERT. He'd been overreacting to simple things ever since he left the front. Hearing a car backfire outside the train station had sent him to his knees. Most of the passersby had given him a wide berth, but a few had looked on with sympathy.

Somehow he needed to convince his brain he wasn't at war anymore. He knew about the symptoms of shell shock. Had certainly seen it in soldiers he'd served with. He wasn't shell shocked per se—not like the guys who went around glassy-eyed and didn't know their own names or what day it was—but he didn't feel like himself all the time. Part of him wondered if he ever would.

Anna came into the kitchen with her hands behind her back. The smile on her face was forced. Somehow he knew the difference between the real deal and a fake one even though they'd just met.

"Did you have a talk with your mother?" he decided to ask.

Her chest lifted in distress before she shook her head. "Yes, I did. Noah, I don't know how to say this, but she's gone back on our agreement to let you stay here. I'm...so darn upset about it, I can't see straight. Oh!"

He stood and crossed to her. "Don't you mind that

one bit. This makes things a bit easier. I'd thought it might be best for me to stay at the YMCA Hotel awhile anyway. We've only just met, and I'm still getting used to being back."

She put her head down, and he could feel her shaking even though he wasn't touching her.

"Anna, I'm having the odd dream here and there," he made himself say. "It would interrupt you and your mother's rest, and I won't have that. This arrangement will be fine. Trust me." If it would help things with Anna's mother, all the better.

"But you can't have that much money after the war," she said. "Noah, you came here at my invitation. I promised you—"

"Anna Sims, I would have come here even if I were as poor as a church mouse." He placed his hand on her arm. "I came to see you, remember?"

"But—"

"I have plenty of money at the moment if it eases your mind. I barely spent my pay during the war, so I have a lot saved up."

He'd sent it back to one of the older bartenders at the bar he'd tended before the war. If Noah hadn't made it home, the money would have gone to the orphanage where he'd been raised. He'd picked up his savings before heading to Chicago.

"That's not the point," Anna said, her chin showing some of that stubbornness Martin used to exhibit. He almost smiled at the image of both of them sticking their chins out like that as infants. Then he remembered the way Mrs. Sims had stuck her chin out when they'd talked on the front steps. The apple didn't fall far from the tree, it seemed.

"Give your mother some time. Seeing me instead of Martin would be hard on any mother. Well, except mine, I guess."

"That only makes me feel worse," Anna said, hanging her head. "My mother should be a source of kindness to you—especially when your own mother wasn't. Martin would have wanted that. He said as much to me in his letters before he died."

"It's early yet," he said. "Besides, I've made it twenty-four years without any maternal affection. Another few weeks won't hurt me none."

That was mostly true. Until the war, he hadn't thought much about his mother, but so many of the guys had written to their mothers or even called for them as they died—like Martin had. It had saddened him to think he'd never have that connection. Perhaps Mrs. Sims would come around in time, but right now his focus was on Anna.

"Noah, she's so caught up in her grief," Anna whispered. "Sometimes I don't know if I can stand it anymore."

He drew her into his arms and felt the parcel behind her back. "You might put that down so I can comfort you." That's all he was doing, he told himself. The last thing he wanted to do was rile up her mother by acting too forward.

"Enough of this." She turned slightly and held out a gift wrapped with string. "A welcome home present."

"You didn't have to do this," he said, but he felt his mouth tip into a smile as he took it from her. When had he ever been given a gift like this, wrapped up and everything? "I have something for you in my bag. Let me get it."

He stepped away and walked down the hall to retrieve it. There was a shadow in the stairway, and he pressed himself back against the wall before he realized it was Mrs. Sims walking upstairs. He let out his breath slowly, his heart hammering. Only then did he realize he'd picked up a candlestick from the entry table. Yes, it would be best for him to stay at the YMCA until he got a hold of himself.

After taking a moment to settle himself, he finally went back into the kitchen. The groceries were gone, and he assumed she'd hastily put them away. Anna had the coffee on, and she was busily wiping coffee cups with a dishtowel as if he were a treasured guest.

He stopped in the doorway and gazed at her. She was so beautiful, what with the lovely dip of her waist and the slender, graceful line of her neck. He'd love to see her hair down, he realized, and that seemed a bit fresh. He reeled himself back in. It struck him that perhaps he could reel in his overreactions to sounds and shadows the same way. Survival was as primal as sex, after all. He'd have to do more thinking on the subject.

"Oh, Noah, you startled me!" Anna said, spinning around.

"I didn't wrap it," he said. "I wanted to give you flowers, but none of the vendors at the station had them." He'd thought about picking a cluster from someone's front yard, but that hadn't seemed right.

"Flowers are rather like sugar," Anna said with a smile. "They might not be rationed, but they're a bit more rare. People started planting things you could eat, what with the war. We didn't know—"

"If the Jerries or the Japs might take the fight to our turf and try and starve us out," he finished for her. "Thank God they didn't." He'd witnessed what hunger could to do a person, bodies grotesquely bloated or sunken in so badly the human skeleton seemed to be covered in parchment paper.

"You open yours," she said.

"Ladies first," he said, untucking the book from his arm.

She took it with a gasp. "*The Secret of the Old Clock!* You got me a Nancy Drew book. Oh, I can't wait to add this to my collection."

He loved hearing the awe in her voice, and his chest puffed out like a rooster's. "It's the first one in the series, which makes it special. Of course, I worried you might already have it since it's one of your favorite series, but this here is a first edition. The lady I bought it from guaranteed it."

"Oh, Noah," she said, pressing it to her chest. "Where did you find this? I mean, you only just returned from the war."

"In Washington, D.C. There are some old bookshops I used to haunt. The war hadn't knocked them out, thank God."

Browsing the slightly musty stacks had made him feel normal again, like he had before the war. Funny how he always felt such a profound peace among books. Had since he'd first discovered them at the orphanage.

"I'll treasure it always," she said, and then leaned up and kissed him on the cheek.

Her lips were soft and warm, and he realized she'd freshened up upstairs. He felt himself blush, wishing she'd kissed him on the mouth. "You're welcome."

"Your turn," she said, keeping the book in her hands like she couldn't bear to put it down.

The string came off easy when he pulled it, and he was careful not to tear the paper. *Robinson Crusoe!* he exclaimed. "You remembered."

"I didn't know if you had a copy of your own since you mentioned reading it in the orphanage."

He did have a copy—in his bag, no less—but he'd never tell her. He'd taken three books with him to war, and that had been one of them. The others were *Tom Jones* and the book that had started his interest in reading and philosophy: a compendium of the great philosophers. He'd taken it out of the orphanage library on his way out. He couldn't leave Francis Bacon and the others behind—although he wasn't sure he'd ever tell Anna about that either. She might not approve.

"This means a lot to me, Anna," he said, feeling the solid weight of the words in his hands. "Books are one of the best gifts you can give a friend. It's like...sharing your soul with someone." He shook his head. "That sounded corny. Especially since you've given me a book you know

I like. Forget I said that. Sometimes I talk crazy."

He'd spoken like this in his letters, but now that they were face to face, he couldn't help remembering that some of the girls he'd liked when he was just getting hair on his chest had made fun of him for speaking like he did. They'd called him a sensitive boy like it was a bad thing. He certainly hadn't blushed while writing to Anna, although at times he'd wanted to cross out the words he'd just put down or hoped the censors would strike them for him. Paper was too precious to be wasted even if it was a V-mail form.

"Don't you dare stop speaking like that," she said, meeting his eyes. "When you talk like that, it's like you're touching my soul, Noah."

She'd called their connection one of words and souls in a letter, but the way she said it now was oddly intimate. He felt that deep spark of attraction for her again and wanted to pull her into his arms and press his lips to hers and never stop.

"All right, I'll keep saying what comes to mind if it doesn't bother you any. Martin didn't mind when I waxed poetic. That's what he called it. Not that we talked about each other's souls or anything."

She laughed. "No, I can't really see Martin talking like that. He hated his catechism, but don't tell anyone."

She had a nice, hearty laugh, one that wrapped around him like an embrace.

"Of course Martin usually told me to lighten up when I got going on all that philosophy stuff. That's what he used to call it."

A smile flickered on Anna's lips. "Martin used to say I waxed poetic too," she said. "And that I was a romantic. Like that's a bad thing. Oh, when you find yourself alone, there's a card inside your book."

Was she blushing? "Why can't I read it now?"

"Because the coffee is ready, and you don't normally make a guest wait this long for a treat. Let me pour us a cup. Do you take milk or sugar or both?"

His gorge rose in his throat at the thought of milk. Suddenly, he was back on a farm in France. A bucket of milk sat on the floor of the barn and thirst drove him to drink from it. He didn't even consider the possibility it might be sour. It didn't look curdled, although the color wasn't snowy white either. A vile tang soaked his tongue. He turned aside to retch, right as someone fired off a shot from an unseen post in the barn loft. Noah spun around and fired back. The loft turned silent again, and he stared at the milk puddle on the barn floor. He retched again when he found the French farmer dead in the loft, decapitated, his blood dripping where the bucket had sat.

"*Noah.*"

Someone was calling his name, and he struggled back. Anna was looking at him with her brow knitted. He couldn't seem to respond to her. It was like a glass wall stood between them, one he couldn't wish away.

You're not in France. That happened months ago.

So why could he still taste that spoiled milk? Fisting his hands, he squeezed with all his might until his head started to clear.

God, in moments like these, he missed the fighting, the physical action of moving forward and taking down the enemy. The endless days of enduring, surviving. Hadn't that been a surprise this past week? But keeping moving, vigilant, and active had kept some of the horror at bay. Most nights he'd been too tired to dream, but now he was home, and it was all flooding back like waves during high tide. How was he supposed to handle moments like these?

Anna deserved better than this from him. She'd turned downright pale.

He cleared his throat and found his voice again. "Black only. It will probably be the best coffee I've had in years. Not that I wasn't grateful for the sludge we had over there." Even cold coffee had been better than none, he'd often reminded himself.

He sat first, and when she took the seat on his right rather than sitting across from him, he angled his chair to be closer to her. He watched as she carefully topped off her coffee with a dash of milk from a small china-painted pitcher that hadn't been on the table earlier. He had to tear his gaze away from it, telling himself it was just plain ol' milk, but his mind couldn't let the thought go.

He took a drink from his own mug and scalded the roof of his mouth. The aroma of the deep roast complemented the bittersweet flavor on his tongue. "I knew you'd make the best coffee."

"My dad used to say that," she said, turning her cup. "Made my mom mad as a hornet. But never mind that. So you stopped in Washington, D.C. Is that where you sent the telegram from? Tell me...everything! I mean, there's so much I want to know. Now that I have you, I plan on hearing all your stories."

The devilish look in her eye confirmed what he'd already known from Martin and from her letters. When she wanted her way, Anna Sims got it.

"I'll tell you most of them. Some don't bear repeating. To anyone."

He wished she wouldn't press him about how Martin died. Mrs. Sims was already upset. What would happen when she found out Martin had died saving him? Would Anna be as upset as her mother? Oh, maybe he should keep it from her. Or delay the telling. Now that he and Anna were together, in person, his fanciful thoughts about her didn't seem so fanciful.

Suddenly, he wanted to hit something. Because he was no coward, and only a coward would shy away from the truth. She deserved to know, and when the time came, he would have to tell her.

She took a sip of her coffee, studying him. "I'm familiar with this way of thinking from the soldiers I've met, but we're...friends."

They were a heck of a lot more than that, and they both knew it. "We are."

"I want you to share things you wouldn't share with anyone else. Like you did in some of your letters."

His mind flashed again to the German camp. To the thousands of dead bodies they'd found piled up like garbage. To the emaciated survivors walking around in dirty striped prison uniforms with numbers tattooed on their wrists. Nothing was ever going to wash away those images or the knowledge of what had been done to the people there. He'd thought he'd seen everything one human could do to another, but he'd been wrong.

"We have plenty of time for stories," he responded, trying to shake it off by focusing on her face. "I've told you more than I've told anyone. Let that suffice for now."

"I hear a warning in your tone, Noah Weatherby," she said, cocking her brow. "It won't deter me. I won't push you to tell me things, but I will encourage it. I've seen too many soldiers fester like they have boils on the inside. If you're having nightmares—"

"I didn't call them that," he interrupted.

She leveled him a glance that was pure schoolteacher, and he recalled how determined she'd been in some of her letters. What other woman would talk so boldly about defying the Jerries by choosing love, not fear? She'd inspired him at so many turns when he'd needed it.

"Martin shouldn't have called you Carrot Top," Noah said, taking her fist and kissing the back of her hand. "He should have called you, 'Tiger,' or 'The Beautiful Reprimander' or something."

She kept holding his hand. "I think I prefer 'Tiger.' Feel free to call me that whenever the occasion permits. And don't think you can distract me with all this flattery. We were talking about your nightmares."

"It's common to have *bad* dreams," he told her, knowing she wasn't going to be deterred. Actually, he kind of liked it.

"Nightmares," she insisted.

"As you wish. I'm still adjusting to being back. Anna, it's a big change for me, to go from fighting in the mud and grime to sitting in your yellow kitchen drinking hot coffee."

"I know," she said quietly. "I'm only saying I won't be relegated to polite conversation. There was so much you couldn't share in your letters, Noah. Now I want to know everything."

Pressure was building in his chest. Part of him wanted to tell her to back off. Push back from his chair and get some air. He took another drink of his coffee instead and waited for the urge to pass. It wasn't like him, this feeling of wanting to strike back or run away.

"I'm sorry," she said softly. "I can be pushy. Martin used to say that all the time. I feel like I've upset you."

"It's fine, Anna," he said, making sure to smile. "It's only part of the readjustment process. So tell me. Are you missing school and your students?"

She tilted her head to the side as if she were considering whether she should let him change the subject. "Some days. But I love being able to wake up a little later. Of course I see my students around all the time in the neighborhood and at church. We're a close-knit community as you saw earlier."

"How far is your school from here?" he asked.

"Oh, about eight blocks," she said. "I can walk, but if we've gotten a lot of snow or it's colder than Billy hell, I take the car if Mom doesn't need it. To appease my conscience, I pick up whatever kids I find walking to school until I'm full up."

He could easily imagine Anna driving slowly down the neighborhood streets, calling out to young kids who were walking to school all bundled up in big puffy coats, their noses red.

"I'm not much for cold myself," he said, thinking of the icy temperatures he'd endured during the war. He had a few spots of numbness on his fingers from frostbite, but he was lucky it hadn't been worse. Anna's St. Christopher's medal had been ice-cold against his skin many times, but he'd never once taken it off.

"Oh, I just remembered," he said, reaching inside

his collar and pulling out her medal. "This is yours. Thank you for sending it to me."

She stopped him from taking it off. "Keep it. I...feel better...knowing you have it."

"But it's yours," he said, gesturing with it. "You and Martin each had one. It doesn't seem right."

She shook her head. "Noah, I want you to have it. Please."

He rubbed the chain between his fingers like he used to do before his unit began their march in the morning. He'd mutter the Our Father like Martin had and then tuck it under his uniform. Though he'd never been a spiritual man, those words and that precious medal—which had once hung against Anna's skin—had made him feel like there was something greater out there watching over him.

"All right, I'll accept it with my deepest thanks," he said and leaned over to kiss her on the cheek.

He felt her jolt from the mere touch of his lips, and again, he had to remind himself to take things slow.

Then she put her hand on his cheek, and he felt something powerful surge between them, something both soft and urgent, stronger than he'd ever felt for another person. It felt a lot like love.

He stayed against her a little longer where he was, unable to bear the loss of that first sweet touch.

Chapter 4

*H*E WAS AS WARM AS A RADIATOR AGAINST HER, AND ALL Anna wanted to do was settle closer. Why was he resisting what they both wanted?

"Noah Weatherby, if you don't kiss me right now, I'm going to come unglued."

She felt a ripple of shock go through him, and then he was leaning back and searching her face. He must have liked what he saw, because his mouth turned up at the corners. Was that a dimple in his right cheek?

"Unglued, huh?" he asked. "That sounds uncomfortable."

Was he making fun of her or teasing? She couldn't tell. She kept her hand on his face, but she stopped her fingers from trailing down to his lips.

"I don't mean to be so...forward. Trust me, when it comes to things like kissing, I'm usually not, but Noah, I care about you more than any guy I've ever met. I understand taking our time, but we're people. Not snails."

"The French really like their snails," he told her.

Now she knew he was teasing her. He couldn't have been Martin's friend if he didn't have a good sense of humor. She leveled him with a look. "Be serious."

"I never knew until you that I liked bossy women,"

he said, raising his hand and pushing a loose curl behind her ear.

Now that was more like it. She wanted to lean into his hand and purr like a kitten.

"There's nothing wrong with a woman knowing what she wants," she told him. *"Woman's Home Companion* says so all the time in their articles." Of course, sometimes their articles on how to catch a man annoyed her.

"Who am I to dispute a women's magazine?"

"You're stalling."

"Your mother is upstairs. That bothers me a bit."

"My mother should *never* be your reason for not kissing me. I'd never get kissed if that were the case. She has strong opinions about what it means to be a good woman. I mean, if I listened to her, I'd be wearing dresses down to my mid-calf."

"I'm not up on the secret language of ladies' hemlines." His lips twitched, and she punched him gently in the arm.

"Are you going to make me make the first move? This should be an easy maneuver compared to the ones you were on during the war."

It looked like he was trying not to laugh. She almost gave up then and there, but she wasn't one to turn tail in defeat.

"I thought it made you happy to make the first move," he said, rising to his feet and gently encouraging her to join him with a hand on her arm.

"Oh, you're insufferable."

He cupped her face, and she put her hand to his chest. Maybe it was time to put it all out there. Forget the slow program.

"Noah, I think I might be in love with you," she said, meeting his gaze head on. "I'm not saying we should rush to marriage tomorrow or anything, but if there's one thing I don't want... Oh, Noah, this war has taught me about carpe diem. Seize the day, the old scholars say. Hey, that rhymes! But in all seriousness, I wish I'd had more days

to enjoy Martin. I can't get more of them now. Not ever."
Her voice was strong, and she'd never felt more sure.

He stroked her face, and she felt a shared grief rise
up between them.

"With you home from the war, all I can think of is
how much time we've already lost. Do you remember how
I told you in one of my letters that—"

*"One letter, regardless of length, can never fill up all
the time in between,"* he said.

Her heart filled with joy. "Oh, I struggled for days
with how to word that! Noah Weatherby, did you memorize my letters?"

"Of course I did," he said. "They kept you close to me."

She laid her head onto his chest for a long minute.
He'd memorized her words, but he wasn't ready to kiss
her? Who was he kidding? "I memorized yours too—
mostly—but sometimes I would pull them out and read
them all. Stack them on my bed like a treasure chest."

"Yours are tied up with string in my bag," he said. "I
always made sure they were with me, wrapped up in cloth
like the picture I carried of you in my shirt pocket."

She wanted to dig into that pocket to see if it was still
there, the picture Martin had carried with him to war.

"Noah, we have everything in front of us. You said
coming home was like getting a second chance in life.
You're *my* second chance."

"Oh, honey," he said, his eyes darkening. "How did I
get lucky enough to be here with you?"

She believed the Almighty himself had arranged
that, with some help from her brother, but she kept quiet,
happy to bask in his gaze.

"Anna, I think I'm in love with you too," he said, caressing her face. "I came here knowing what I felt and
what it could mean. For both of us. Now that I know you
feel the same way…"

He gave her a pointed look, and she gave it right back
to him. "I don't do slow well, obviously," she said. "Deal
with it."

"Be my sincerest pleasure," he said with a small smile. "There are some things I'll need to figure out. You know that, right? I still have some...junk to sort out in my own way about the war and what I want to do with my life. But we can talk about that another time... Right now, I do want to kiss you."

"Then kiss me, you silly man," she said, tilting her head up.

He lowered his mouth to hers, and she felt the punch of his touch all the way down to her toes. Her body rocked back at the power of it, but his hand came around her waist to balance her gently against his tall, lean body. Even in her heels, she needed to rise up on her tiptoes to continue the kiss. Now that she had him, she wasn't going to settle for anything less than being kissed senseless like she'd seen in the movies.

Seeming to understand her wishes, he cupped her cheek with his other hand and angled her mouth until their connection was even more perfect. She felt his muscles tighten, and then he tugged at her bottom lip. Oh! That hadn't been in any of the movies she'd seen, but good heavens, how she liked it. Eager for more, she leaned into him.

He settled back to kissing her lips, and to her astonishment, she found herself hoping he'd tug on her bottom lip again. It seemed too bold to ask. She hadn't kissed many boys before. Three, in fact, and none of them had kissed her like this. Noah made her want to do more than kiss, which was both alarming and exciting. She finally understood what it meant to feel desire—the kind of wanting that could weaken the knees.

She loved feeling his breath against her mouth. Oh, she'd kiss him every day if he'd let her. She twined her hands around his neck, loving the feel of her breasts pressed to his chest. It was another new feeling, but one filled with discovery and excitement.

His tongue slid across the seam of her lips, and she jolted.

"Too much?" he whispered, angling back to look at her face.

"Ah...no. Only...different." Of course, she'd heard about it.

"So much for not going fast," he mused.

The hand on her waist loosened, but she wasn't ready for him to put distance between them. "I...I've never been kissed like that before. But I think I like it. Do it again." She wasn't one to walk away from a challenge or a new experience.

He took his time, and she could see him thinking. Considering, more like, she decided.

"Maybe we should stop," he said.

"Not yet. Please, Noah. Just a little more, and then I'll start your blueberry pie."

His chuckle was soft and the sound filled her heart with joy. She'd wondered about the quality of his laugh so many times. It was deep and seemed to rumble in his chest.

"You're a regular negotiator, aren't you? Martin was good at that too. I'll bet you were invincible together."

"We were," she said, remembering how they'd double-teamed their dad for ice cream in return for doing their chores faster. "I'm glad we can talk about him. In a happy way. I...need that, Noah."

Her mother only mentioned him when she was railing at God for taking him away, and it had felt like his beautiful memory was slipping away with each day in the house.

His hand caressed her cheekbone. "So do I, Anna. Now come here."

She rose onto her tiptoes, offering her lips to him, and then his mouth was moving against hers in the most delicious way. Slow. Sensual. Oh, yes, this was more like it. When his tongue caressed her lips, she opened them for him like she'd heard other girls talk about. When he slid it inside and rubbed it against hers, she shivered and felt something warm and urgent spread in her belly. No wonder so many girls had trouble waiting for marriage. She might be in trouble herself.

They were both breathing hard when he stopped kissing her, but he didn't let go. His arms stroked her back, and she laid her head against his chest. The love she felt for him was stronger than ever.

"I can't imagine doing without you," she whispered. "I was so afraid you might die, and we'd never have a moment like this. Thank God you were spared. Oh, thank God."

There was no way the relief she felt now could ever erase all the worry and sleepless nights of the past years, but she was glad they were behind her. She'd have to say some extra prayers of gratitude tonight at bedtime and light some more candles in the church if she could find any. They'd run out of votives. People had started to bring any candles they had at home to light for loved ones, but the shortage had become such a problem that Father Shaughnessy had found an unorthodox way to handle it by deciding to keep bees, even though it would take a while to harvest the fruits of his labor.

"I told you that your strength was what got me through the war," Noah said, "and I wasn't lying. Anna, there were days when I was so tired or horrified at what I'd done or seen someone else do..."

She hugged him tight, hearing the pain in his voice. "Our letters saved each other, I think. Sometimes I wonder if I'd be like my mother if it weren't for you."

He looked down at her. "I mean no disrespect to your mother, but you could never be like that. Your heart...and your will are too great. Even though I'm not a religious man, I thank God for it."

"We'll figure things out, Noah. *Together.*"

And she kissed him softly on the lips one last time as though to seal the promise.

Chapter 5

*T*HE FOG-COATED COUNTRYSIDE WAS GOING TO BE A BITCH TO navigate. Noah crouched down next to Martin. He looked at Henry and David and signaled for them to stay low and head east. Hopefully the tree line would continue to give them cover. One of the scouts had reported there was a farm ahead, filled with Jerries. They were supposed to take them out so the company could move forward. Noah was in charge. His commander had promoted him again due to his good instincts for how to take out the enemy.

The other guys weren't crouched down like they were supposed to be as they started to move out. He gestured to them with their pre-arranged hand signals, but they didn't heed him. What were they doing, standing up straight and walking like that? The Jerries didn't need any help putting them down.

Martin started to veer away from the tree line, and Noah cursed. What in the hell was his friend doing? Usually he was completely focused, his weapon at the ready. But Martin headed straight into the field, and the fog started to cover him. Noah turned to Henry and David, but they were both gone too.

What the hell? His commander was going to have his hide for this clusterfuck. He went after Martin since

*he knew his friend's last location. Part of him wanted to
call out to him, but he knew better. Sound traveled, and
he didn't want to give away their position.*

*A small hill came into view, and Noah saw Martin
walking toward it. Noah picked up the pace, his pack
heavy on his back, but by the time he reached the hill,
his friend was already gone. He turned around to scan
the area and nearly jumped out of his skin.*

*A woman in black stood a few feet away from him,
and his weapon rose instinctively before a clearer head
ruled the day. It was Martin's mother. Anna's mother.
What in the hell was she doing here? He put a finger to
his lips to signal she should be quiet. Even though he
wanted to know how she'd gotten here, he knew better
than to ask. Best get her to safety and then find Martin
and the other guys.*

*She slowly shook her head when he pointed in the
direction he wanted her to go.*

*"My son should have lived," she said in a voice that
carried across the fog. "Not you."*

*Then she stepped aside. A Jerry was behind her,
his gun pointed at Noah. He heard the shot before it hit
him square in the chest.*

Noah lurched up in bed, clutching his heart, sure
the bullet had gone through. Darkness closed in on him,
and he dove to the floor, his breath heaving. Where was
his gun? He huddled next to the mattress and patted the
floor.

There was laughter in the corridor, and he strained
his eyes to make sense of where he was. Then he remembered.

Chicago. The YMCA Hotel.

A dream! Another stinking dream. He tried to push
off the floor, but he saw stars as the adrenaline roared
through his system. His body started to tingle, and he
fought for breath. Oh, God. So real. He could almost
smell the overgrown lavender on the hill, its fragrance
somehow more pungent at night.

But it wasn't real, he told himself, reaching for his strength. Martin hadn't been in France with him. Neither had Henry or David. They were dead. They were all dead. All but him.

Mrs. Sims wasn't dead, though. It had felt so real when she'd stepped aside to let the Jerry shoot him square in the chest. Why would he dream something like that? Sure, she wished her son were alive instead of him, but she wouldn't want him dead.

She doesn't want you to die yet, but she might when she learns that Martin took the bullet meant for you.

He squeezed his eyes shut and bit his lip, fighting the urge to be sick.

Think of something else.

The image of Anna filtered into his mind as easily as sunshine through a window on a sunny day. Her blue eyes were smiling, matching the dress she'd worn yesterday. So pretty. She'd made him blueberry pie, and the tangy sweetness had made him close his eyes in appreciation. Her pot roast had been equally delicious, but not even close to the deliciousness of her lips.

Oh, how they'd kissed, on and off for the rest of the night, first in the kitchen and then later on her front porch. The rest of the time they'd talked in a world all their own. Mrs. Sims had come down from her room to make herself a plate for dinner, but she'd left them alone.

The easiness he felt with her was remarkable, but even more so was the feeling of connection between them when the words fell away and they simply stared into each other's eyes. In those silent moments, it felt like a deep knowing existed between them.

They'd danced on the porch too, the soft music from the radio streaming through the open window. She'd been like a flame in his arms, her body as warm and inviting as the night, and he'd struggled with his desire for her.

Anna had told him she loved him before they parted

last night. And he loved her too. Part of him had known it from the get-go. How could he not have fallen for her? He'd never met or spoken to a woman like her. With each letter, she'd unfurled more feeling in his numb heart. Her jokes. Her stories. Her sheer vibrancy. The fact that she'd decided to be a teacher after teaching a neighborhood girl to read when she was nothing but a girl herself. The way she quoted St. Augustine, a philosopher he much admired.

Billie, his buddy in the unit, had teased him about Anna, and no wonder—he'd mooned over her for years.

The night had been more romantic and meaningful than any in his life, and as the memories continue to play in his mind, he felt his heart rate begin to normalize, his breathing become less shallow. The back of his throat still tickled with nausea, but the worst was over. He leaned his head back against the mattress and opened his eyes.

How many hours did he have to wait until he'd see her again? God, he hoped it wouldn't be too long. She'd promised to pick him up at ten after breakfast in the hopes he would get a good night's rest. Call him old-fashioned, but he hadn't been keen on the idea of her driving him around, especially since he suspected she'd insisted on it out of guilt that he wasn't staying with her.

Her mother's image rose in his mind, surrounded once again by the thick white fog.

Sleep didn't seem possible, so he rose and turned on the lamp. The clock said it was three thirty-seven A.M. He sighed. It was going to be a long night.

Anna's gift of *Robinson Crusoe* was on the bedside stand. He opened it, remembering she'd mentioned a card, and retrieved the white handmade card with the red-paper heart on the front. The words she'd written made his heart turn over in his chest.

> *Welcome home, my beloved friend from*
> *across the sea! To all the grand adven-*
> *tures you're going to have and every-*

*thing you'll learn along the way. I'll
be by your side through it all. That's a
promise you can count on.*

Love, Anna

He traced the last line, feeling a messy swell of emotion, then set down the card and picked up the book.
He'd read it many times, but it struck him that he no
longer felt as much of a similarity to Robinson, the hero,
the sole survivor of a shipwreck. For the first time in a
long time, he didn't have to do it alone. He had Anna,
and she had him. The thought comforted him.

Morning came. He showered, savoring the feel of
hot water on his skin even though the hotel had mentioned the rationing of water and shampoo. He'd missed
being clean. The orphanage had been a stickler for it,
and he'd heard more than one person say "cleanliness is
next to godliness." He still didn't know what that meant.
But damn if a hot shower, albeit a short one because of
the rationing, didn't feel awesome.

After shaving and dressing, he touched the book
Anna had given him and left to meet her downstairs.

She was waiting for him in the lobby already, this
time in a red dress that matched her lipstick. A soldier
was talking to her, and while she was responding, her
stiffness conveyed her discomfort. He crossed to her
quickly.

"Anna!" he called.

"Noah," she said, turning, her whole demeanor soft-
ening.

The soldier shot a hostile look at him, and Noah
raised his eyebrow. *"Private.* Thanks for keeping my girl
company. You ready to go?"

She nodded, her hairnet bobbing in the back, and
he took her arm and led her outside.

"I had it under control," she told him.

"Yeah, you weren't tugging on your earring," he said
dryly, looking around for her car and finally spotting it.

"I know you did, but it made me feel better to dress him down a little."

"The way you said 'private' was inspired. All tough and manly. I'll bet you can be fierce when the situation requires it."

He thought of the war. "When I need to be."

"This is a new side of you."

"Hopefully not one you'll see very often."

She reached into her purse and threw a set of keys at him. He caught them against his chest.

"I realized you were uncomfortable having me drive you home last night, so you can drive me today. Male egos! I'll tell you where to go if you can follow my directions."

There was some sass in her voice, and he found himself smiling. What she didn't know was that he'd already studied a map of Chicago and had a good idea how to get to her house on South Side. Old habits from the Army died hard. He liked knowing where he was at any given time. "It's not that I'm not grateful..."

"But you're the guy," she finished as he opened the passenger door. "I'm okay with that. There are a lot of articles in the women's magazines about men coming home from war. We've gotten used to working and taking care of the home front, you see, so we should expect some friction."

"Honey, if this is friction, we're in good shape." He shut her door and came around. "I'm going to be cutting the grass and taking out the trash too. Any objections?"

She fairly beamed with delight. "Not one single little objection. Brendan Dougherty will be over the moon about the grass. Thank you, Noah."

He was glad she wasn't going to fight him on that. Martin had asked him to look after them, and to Noah, that meant doing what his friend would have done if he were still alive. "Any other things that need doing around the house—"

"I'll make a list if it will make you feel better," she said, angling her body toward him. "First things first. Aren't you forgetting a hello kiss? It *is* the proper greeting between two people who are going together."

They *were* going together, he realized. His slow program had been doomed from the start, and in the light of day, he honestly didn't give a damn. Last night, while he was dancing with her, tasting the lingering notes of blueberry and coffee on her tongue, and listening to her words in her beautiful voice, the war had seemed so far away. For a few moments, it was as though it had never existed. Like he and Anna had been together forever, enjoying dance after dance after one of her mouth-watering dinners.

He leaned over and kissed her sweetly on the lips. "Any more kissing than that and we might get arrested."

Her eye roll told him what she thought of that. "You'd be surprised how lax those public kissing rules have become, what with the war and all. With so many people saying goodbye, kissing has become a happy epidemic. But a few months back I was walking through the park, and I came across a couple that was really going to town. His hands were inside her coat and everything. That was the only time I thought about telling them to get a room."

As Noah turned on the engine, he thought about that man. Talk about lucky. He'd like to get his hands inside Anna's coat if he were being honest, and yes, get a room, as she'd called it. But she was a lady, and a virgin surely. She hadn't said the words out loud, but if she'd never French kissed anyone... Plus, she was a good girl—someone who wouldn't do something taboo.

Maybe it was his lack of religious conviction, but he didn't see sex outside of marriage as a problem so long as both parties were responsible and on the same page. He'd been with a few women like that. Never prostitutes though. A few girls had gone that route after leaving the orphanage, thinking they had no other way to support themselves. Desperation had driven plenty of women to do the same across Europe. Some of the guys had teased him for being a prude—even more so for giving his cash to prostitutes without asking for anything in return—but he hadn't paid them any mind.

He hadn't been with a woman since before he left for the war, in fact. Too damn long, if you asked him. But Anna was different, and he needed to be respectful. Wanted to be. Despite how bossy she got about kissing.

"I thought I'd show you a few sights today," she said, settling back as he drove away from the hotel. "I've been saving my gas rations. I want to give you a better sense of your new town."

They'd talked about that—the possibility of him settling in Chicago. But the war in the Pacific still loomed large in his mind, and he didn't want to promise anything just yet. Those boys might end up needing his help, or the War Department could call him back into service. Until the war was completely over, his life wasn't entirely his own.

"You sure do make a pretty tour guide," he said, wanting to put his hand on her knee.

Her head rolled to the side, and he fought the urge to stare. Still, he couldn't help but dart glances at her. That luminous creamy Irish skin and those blue eyes were so captivating. Then there was her auburn hair. God, he couldn't wait to see it down around her shoulders. That blonde bombshell actress, Veronica Lake, might have done the War Department a favor by launching the Victory Roll to keep women safe from accidents in the factories, but it was hell on the male imagination.

"Only one thing about driving," she said. "I'm not sure if you're a speedy driver, but if you could keep to the limit, that would be best. If you get picked up for speeding, you lose your gas card."

"Sounds like a fair punishment to me," he said. "Don't worry. I'd never speed with you in the car. Precious cargo."

She kicked out her feet and tugged her dress down when it inched up. "I like it when you talk so sweet."

He followed her directions, and soon they were on a

main thoroughfare. The size of the city awed him. Washington, D.C. had a strict height limit—nothing could be built taller than the Washington Monument—so the city never felt overwhelming. Chicago had buildings great and small, packed together like sardines in some places, yet it still felt grand, what with the wide thoroughfares of Michigan Avenue and picturesque bridges crossing the Chicago River. Anna made a point of showing him the Chicago Trade Building and the Field Museum of Natural History. The size of the public library blew his mind.

"I'll take you there soon," she said. "Today is about giving you a lay of the land."

"I was planning on asking you about the local library," he told her. "I have some things I want to research."

"Then you're going to love Chicago," she said. "We have tons of libraries."

He turned right as she instructed, but he still watched the red brick building until it faded in the rearview mirror. What kinds of new books might he discover inside that giant building? Oh, his hands itched with the possibilities.

"Do you like baseball?" she asked, rolling the window down.

He followed suit, glad she wasn't the kind of woman who worried about the wind blowing her hair. "I've taken in a Washington Nationals game from time to time, but I'm no die-hard fan. That's probably unpatriotic, although I don't know who decided baseball was America's national pastime. No one asked me."

"Whew! I'm not a big fan either, although I like going to the games sometimes. White Sox. Not the Cubs. That's really important. Chicago has two teams and you have to choose a side."

That was news to him.

"The White Sox play at Comiskey Park and have this wonderful player called Luke Appling whose nickname is Aches and Pains. People are going to ask you about stuff like this. You can tell a lot about someone by whom they root for."

He wanted to ask 'like what,' but the car in front of him slowed down abruptly and he needed to brake. There was so much to take in and remember, and suddenly it all felt like too much. He took a deep breath in, then out. Repeated it. A quick glance at her helped settle him.

"Do you like any other sports?" he asked.

"The Bears," she said. "They're football, you know."

He had to purse his lips not to laugh. "I know about football," he said in a simpleton's voice.

She gave a gusty laugh. "You're funny. I like that."

Looking over, he couldn't help but smile. "I thought the war had broken my funny bone." He bent it at the elbow and shook his head. "Looks to be normal."

"Okay, back to the Chicago sports lesson," she said in a strict teacher voice. "The Bears are like titans around here. Everyone is a fan! I mean, who doesn't like a team of world champions filled with good-looking men in tights?"

"I remember Martin being ecstatic after they won the championship in '43."

"You need to memorize the name Sid Luckman. He's the quarterback. Some of the players fought in the war and some served stateside, working during the week to help the war effort and then coming home on the weekends so they could play on Sunday. It kept the morale up, you know."

She sounded like she was spouting a military pamphlet, and very adoringly, if you asked him. He was of the mind that every able-bodied man—especially those in top physical condition—should be serving actively on the front, but that was something they could talk about later, when they knew each other a little better. Right now, he was in a car with a beautiful woman, and he wasn't going to spoil it by being too serious.

Instead, he asked, "Is there going to be a quiz?"

She turned quiet for a moment, and he looked over to see why. "What is it?"

"I'm sorry. I should have thought about how new all of this is to you. Of course there won't be a quiz. I'm being silly, is all. I'll just pipe down and let you get a sense of your new town on your own. If you have any questions, just ask."

She seemed as deflated as an old tire. "Anna, it *is* a lot to take in, but that doesn't mean I don't like your enthusiasm. I mean, I knew Chicago was the second largest city in the nation, but seeing it..."

He'd been in other large cities during the war—Paris, Rome, Berlin—but none of them were so bustling. Maybe in their heyday, but the war had changed them.

"Mayor Kelly wants Chicago to be the friendliest city in the world," Anna said in her sweet tour-guide voice. "I'm doing my part at the USO, so I know a lot. Come on. Let's head closer to Lake Michigan. That's always a nice view. Of course, we have a lot of boats on the lake these days, military ones like the *USS Wolverine* and *Sable* and a slew of ones carrying iron ore and coal. I thought you might like to see them."

He continued to follow Anna's directions and took the main road along Lake Michigan. Tents and pavilions dotted the stretch of blond sand, and there were people everywhere he looked. Some of them were swimming in the dark blue water, while a group of soldiers in uniform were playing horseshoes in what looked like a park to the left. He almost scoffed. Horseshoes! When a war was going on in the Pacific.

"That's the Summer Recreational Center or what we locals call The Serviceman's Club," Anna told him. "It's something like twenty acres, if memory serves, and all for the distinct enjoyment of our servicemen. Ruffled some feathers, let me tell you, what with it being lakefront property and all. But Mayor Kelly wanted soldiers to have a place to blow off steam. I mean, Chicago is one of the biggest training centers for military personnel in

the country. That's why we have so many places for servicemen and women to enjoy."

It was like a vacation postcard for military service.
Part of him understood what they were trying to do. Blowing off steam was important, but this just felt wrong. It
stuck in his craw that they were acting like this, so light-
hearted in their uniforms, when their brothers in arms
were still out there risking their lives.

"I'm not sure I like all this...appreciation."

She reached across the space between them and put
her hand on his arm. "When I look at it through your eyes,
I can see why it bothers you. This must look like a playground compared to where you've been."

He thought about the stacks of bodies they'd come
across in villages and the ovens... Bile rose in his throat.
No, he shouldn't think about that right now. Not when he
was with her.

"I can't believe we wear the same uniform," he said in
all honesty.

He heard her sigh. "We're not perfect, Noah, but I try
to look beyond that and see a city coming together in an
amazing way to keep our boys' spirits up before they ship
back out."

He felt small when she put it that way. "I remember
your letter about looking for a silver lining in everything,
even when we have to squint. I just have to squint a little." He made a show of doing so, but she didn't laugh. "I
shouldn't judge just because these guys look to be getting
the cushy treatment, while I was in Anzio and Normandy."

God, in that one horrible day at Anzio, they'd lost
more men than any of them could have imagined. And
then on that damn beach in Normandy... He'd thought
he'd seen everything a machine could do to a human body,
but he'd been wrong.

"So you were in those terrible places! Oh, Noah! I
knew you couldn't say in your letters, but I just felt it. I
can't imagine what that must have been like. The broadcasts said it was horrible."

Horror was too small a word for the sight of blood and guts spilling out from good men. Limbs scattered across the ground. The screams. "It was. Where to next?"

He hit the brakes when he saw the brake lights of the car in front of him. He'd noticed them at the last instant. Anna lurched forward, and his arm shot out to stop her from crashing into the dash.

"Dammit, Anna, I should have been paying attention. Maybe you should drive."

"No, it's okay," she said, patting the arm he had around her. "I shouldn't ask you questions like that when you're driving."

He lowered his arm, biting back the request that she not ask him those questions ever. Rather than speak, he put the car in second as the car in front of him sped up again.

"We have traffic," she said absently, as though she didn't know what to say just now.

He had made her feel that way. "We have it where I'm from too," he told her. "Anna, I'm sorry I was cross. I haven't been decent company since the war started, and I've been around mostly men for the past couple years. Most of us only growled and barked at each other." Or yelled "incoming" or "snipers."

"I don't think you're rough around the edges," she said. "How about I show you my school?"

He wondered if she was concerned about how her mother would react to seeing him again. Anna had mentioned Mrs. Sims worked five days a week from eight until three, but that left a lot of time in between. "I'd love that."

They headed back toward South Side, and he did his best to catalogue the landmarks they passed. Some hadn't been on the map he'd studied. "How is it your neighborhood seems so nice? I mean...Billie got your neighborhood wrong, didn't he?"

She nodded. "Yeah, we don't live in Irving Park like he figured, but I didn't feel the need to correct you."

"Why not?"

She worried her lip. "Well, some people in Chicago have strong opinions about other people's neighborhoods. I worried Billie might have a chip on his shoulder about my neighborhood, and I didn't want him to influence you."

"Influence me how?"

She looked away. "I know he's your friend and all, but people in Chicago sometimes talk badly about each other. Like real bad. Racial slurs and such. The war has helped that, I think, but..."

"Okay, I see where you're going with this," he said, and she exhaled harshly in response.

She wasn't wrong. Billie had strong opinions about a lot of things, from the shit quality of cold coffee to the staleness of an old cigarette. Noah usually ignored him when he got his juices going since it hadn't happened too often. They'd been too focused on the push into France and later Germany to have much time or energy to get bent out of shape about trivialities.

If the war ended soon like everyone hoped, Billie would be in Chicago soon too. His friend had suggested they could work together, although he hadn't elaborated on the details. They'd have to talk that out thoroughly before Noah committed to anything. Billie had a way of talking pie in the sky sometimes, and Noah wanted something he could wrap his mind around, if not his hands.

"If Martin told me about the different neighborhoods and the...strong opinions, I can't say I remember. But Billie did seem to think South Side is a pretty tough place. That's not your neighborhood."

"No, we're in a more...upscale part of South Side now," she said. "My dad saw to that. He and my mom grew up in that part and didn't want it for Martin and me."

"So Billie was right about some of South Side?" he asked.

"Partly, but there's a lot of hatred in Chicago, and I'm here to tell you I don't like it. No, not one bit. You see, there's prejudice between North Side and South Side, and every neighborhood in between. You have the Polish and the Irish and the blacks and the Jews, and the Italians, of course. Despite what the papers say, they aren't all in the mob. Of course, ask nearly any Irish and they'll tell you differently. I guess I'm a little touchy about that."

"I'm not fond of prejudice either," he said. "Washington has a lot of blacks, and they aren't any better or worse than white people, if you ask me."

She made a rude sound. "Some people just like to *think* they're better than others. Well, my father taught Martin and me not to judge a man—or woman—that way. He worked with a lot of different people when he was a railroad man, as he liked to call it. It was because he was good with people that he got promoted."

Noah wasn't surprised. Martin had possessed that same ability to charm people.

"He made a good living, and so he moved our family to a nicer neighborhood when Marty and I were five. Like I said before, he wanted a newer house away from some of the more...unsavory elements. Not people who were simply different from us, mind you, but gangsters and criminals. Goodness, if you voted for a candidate who wasn't a Democrat, you wouldn't have your garbage picked up for six months."

"Seriously?" he asked, tucking that tidbit away. He wasn't overtly political, but he voted as a citizen.

"Yes," she said, shaking her head earnestly. "Dad used to say moving us out of his old neighborhood was one of the best decisions of his life. Other than marrying my mom." She paused, then added, "Don't be fooled by where we live, though. My dad worked hard, and so do my mother and I. I mean, we have the insurance money and his pension to support us, but we wanted to carry our own water, so to speak."

He'd wondered about the status of their finances, especially given Martin's passing. "Thanks for telling me all that. I know it's not polite to talk about things like money."

"It's important for us to talk about such things, what with us being together and all. But that's not for now."

Funny how they were getting to know each other better on what he'd thought would be an easy car ride. She was showing him the same strong and heartfelt woman he'd fallen in love with in her letters.

"Go ahead and take the next left, but be careful. It's a blind curve up ahead."

She guided him the rest of the way, and finally he pulled to a stop in front of St. Patrick's. The church was a building of red brick with large stained glass windows, two belfries, and a cascade of stairs leading up to a set of thick double doors. It was larger than Noah had expected, but he wasn't exactly an expert on churches. The school was to the side, across a perfectly cut lawn, and also had red brick siding. It stood two stories high with large louver windows gleaming in the sunlight.

"How many places are named St. Patrick's in Chicago?" he asked dryly.

She shrugged as he shut off the engine. "Probably bunches, but this is the only one that matters to me. I made my First Communion here. Ducked through a window and climbed onto the school roof when Kelly Kincaid dared me. Danced with my first boy here in the parish hall. Paddy O'Shea."

He found himself smiling as they left the car. It seemed natural to take her hand. "I'm not going to have to fight him for you, am I?"

"Heavens no," she said, her eyes darkening. "He died in France."

He wanted to curse. "I'm sorry," he said. "I didn't think."

She got teary-eyed. "So many of the boys in the neighborhood have been killed. It makes me sad when I think about it, but then I pray for them and try to let it go. I think about being happy instead. Still, I'm really glad I was the first girl Paddy danced with."

"You keep those memories, Anna Sims," he told her,

raising her hand to his lips. "They're important."

"Anna!" someone called, and he looked over to see a white-haired priest walking toward them.

"Father!" she said, her entire demeanor transformed. "Come meet Noah."

The older man hustled forward, a welcoming smile on his round face. "Why do you think I'm running this way? I don't do that for everyone, you know. It's hot in these black garments. Noah, it's so good to finally meet you. I'm Father Shaughnessy."

Noah took his hand when he held it out and pumped it warmly. Maybe he wasn't one for religion, but he'd heard quite a bit about the priest from Anna. He'd figured prominently in her letters, much more so than anyone else save Martin and her mother.

"We're all so glad you made it through the war unscathed. You've been a blessing to our Anna here. Made her smile when times were tough. Not an easy task. I struggle with it every Mass."

"Oh, no you don't, Father. No one gives a better homily than you do."

The priest's wink was downright cheeky. "It's important to start the homily with a joke or a good story. Reels people right in."

Anne kissed his cheek, and he put his hand around her shoulders. Their affection was palpable, which caught Noah off guard despite all the praise Anna had heaped on the man. He'd thought a priest would be more formal with the people in his church.

"I'd heard you arrived yesterday," Father said. "I was planning on coming over tonight to pay my respects. How's your mother taking it?"

Anna shrugged.

"That great, eh?" he asked, rocking her in place. "What did she do? Give you a cold shoulder like she's been giving me since our little talk?"

"No, Father," Anna said, meeting his gaze. "She said Noah couldn't stay with us."

Noah shifted on his feet, uncomfortable with being discussed as if he weren't there.

"No! She wouldn't..."

When Anna didn't respond, he clucked his tongue. "Well, she's a work in progress like the rest of us. I'll keep praying for her, but in the meantime, Noah, I want you to stay with us at the rectory. We have a few spare rooms and a wonderful cook when you're not eating at Anna's."

Stay at a church? "That's very kind of you, Father, but I'm staying at the YMCA downtown."

He waved his hand. "That's quite a ways, and you don't have a car, I would imagine. Gas ration cards are hard to come by. If you stay here, you can walk to Anna's house in five minutes or less. Please, Noah, it would be a treat. Anna tells me you are well read in the classics, and that's one of my passions. Besides, Father Wilson is a good man, but he's literally as quiet as a church mouse. Spends all his spare time in prayer or in his room. Not that I have a problem with that, but being a priest is about being with the people."

Anna's mouth twitched. "Father Wilson is new to our church, Noah, and he's been a little hard to get to know."

The priest jostled Anna playfully. "Turns down family dinners with parishioners, which I would never do. Right, Anna?"

"You do love a good meal," she teased.

"Forgive my ramblings. Noah, I would really love for you to stay here. You'd have plenty of privacy, I promise. Besides, some say I have the best whiskey in the neighborhood."

Noah could sense the steely determination under the man's easygoing demeanor. That meant something. Like maybe that he'd try to get Noah to come around to his way of thinking. He wasn't sure staying with a priest, even one Anna seemed to like so much, was a good idea.

"You know I'm not Catholic, don't you?"

"Yes," he said, his eyes narrowing. "Should that bother

me? I don't ask people what church they go to when I offer help. Do *you* have something against Catholics, Noah?"

The man would be a good debater, Noah imagined. No wonder he and Anna were as thick as thieves. "No. Like I was telling Anna earlier, I figure people are people. Some good. Some bad."

Father nodded. "Exactly. Could I persuade you with the use of our private library? I used to lend my books out to anyone who asked. But after a few books weren't returned and others were handed back with dog-eared pages and ruined spines, I found myself having very uncharitable thoughts. I had to prescribe some serious penance for myself. A couple years ago, I decided to stop that nonsense and save the books for those who could appreciate them. But you look like a man I could trust with a rare book of Thomas Aquinas' sermons."

The glint in his eye had Noah smiling finally. "You drive a hard bargain, Father."

Calling another man Father felt odd on his tongue, even if the man looked to be in his fifties. He'd never had a father—or a priest—in his life. He looked at Anna, and he appreciated that she didn't try to offer any persuasion of her own. He caught the conspiratorial glance between the pair and decided to play along. This man wasn't at all what Noah had expected.

"I can't turn down a rare book," he said. "Thank you for the offer, Father. I'd be happy to stay with you for a while."

But as soon as he said it, he wanted to take back his consent. What would happen if he had a nightmare?

Father suddenly put his hand on Noah's shoulder and looked him straight in the eye. "It's going to be fine, Noah. Who knows? You might even have some fun. I might be a priest, but that doesn't stop me from having a good time. Every day is a gift. I figure the war has taught us that if nothing else."

"Can you see why we all love him so much?" Anna said, kissing the man's ruddy cheek.

"Well, I need to get in for lunch or Mrs. Hughes is going to tan my hide. She hates to see us eat cold food and hems and haws about keeping it warm for us. It dries out, you see. Noah, come over with your things any time. I'll tell Mrs. Hughes to look out for you."

"Thank you, Father," Anna said. "You can't know how much this means to me."

"Oh, hush now, lass, it will be fine. Be good for both of us, I expect. And this way you won't worry as much."

Anna's eyes widened.

"Haven't I known you since before your First Communion? Our Anna here has one of the biggest hearts in the whole parish, and she needs to let others help her more. I'll talk to your mother again when I feel the time is right. We'll bring her around, don't you worry. Looks like there's more than letter writing in your future. It will be fun having a ringside seat. Okay, I'm off."

He hustled across the lawn, his black outfit billowing behind him, and then disappeared into a large two-story red brick house on the opposite side of the church from the school.

Anna turned to him, her eyes scanning his face. "He's wonderful, isn't he? I hope he didn't put you on the spot. I mean, staying here would be closer, and he's right. I wouldn't worry as much."

He didn't know why she would worry. It wasn't like he was fighting in the war anymore. But he didn't want to hurt her feelings. "I'm sure it will be fine." And if it wasn't, he would make a polite excuse and go back to the YMCA.

"Father is one of those rare people who's good with everyone. He can soften an old battle-axe or open up a kid with a chip on his shoulder. He tells the best stories. Oh, and his jokes..."

He *did* want to get to know the man Anna valued so much. Plus, it wouldn't be bad to have an ally when it came to Mrs. Sims. That dream he'd had still gave him a chill when he thought of it.

"I suppose I should check out of the YMCA then," he said. "How about you show me the school and your classroom first and then we can grab a bite to eat before heading back downtown?"

She hugged him briefly, and he savored both the spontaneity and sweetness of her affection. "Sounds like a plan."

She took his hand, and together they set off.

Chapter 6

THE DINING ROOM TABLE WAS COVERED WITH BAKING DISHES and cakes and pies when Anna walked in after returning from downtown. She felt Noah still behind her, his hand coming to rest on her waist.

"*Oh, my goodness!*" she breathed, putting her hands to her cheeks.

"There's more in the kitchen," she heard her mother say. "The neighborhood seems to think there's something to *celebrate*. I've been greeting people all day, and it's given me a headache."

The pocket doors were open, and she could see her mother's black shoes crossed at the ankles on a footstool. She walked to the parlor doorway. Her mother was knitting a blue scarf for her Victory Knitting group.

"How nice of everyone," Anna said, trying to keep her tone light. Her mother had always loved their neighbors' generosity in the past.

"They're acting like Noah is part of this family." Her mom said it like it was a bad thing.

Anna glanced back to check on Noah. He was standing by the dining room table, staring at his uniform hat in his hands with a dejected look on his face. Anger rolled over her.

"Mom, Noah is more than a friend. He was like a

brother to Martin, and now he's officially my beau." There, she'd said it.

"Well, isn't that nice? That makes you like every other rash girl out there, Anna. I expected better of you."

The words seemed to pummel her in the midsection. "I'm not being rash. Neither is Noah. We've been writing each other over a year and half now. But that's not something we should discuss right now." She would explode and say things she would regret. Besides, it was easier to catch flies with honey. "I'm going to spread the news that we're having a party tonight to welcome Noah." She'd planned as much anyway. Better to do it with the food fresh.

"Seems the neighborhood has already issued the invitation," her mother said. "Mrs. Flynn used up her ration cards to make her special buttermilk chocolate cake, and she's as tight as they come."

Usually the woman had a demeanor as sour as her buttermilk, and yet she'd done more to welcome Noah than Anna's own mother had. "How kind of her. It's kind of all of them," she said pointedly.

"If you say so," her mother said. "I'm going up-stairs."

"You're really going to turn your back on our neighbors when they come to this house?"

"No, I'll come down and make an appearance even though my head hurts," she said, rising from the couch. "But I still think you're moving way too fast, young lady."

Anna clenched her hands at her side. She was old enough to make decisions for herself. Other people saw that—why couldn't her mother?

"Father Shaughnessy has asked Noah to stay with him and Father Wilson at the rectory."

Her mother had to know what an honor that invitation was. The rest of the neighborhood surely would. And Father wouldn't have invited Noah to stay so close to Anna if he hadn't also approved of their courtship. *Take that, Mom.*

Her mother stooped to pick up her knitting and tucked it under her arm. "He's a big-mouthed meddling fool. Keeping those bees must have addled his brain."

"*Mother!* He's been good to this family as long as I can remember."

Silence was her only answer. Her mother had walked away.

"Maybe I should go," she heard Noah say softly.

She spun around. "No! Don't you dare let her... headache discourage you." She waved her hand, searching for the right words. "Noah, I want you here. The neighborhood wants you here."

His hands settled over her arms. "Anna, I want to be here, but she's your mother."

She'd been feeding herself that same line for over a year now. "It's her choice if she wants to stay upstairs for most of the party," she told him. "The rest of us are going to have a good ol' fashioned party. Have you ever seen the Irish party, Noah?"

His eyes were troubled, so she touched his cheek. His eyes closed for a moment as if he too were unbearably saddened by what had transpired. And why wouldn't he be? Her mother's words had to feel like a rejection.

"You look at me. We're going to have a gay time tonight. Trust me. Will you help me set up the card tables outside? They're in the basement."

"If you're sure..."

Anna threw her arms around him. "Noah Weatherby, I love you and you love me. The war couldn't keep us apart, and neither can anything else. No force on earth can. Time to get used to the idea."

The thought of all they'd overcome so far made her feel like breaking down and crying on his shoulder, so she squeezed him and set off for the basement. Noah followed her down the squeaky steps, and by the time she pulled on the string at the bottom, illuminating the space, he stood beside her. The canned goods she and her mother had put up were mostly gone from last summer save a couple jars of beets, which neither of them loved. Martin's old bicycle caught her eye. The tires were gone, part of the tire drive for the war.

"After this war is over, we'll get new tires for Martin's bike and you can ride it around if you'd like," she said, pointing to it in the corner. "It's a nice neighborhood to take a turn in. Martin used to put me on the handlebars and pedal as fast as he could until I begged him to let me off."

He grimaced. "I...ah...don't know how to ride a bike."

Right. The orphanage. Sometimes she needed to remind herself that he hadn't grown up in a normal home with two parents like she had.

"I'll teach you. My bike is in the garage. But no matter. Let's get these card tables."

"Where are they?" he asked.

She showed him and tried to protest when he picked up all four. "But you're—"

"If you knew how much my pack weighed... Anna, go on upstairs and hold the door. I'll be right behind you. Then you can show me where to put these."

They headed out to the backyard, and he set them up where she instructed. "The others will bring more tables and chairs. Noah, I hate that you have to be lifting things, what with you just getting in yesterday and all."

"Anna, if you knew the last time I was at a party... The generosity of your neighbors overwhelms me. I mean, your mother is right. I'm not family."

She poked her finger in his chest. "Are you not my beau? And the man Martin thought of like a brother? Trust me, Noah Weatherby, that makes you good and special." She couldn't say family yet. They hadn't spoken explicitly of marriage, but she had a feeling they would get there.

Sure enough, the closest neighbors saw them out in the backyard and started to carry out more tables and chairs. She introduced Noah to the ones he hadn't met and whispered the names of the ones he'd briefly encountered the day before.

The sun was warm, and she hustled inside to pour a few glasses of iced tea. She heard a knock on the front door, so she headed that way. When she opened the door, she couldn't help but smile.

"Hiya, teacher," Willie Buckley said. "Mom sent me over to help you and your fella get ready for the party."

She loved hearing Noah called that. "That was nice of her," Anna said, although she knew Mrs. Buckley had probably jumped at the chance not to have him underfoot.

Willie was one of the students she shared a special bond with. Like her, he'd lost his brother in the war. He'd gotten into loads of fights at school, but his behavior had improved drastically after Anna sat him down to talk. They'd spoken about their brothers and how upset they both felt, and Willie had broken down. He hadn't gotten into another fight at school, although she knew he sometimes still did in the neighborhood.

"You know Mom," Willie said. His eyes darted to the table. "Wow, you have as many cakes and pies as the church bake sale. Can I have a piece now?"

"No, you can't," she said. "But maybe after you help awhile, I'll make an exception. Come and meet Noah."

"Mom says he's a real hero, what with serving with Audie Murphy and all."

Anna stopped short. Audie Murphy was the most decorated solider in the war. He'd been on the cover of *Life Magazine* last week, looking handsome as all get out in his uniform. She hadn't read the issue, but she'd seen it at newsstands downtown.

"I...somehow had forgotten that."

Noah had never said anything about him in his letters, but he hadn't mentioned too many of the boys in his unit. Most of the ones he'd talked about had died. Only Billie, his friend from Chicago, was still alive, and even he'd been wounded. It struck her that Billie would likely be coming home soon. Hopefully he would give Noah one more reason to consider staying in Chicago.

"You said he was 3rd Infantry Division, right?" Willie asked.

"I did," she said, crouching down. "But Noah doesn't like to talk about the war. You might...ask him about something else."

"No one wants to talk about the war," Willie said in a voice laced with regret. "I just don't understand it. We licked those Krauts something good and—"

"Willie, please don't use that term," she said. "You know we have Germans living in Chicago. It's...unkind."

"Doesn't make them stop calling me a Mick when they see me downtown," he told her.

"Willie Buckley, did you just roll your eyes at me?"

"Sorry, Miss Sims," he said. "I'm going out back to help your fella. I promise I won't ask him about the war."

He slowed down as he walked by the dining room table, as if cataloguing the goods. Moments later, he was running through the house, and then the back door slammed. She thought about going out there to introduce him to Noah, but Willie would do just fine. She needed to pour the iced tea.

But the doorbell rang again and again, with neighbors delivering more food or chairs for the party. When she finally got back to the backyard, she spotted Noah surrounded by a cluster of boys, a few from her class like Willie. He had a bottle of Squirt in his hand, and he was smiling as Brendan Dougherty talked with his hands, likely telling a tall tale. He was ten years old now and told her she was pretty every chance he could, the little charmer.

"How's everything going out here?"

"Hiya, Miss Sims," Brendan said, rushing over and grabbing her hand, only to pull her closer to their group.

"Your fella gave me ten dollars for cutting your grass. I love him!"

"He did?" Her gaze flew to Noah's. "But your mother wouldn't let me do anything for you."

"She's crazy sometimes," Brendan said, circling his finger at his head.

"*Brendan Dougherty!*"

"Sorry, Miss Sims."

Noah shrugged. "Work deserves compensation. And that's enough of that."

She decided not to pursue the matter. Part of her thought it was downright sweet of him. Like he was taking care of things as the man of the house—just as Martin had wanted.

"He told us that the Japs don't eat little kids like you hear about," Willie Buckley said with a grimace. "Can you believe that?"

Her mouth parted in surprise. "I didn't know you actually thought that, Willie." Of course, she'd heard a lot of things said about the Japanese, but she hadn't taken that one seriously. "You know cannibals don't really exist any more."

"Only in books like *Robinson Crusoe,*" Noah said, flashing her a smile.

"Do you know that book?" Willie asked, slapping his hand to his forehead. "I love that book! Miss Sims read it to us for a few weeks. It's crazy."

"It's one of my favorites," Noah said. He seemed more relaxed than usual. Not that she'd seen much of him in person, of course, but there was less tension in the way he carried himself.

"Miss Sims, we're not asking Noah any questions about him fighting or anything," Willie told her, his hands sticky from his Coca-Cola bottle.

She wondered who had brought the sodas out back.

Noah raised his eyebrow at her, but she only smiled. "I'm going to brew up some more tea for iced tea."

"Don't worry about drinks," Brendan said. "Dad said

he and some of the guys were bringing more sodas and other drinks."

"That's nice of him," Anna said. Shifting her gaze to Noah, she explained, "Brendan's father owns one of the pubs in the neighborhood, and he's just back from the war."

"My dad is known for pulling the best pint out of all the bartenders in town," the boy said with a grin. "Of course, my mom kept it running while he was in Europe, but now that he's back, she's going to take a breather. We're a handful."

That sounded like Mary Dougherty, Anna thought, but she wasn't wrong. "Noah used to be a bartender," she told Brendan.

"Cool! You should tell my dad that. He could hire you. Mom says we need to do everything we can to help our boys get back on their feet. That's why I'm not supposed to tell my dad if he's wrong about where something is in the house. Mom moved a lot of things, and he's been upset about it."

Noah cleared his throat. "Your mom sounds like a nice woman, Brendan, and I can't wait to meet your father. Boys, I'm going to help Anna for a while. Do you think you can keep a handle on everything out here?"

The boys all nodded, even four-year-old Robbie Dougherty, who followed his older brother around like he was his hero. Little Robbie was born just before Pearl Harbor, so he had no memory of his father. Mary had told her in confidence that he'd cried the first time Brian tried to hug him. The poor woman had cried too while telling her about it.

"Willie, I want a tally of the number of soda pops we have so far. Brendan, I want you to count all the chairs and then add up how many people you think are coming tonight."

Noah continued to fire off orders to the boys, and she loved seeing the respect he'd already garnered from them. He was a natural leader, something Martin had mentioned in his letters to her—and a natural with kids too.

When they went inside, she looked around to make sure no one had come inside the house to drop anything off while she was out back. Satisfied, she put her arms around Noah's neck and pressed her mouth to his.

He jerked in surprise, but then his hands slid around her waist. His lips softened and started to move over hers.

"They adore you," she said against his mouth.

He eased back and traced her cheek. "They miss having men around, I expect. I'm glad Brendan and Robbie's father is back. That helps. So you told the boys not to ask me about the war, huh?"

Was this dangerous territory? She couldn't quite tell. "Willie remembered you were in the Third and asked if you knew Audie Murphy...and..."

"I see." He straightened his spine, almost as if the mere mention of the solider had him standing at attention. "I don't like to mention it since people know so much about him now. After Holtzwihr..."

Even Anna knew that story. Lieutenant Murphy had saved dozens of lives while taking out a bunch of Germans in the process.

"He's a great man," Noah said. "I respect him and was honored to serve with him and under him. But you're right. I don't much like to talk about what we did over there."

He hadn't told her much in his letters, although he'd told her more than many men probably did. Sure, it hadn't been anything battle-oriented. That wasn't allowed, and for good reason. But he'd told her plenty of hard truths about the strain of war on a person and the moral struggles he faced doing his duty.

"Have I told you today how much I love you, Noah Weatherby?"

His smiles were coming more frequently now. In moments like this, she could feel the changes happening inside him, like old pieces of him resurging and coming together. She liked to think it was partly her love that was doing it.

"I believe you whispered it to me at the sandwich shop earlier," he said, taking her hand and kissing the back of it. "I almost choked on my roast beef."

"Now that you're finally here in person, I find I don't want to hold anything back."

Part of her was scared at the urgency she felt to share everything with him, but it felt right. The war had given her that urgency, and she tried to think of it as one of those silver linings she'd written to Noah about.

"Things are going to get a little crazy tonight, I imagine," she said. "I tried to warn you earlier. We Irish know how to party."

"I'll manage," he said, kissing her cheek.

Hours later, as she watched Noah dance with Mrs. Fitzsimmons, she found herself smiling and swaying to the music. Her heart was happy. The war seemed so far away tonight. No one had on the nighttime broadcast, something you could usually hear through people's open windows as you walked past their houses in the summer, and everyone had come together to celebrate Noah.

"He's wonderful, Anna," Father Shaughnessy said, appearing beside her. "Martin was always a good judge of character. I can see why they became brothers. And I can see why he would catch your eye. He's an old soul."

Even thoughts of Martin couldn't dim her mood. She could feel him watching from heaven with a smile on his face. He'd have loved tonight.

"You're right about Martin. He was friendly with everyone, but he only had a few close friends. Always said a guy had to have your back or he wasn't worth anything. My dad said the same."

"Noah would stand up," Father said. "I'd want him to be on my side in a fight."

"I pray his fighting days are over forever," she said.

"I want to thank you for offering him a place to stay at the rectory. I know what an honor it is."

Father sipped his whiskey. "I expect a few people will hem and haw about him not being Catholic, but I'll deal with them. You might have to as well, but I imagine you've thought of that."

She actually hadn't. "The old guard is pretty traditional about things." And her mother was one of them.

"Why that should matter so much to some people, I'll never understand," Father said, "I may not be traditional in my thinking, but I've preached about it before and I'll preach about it again. As if our Lord would have asked what religion someone was before performing a miracle. Balderdash."

She linked her arm through his. "My mother barely stayed past making up a plate for dinner. I know people noticed." God, she hoped they weren't already gossiping about Noah's background and her mother's reaction to it. It wasn't like she could explain her mother objected to him for other reasons.

"Maybe she was living by the old adage of 'if you don't have anything nice to say...'"

"It still doesn't make it right."

"No, it doesn't," he said, his mouth twisting as if the thought was bitter to him. "Too bad she didn't take me up on my invitation to dance. Dancing lightens the mood of most people, even grieving ones."

"You're so Irish, Father, and the good kind," she said, bumping him a little. "*Dancing.*"

"Yes, dancing," he said, leading her in a merry circle to the music. "Speaking of which, you should go dance with Noah before one of the other women grabs him. Maybe you're right, and it's the Irish in me that thinks so, but it's pretty clear people have missed dancing. Maybe I need to host a dance at the parish hall. I know we haven't beat the Japanese yet, but we all see the light at the end of the tunnel, thank the Lord. That's something to celebrate."

The war had stopped all of the celebrating for a spell. Halloween had been suspended for the last three years, something she'd been outraged about on behalf of the children. When the White House had forgone a Christmas tree, so had nearly every American family. The few weddings she'd attended had been serious affairs, what with the men going back to the war.

"It's like all the joy in the world disappeared during the war."

Father gave her a mischievous wink. "Yes, but we can always change that. I'll do some thinking on this parish dance. Now I'm going to do some dancing myself. Come, I'll take Mrs. Fitzsimmons from your beau."

They walked to the center of the backyard, which was functioning as an informal dance floor. Everyone had danced tonight—even Old Mr. Dunne. Her mother would complain about the footprints and any divots in the lawn, Anna knew, but she would fix what she could tomorrow. The grass would mend easier than her mother's heart, it seemed.

"Noah, I brought your sweetheart here," Father said as the song ended. "Mrs. Fitzsimmons, would you care to dance with an old priest?"

"I'd be happy to, Father," the woman said. "Anna, thank you for allowing me to dance with your young man. He's a keeper. I can see why he and Martin took to each other."

"Your lady," Father said, spinning Anna in a circle and leading her into Noah's arms.

He held her gently around the waist. "Thank you for the dance, Mrs. Fitzsimmons. I'll let you know when I can come for tea and that wonderful pound cake of yours."

Father set his drink down on one of the side tables, and Anna gave Willie a look when she saw him eyeing the half-drunk whiskey. She would bust his chops if he tried sneaking any of it. Sure, some of the boys did such things at parties, but they weren't going to do it under her watch.

"You have your tiger look on," Noah said softly,

leading her to the orchestra music.

"Some of the boys look like they're liable to sneak a lit-tle whiskey or beer from the abandoned glasses," she said.

He chuckled. "I remember doing stuff like that."

"You? I'm surprised. You don't even smoke."

"I did before the war, but like I told you in one of my letters, I didn't want to be shot because I was out taking a smoke. The guys ribbed me about it at first. Then we ran out of fags, and they wished they'd quit sooner too."

She'd smoked less as the war had gone on too, most-ly because there had been cigarette rationing. Of course she could have taken some from the USO like many of the girls did, but she didn't feel okay about it. Receiving gas rations was one thing. Transportation to the USO was part of the job.

"Well, aren't you a smart one?" she said, loving the feel of his body against hers. Of course, they needed to keep a little more distance between them with everyone around. Last night after dinner, they hadn't needed to observe such proprieties.

"You're the teacher," he said. "Everyone has been telling me how great you are with their kids. Willie's mom said you single-handedly taught her son addition, which his earlier teachers couldn't do."

She shrugged. "Some teachers brand kids as smart or challenged and then treat them accordingly. I don't do that."

"To your credit," Noah said, turning her slowly. "If I'd had a teacher like you, I might have finished high school."

He'd alluded to being mostly book learned in his letters, but hadn't elaborated. "Why didn't you?"

"I couldn't take the rules anymore, so I ran away at fifteen. I made sure I had a job first—I found one at a lo-cal bar a few days before I left for good. Some of the boys and girls had run away earlier, and they'd fallen into... difficult circumstances."

She thought of how safe her upbringing had been. "I

hope the first thing you did when you left the orphanage was get an ice cream."

He spun her around. "You remember that story, do you?"

"Of course. You got busted for sneaking out, only to discover the great thinkers because you had to clean the library. How could I not remember a thing like that?"

His hand gripped her waist. "I remember all of your stories too. When I couldn't sleep or we were hunkered down in a foxhole, waiting for orders, I'd replay them in my mind."

"I'm glad."

"I told you they kept me going," he said, his green eyes intent on her face. "*You* kept me going."

Her heart welled up with feeling, and she didn't care that others were looking. She laid her head on his shoulder. Everyone knew he was her beau. A few of her friends had even asked when they were getting married. Alice seemed especially determined to get them hitched. Her argument was no-nonsense and straight to the point, so Alice: *If you don't marry the guy you've been writing letters to for a year and a half now, what's wrong with you? Heck, what's wrong with him if he doesn't ask you right away?*

Not wanting to stir the pot, she'd put them off, saying he'd only just returned home. Soon Noah would have to meet everybody in her life, but it seemed wise to make it gradual. The neighborhood was plenty for the moment.

"You also didn't tell me I'd have a welcome committee like this," he said in a voice only she could hear.

"I guess I didn't really think about it. I was so focused on getting you here." Home to me, she thought but didn't say.

Last night she'd thanked God again for bringing him home safely. She had a feeling she was going to be saying that prayer for some time.

"Me too, Anna," he said. "Thank you. I...never imagined I'd feel so welcomed. These people...they've made me feel like one of them."

She lifted her head. "I'm so glad you're okay with all of this because...well, this is my life. This is how it is here."

This is what it would be like if you married me.

His mouth turned up. "I like your life, Anna Sims."

Oh, how she wanted to stroke his face, that slight dent in his chin. It wasn't as marked as Cary Grant's or anything, but it was still charming. Someone bumped into her from behind, and she heard a chair slam to the ground moments afterward. Noah jerked in her arms. His head swung in the direction of the sound, and she felt his muscles bunch as if in preparation to spring.

"Someone knocked down a chair," she told him, carefully watching his face as he struggled with his war instincts. "This is what I meant by things getting crazy. Some people drink until they're three sheets to the wind and then..."

His heart was pounding. She could feel the loud, angry beats against her hand. And was that sweat running down his temple? He didn't look like he was breathing.

"Noah, let's grab a drink," she said, tugging on his hand to lead him away from the dancing.

Sure enough, Robbie Murphy and Johnny O'Hara were so drunk they were holding each other up as they laughed raucously by the large tree flanking the alley. If anyone ended up throwing up in their backyard, she was going to give them an earful and make them clean it up with a water hose. But right now, she needed to do what she could to help Noah.

His hand was protective, positioned on her lower back, and she could feel him straining to keep control of himself. Opening the back door, she smiled when she saw some of their older neighbors playing gin rummy at the kitchen table. His muscles seemed to lock, and she knew he was hanging on by a thread.

"Noah, why don't you go to the front porch? I'll grab you a drink."

He nodded at everyone before exiting the kitchen.

"It's a great party, Anna," Mrs. O'Shea said, shuffling the cards. "Your dad and Martin would have loved it. Your mother should have taken some aspirin for that headache."

A few people nodded while a couple others looked away, as if they didn't want to make eye contact.

"I did take some aspirin, Margaret O'Shea," she heard her mother say from behind her. "Of course, with all the ruckus going on outside, it's not helping my headache none. I might as well play cards."

She gave Anna a pointed look before pulling an empty chair to the table. Anna had to soften her mouth. Somehow her mother's appearance didn't make her feel better.

"Paddy would have loved this party if he hadn't died in the Pacific," Mrs. O'Shea continued, laying her cards face down on the table. "Mary, it seems to me like it's up to those of us who've lost sons in this war to celebrate the boys who come back."

A pin could have dropped and no one would have noticed. Anna watched Mrs. O'Shea stare her mother down.

"Anna's beau is a good man from what I can tell, and that's no surprise given her good sense," the woman continued. "He's a real hero."

"Hear, hear," old Mr. Dunne said, thumping the table. "Martin wouldn't have picked a know-nothing for a friend, and Anna sure as hell wouldn't have fallen for one. You raised your children right, Mary Sims, and don't you forget it."

Given her mother's earlier comments about her poor judgment, she appreciated their support. She felt tears gather in her eyes.

"Thank you," she said. "Speaking of Noah, I promised him a drink. Mom, I hope you have fun playing cards. Maybe it will make your headache go away."

"One can hope," her mother said. "Margaret

O'Shea, you'd better stop jawing at me and deal the cards."

Exiting the tense room seemed like a good plan. Looking in the refrigerator, she pulled out two Squirts. She'd seen Noah lift a drink with Brian Dougherty and a couple of the other men freshly back from Europe, but he didn't seem like much of a drinker. A toast was something special, and she had a notion they'd been drinking to their fallen comrades.

When she reached the front porch, Noah was standing with his back against the brick wall, facing out toward the street. His tough-guy stance made her wonder what memories were filtering through his mind.

"I have your drink," she said, sitting in a chair.

She felt a pinch of guilt for stepping away from their guests, but she wanted to be alone with him, if only for a while. Right now he needed it, and she realized she did as well. Seeing her mother stand off with Mrs. O'Shea had left her unsettled even if she wanted to kiss the woman for speaking her mind.

Noah stayed standing, and she wondered if that was because he *couldn't* sit yet. He didn't take a drink of his soda either.

"You don't drink much," she said. "Alcohol, I mean."

"There are two kinds of bartenders in the world. The ones who drink like fishes and the ones who don't give it much thought. I'm the latter."

"I'm kinda glad. I'm not happy when the men get to the falling over stage."

"I don't fall over," he said simply.

No, he wouldn't. Even though he was still so thin, he was strong as an ox. She'd felt his biceps when she'd touched his arms.

"I'd try to catch you if you did, but then I'd have to beam you in the head with a cast-iron frying pan the next morning."

"A cast-iron frying pan?" he asked, easing into the chair beside her.

She swallowed her sigh of relief. She'd noticed how he'd stand for a while until he felt more comfortable. It was like the solider in him had been assured everything was safe before he relaxed. *Please God, let that go away soon.* She hated to see him so torn between what he'd been and what he might become.

"In my family, the women are known for chasing their, ah..." She couldn't use the word "husband" quite yet. "The men in the house with a frying pan. It's an Irish thing, I think. My grandfather gave my mother a pan like that when she married my father, and it always sat on one of the stove burners, part joke, part threat."

After her dad died, her mother had clutched that silly frying plan to her chest and then dumped it in the trash. Somehow she'd forgotten that. Anna wondered who was going to give her a frying pan. All the significant men in her life had passed, and she didn't imagine her uncle would remember unless her aunt reminded him. But even though they saw them at holidays when they drove up from Champlain, they weren't close. Well, she could buy her own frying pan if she wanted to.

"I would appreciate not having a threat like that around," Noah said softly. "I...can't guarantee how I would react. What with the war and all..."

Oh, how stupid of her. "Of course," she said, leaning forward and looking him in the eye. "I can't imagine needing to keep you in line like that anyway. That didn't come out right. I didn't meant to imply—"

"I know what you meant," he said, extending his hand.

"Seems silly talking about frying pans, doesn't it?" she asked, taking it.

"And yet, when you talked about the tradition, your eyes filled with light, even in the dark. Then they grew sad again."

She waved a hand. "Memories, is all."

"Memories are powerful," he said. "Too powerful, in some cases."

He was referring to the war, she imagined. "Noah."

"What?" he asked.

His hand was warm, and she curled her fingers around it. "I only wanted to say your name. I'm so glad you're here."

"Me too," he said, rubbing the back of her knuckles with his thumb. "We should head back. Your neighbors will be wondering where we've gone off to. I don't want there to be any untoward talk."

"They know we're on the porch, trust me," she said. "No one has any secrets in this neighborhood. When you sneeze with the windows open, someone next door says, 'God bless you.'"

He chuckled. "Good to know. I'll make sure to muffle my sneezes. Come on. Let's dance a little more. What time do people normally clear out?"

The grandfather clock in the parlor had indicated it was close to midnight when she'd walked by it. "With school out, it might be two-ish? Of course, some of the older people might head on home soon."

The ones with young children had already left. Anna thought about the older neighbors playing gin rummy with her mother. Who knew how long they'd keep playing? Would her mother stay until the end? Anna hoped so. It didn't make up for her earlier behavior, but at least it was something.

"What about Father Shaughnessy?" he asked. "I don't want to bother him or the other priest, especially on my first night."

"Oh, Father can party with the best of them, but he has the morning Mass at seven. He might head out early. We can ask him."

He stood and pulled her out of the chair. Needing to touch him, she moved in and hugged him. His arms came around her too, and they swayed to the music coming through the windows.

Earlier, just as the party was heating up, she'd pushed the radio in front of one of the back-facing windows and cranked up the dial. The news updates on the war in between the songs had brought quiet to the party every time they aired. Noah had looked down at his feet, his hands clenched by his sides. Maybe he was frustrated to be listening to the news now that he was no longer part of it. While he hadn't said it, she suspected he was bothered to be home before the war was truly over.

Please God, let it end soon and bring all our boys back.

"I love you," she whispered against his neck.

"I love you," he whispered back, his hands clenching on her waist for a moment.

Oh, how she loved the way he squeezed her like that. "I want to send them all away and be with you," she said.

"But that wouldn't be neighborly. Besides, they've been so welcoming to me. I would hate to offend anyone. Come on. We'll dance some more. The time will fly."

The time did fly, but Noah ended up going off with Father after the two of them helped her clean up, something her mother had failed to do, having gone up when the card playing ended.

Anna watched them until they disappeared from view, then shut the front door and leaned against it. Seeing him walk off had pulled at her heart strings, but it wasn't like he was going off to war again.

Soon, she hoped they'd be closing down parties together, only to retire to the quiet sanctuary of their bedroom.

Chapter 7

NOAH AWOKE GASPING. THE IMAGE OF HENRY'S GUTS spilling out continued to play in his mind. Oh, the gore...

Sweat rolled down his face, and he pressed his hands to his chest in the hopes it would help him breathe. He closed his eyes, but the images continued their haunting repetition. Blood. So much blood. Spurting. Gushing. Internal organs pink and pulsing.

God! He shoved the covers off and stood up, clutching the bedpost for balance. These dreams were pure agony. His friends and brothers at arms dying over and over again around him as he watched, helpless to save them.

His room felt like a small cage, and he couldn't ignore the urge for more breathing room. If he was quiet, he could make it down to the library. Maybe he could find solace in a book until dawn broke. Father Shaughnessy had shown him the way of things earlier in a brief tour before bidding him a congenial goodnight likely fueled by Brian Dougherty's whiskey.

Noah scrubbed at his face, wiping away sweat droplets, and made his way out. The house was quiet save for a man's snoring coming from Father Wilson's room. His heart still thundered like a German tank in his ears and he fought the urge to run. His body and mind were at war, and all he wanted to do was charge down the stairs and out the front door to fight. Something. Anything. But the enemy wasn't outside...

The enemy was inside now, and he felt powerless in the face of it.

Light shone in the library's doorway. Had someone forgotten to turn off a lamp? When he entered, he stopped short. Father Shaughnessy was sitting in a wing-backed chair with a book open in his lap. His cheeks were less ruddy than they'd been.

"Noah!" the priest said. "Come join an old man. Sometimes I have trouble sleeping, and I come down here when it's clear no amount of praying will help me rest."

He wasn't suitable for company. "No, I'll—"

"Sit right here," the priest said, standing and crossing to him. "I won't bother you, I swear. We can read in silence. Please, choose a book and make yourself comfortable."

The man stood silently before him, as if waiting for Noah to make a choice. He couldn't face his tiny room again. It was either stay here or wander outside and sit on the front porch, but he desperately wanted something to focus on instead of the way he was feeling, and books had always been an escape for him.

"Thank you," he said, breaking off to the bookshelves.

Father shuffled back to his chair and resumed reading. Noah looked at the leather-bound books and felt his heart rate slow. By God, the man hadn't been emptily boasting. He had an incredible collection of philosophy.

"Have you read John Stuart Mill's *Principles of Political Economy*?" Father asked. "A quote from it came to mind earlier, one that might interest you. 'A man who has nothing which he is willing to fight for, nothing which he cares more about than he does about his personal safety, is a miserable creature who has no chance of being free, unless made and kept so by the exertions of better men than himself.' I pulled the book when I came down so I wouldn't forget. It's on the table by the other chair."

A man who has nothing to fight for... "That does interest me. Thank you."

He moved slowly to the chair, his eyes resting on the navy leather-bound book stamped with a gold title. Father crossed his ankles and sank deeper into the chair.

"Of course, he talks about justice and the misery of war and some other things. See what you think. Oh, and turn on that other lamp. No need to strain your eyes."

"I will. Thank you." He realized he was repeating himself, so he opened the book.

The mantel clock ticked in the background as Noah started reading. The outer world faded, and he found himself in a space that had always comforted him. It felt as if Mill was speaking to him, and only him, his ideas coming to Noah as if they were seated side by side.

"How are you finding Mill?" Father Shaughnessy asked after a while.

Noah had to shake off the reverie. He looked over. The priest was regarding him in the soft lamplight. The man had a way of making his body completely still, even though he was actively listening. It practically compelled a person to talk, and the priest didn't miss much of what was said to him, Noah imagined.

"There's a lot on economics and how it drives the world. Honestly, I've skipped some of that. I was more interested in the economic impact of war. The way Mill describes it...well, it looks very different when you're in the face of it."

He thought of the devastation he'd seen. Ancestral homes demolished. Towns in existence since the Romans leveled. And one of the deaths that haunted him most— the little boy who had shined his shoes in exchange for a chocolate bar lying dead on the ground without legs after enemy mortar fire. Noah had told Anna about that boy, but he hadn't told her that he'd found him two days later, his life snuffed out. The boy had been the same age as her students, and he knew the truth would devastate her. If he'd cried, surely she would. Why cause her the pain?

There had been so much devastation, human and physical. How could it ever be rebuilt? Sure, Mill also talked about the money war generated, in terms of weapons and industry, but the very thought of someone profiting from war left a bitter taste in Noah's mouth.

"I imagine war looks very different than Mill writes," Father Shaughnessy said. "Seems like every line of morality is blurred in times of war."

"Is morality ever that clear?"

Father closed his book and then crossed his hands prayer-like in his lap. "I could tell you Jesus and others in the Bible outline morality rather nicely, but you might say there are some contradictions even there. I might even agree with you, but don't tell the bishop."

So the priest had a boss too? No one seemed to be their own man these days. "Yeah, the Old Testament talks about an eye for an eye while Jesus talks about turning the other cheek, if I recall. The orphanage schooled us in the Bible. Said it would help us get over our unfortunate births and not turn into bad seeds."

"That gets my fire up," Father said. "Why people talk such ways to children, I'll never know. Most children are as pure as any saint, but I digress. Back to morality. In my experience, most men of faith exhibit both tendencies, forgiveness and revenge. I rather like Marcus Aurelius' saying about the matter."

Noah loved that Roman philosopher. He'd devoured *Meditations* when he'd found a copy. "Which one?"

"'Waste no more time arguing what a good man should be. Be one.'"

"That's a good one," Noah said. "One of my favorites is 'You will find rest from vain fancies if you perform every act in life as though it were your last.' The war sure as hell—sorry, heck—taught me that. I'm surprised you're so versed in a Roman emperor and philosopher. Didn't he persecute Christians?"

"Son, if I only read men who hadn't persecuted Christians, I wouldn't have read some of my own church's history."

Noah almost chuckled at that one. "You seem rather open-minded..."

"For a priest?" The man bellowed a laugh, a loud boisterous one that had him clutching his belly. "People have such stereotypes about so-called men of God. When I first heard someone refer to me that way, I looked over my shoulder to see who they were talking about. Then I realized it was synonymous for priest in their vernacular. Ridiculous, if you ask me. I'm no more a man of God than anyone else trying to be."

Noah was starting to like this man more and more.

"That's why I like Aurelius' quote in *Meditations*. It's a simple statement of what I was raised to believe, I suppose. My father always did what he thought was right and taught us to do the same. If he had any confusion about the best course to take, he would research the alternatives, pray on it, and come to an answer that gave him ease if not outright peace. In Catholic terms, we call that a well-informed conscience. It's something I live by."

That was a new term to Noah. "What if you have to do something you believe is wrong?"

"Such as?" the priest asked.

"Like killing a man in the line of duty," Noah said. "When I first signed up—right after Pearl Harbor—I believed it was the right thing to do. That we needed to take down the bastards who'd bombed the *Arizona* and killed our boys. Sorry about the language, Father."

He waved a hand. "You can't offend me. Keep going."

"Well, there were people I killed who I can justify having killed. They were going to kill me or one of my guys. You just do it, you know. In the moment." He suddenly could feel his pack on his back. Feel his gun in his hand.

"And now?"

He struggled for words. "I...feel haunted by it all. The killing. The friends who went down next to me. I figure...I would feel different about it if I believed it was completely justified."

Father said nothing, and for a moment Noah waited for him to respond. When the silence lingered, Noah shook his head. Maybe the priest didn't have any answers either. Maybe no one did.

"Some of the men I shot would call out for their mothers. *Mutter* and *madre* are easy to make out. Then there were other women's names. Maybe a wife or girlfriend. Even a sister."

Hadn't Martin called out for Anna and his mother in the end? "It was hard to shake the feeling we were all caught up in the same kind of hell. They were taking orders just like me, and all because some guy had decided to take what wasn't his. They got caught up defending it, whether they wanted to or not."

"And it was your duty to stop him even though he wasn't the one who'd started it in the first place?"

"Yes," Noah said immediately, and then felt a familiar stab of confusion. "No. I don't know. That's the problem. I can see both sides. Hell, part of me wishes our side hadn't beaten Germany up so badly after World War One. Some say Hitler could never have done what he did if the conditions hadn't been right. But that doesn't matter, does it? What's done is done."

"Yes, it's done," Father said. "Millions of people have died in this war, and some will still die before we beat down the Japanese, God willing. Are we better off after it all? I want to tell myself we stood up to yet another bully in history, and I believe that's true, yet I could name you twenty war widows. Now I have good men I've known since they were born coming back home and going to confession, crying their hearts out as they share the gory details of the things they had to do in war. I'm struggling for answers as much as they are."

Noah wondered if confessing had helped any of the men, or if they continued to be haunted by their memories.

"Back in my old neighborhood," Father continued, "we had a saying about the ends justifying the means. As I grow older, I'm not so sure that's appropriate for every situation. But I'm also not sure that merely loving someone as Christ would will preserve justice and order in the world."

"So you're just as messed up as I am," Noah said before grimacing. "Sorry, Father. I'm not fit for polite company. I've done nothing other than fight for the past few years."

"Yet you managed to make a beautiful young woman like Anna Sims fall in love with you," Father said. "That seems to suggest you haven't lost all your faculties."

"Letters aren't exactly the same as keeping company," Noah said. "She might well change her mind."

"I doubt that," Father Shaughnessy said. "Anna is a good judge of character. So was Martin. From what I can see, you're very good company. You ask good questions. You have strong feelings about the important things. That makes me like you all the more."

He found himself blinking in surprise at the man. "Thank you, Father."

"Please call me Niall," he said. "You're not Catholic, and it must seem weird for you to use that word for a man who isn't your father."

Noah had never called *any* man father, but he refrained from saying so.

"Besides, I have a feeling we might come to be friends. Certainly it's nice for me to quote men like Marcus Aurelius without getting into trouble with the bishop." He laughed. "Some narrow-minded people think we priests should only read Catholic theologians. Again, my father taught us to read everything we could on the topics that interested us."

"What was his profession?"

"He was a history teacher at Loyola University here in Chicago," Father—no, Niall—said.

"He sounds like a good man. I imagine he left a legacy," Noah said.

"He wouldn't have called it that," Niall said. "He only did what he felt was good and right. His passion was helping young people learn more about the world's history and how it impacted their lives and minds today. He wasn't thrilled about me becoming a priest. Thought it would be too restrictive for my mind, but I've managed to navigate the sometimes narrow corridors of the church all right."

"What is your passion then?" Noah asked.

"Serving people in the most joyous and horrible moments of their lives, from a baptism to a death. People say I have the best shoulder to cry on." He waggled his brows. "In case you ever need it."

Noah almost laughed. "I'm good, but thanks."

"So, Noah, what is your passion?"

"I'm hoping to discover it," he said. "I told Anna I started learning things, reading books and the like, when I came across Francis Bacon's saying that knowledge is power. An orphan doesn't have much power."

"And what's up here can never be taken away," Niall said, tapping his temple. "Smart of you to realize that. You can't be persuaded to do something against your own good if you have knowledge. People can make bad choices, but those mostly come from ignorance, malice, or fear. Someone with knowledge learns how to make decisions from a different place, and when coupled with the heart, you can't go wrong."

Noah had never heard a man talk about the heart like that. "You're right, Niall. I have a feeling we are going to be friends."

The man stood. "I'm going to head up to bed and see

if I can sleep a little more before morning Mass. Please feel free to stay as long as you like. As I said last night, think of this place as your home."

As he watched him walk off, Noah sat up straighter in his chair. "Thank you, Niall. For the company."

At the door, Niall turned. "I heard you call out earlier. I came down thinking you might need a friend. Turns out, I needed one too. Thank *you,* Noah."

Noah could only lean back in astonishment as his new friend closed the library door.

Chapter 8

ANNA WAS MAKING COFFEE THE NEXT MORNING WHEN HER mother came into the kitchen.

"Margaret O'Shea is a meddling busybody," she said, her tone filled with angst. "She kept me up all night with her interfering opinions."

Turning around, Anna leaned back against the counter. She searched her mother's pale face. Had her conscience bothered her? "Mrs. O'Shea has been your friend since the day we moved to this neighborhood."

Her mother pulled out a chair and sat down. "My on-and-off friend, to be precise. That woman can push at you something fierce when she has a mind to. She couldn't talk enough about how happy you looked, dancing with your fella. Everyone playing cards was on the edge of their seats, wondering what I was going to say in response. She embarrassed me in front of them."

So this was about embarrassment? "She means well, Mom. They all do, you know. Our friends have had always had our backs. Do you remember how old Mr. Dunne helped you collect Dad's pension after he died? Or how Mrs. Fitzsimmons organized all the food for Martin's wake?"

Her mother placed her elbow on the table and rested her face on her palm. "Yes, I remember all of that, Anna, and it's not that I'm not grateful. But to call me out in my own house. God knows what she's saying elsewhere."

This conversation wasn't raising her hopes. "She's not a gossip, Mom. You know that. Everyone is just worried about you. That's why they've been talking like that." She sat down at the table and held out her hand.

Her mother took it, and Anna had to blink away tears of relief. "If Father Shaughnessy and Margaret are any indication, people are worried indeed. I've never seen so much meddling."

"It's an Irish thing," Anna said. "You know that. We meddle and push at each other out of love. Dad always used to say that. Remember?"

There was an audible sniff. "That man could push like no one's business. I'm not sure I would have married him if he hadn't harangued me into it. Oh, I miss him, Anna. Ever since Martin died, I've wished I could curl up in your father's arms and hear him tell me everything was going to be okay."

Anna couldn't fight the tears streaming down her face. "I miss him too, Mom."

"Then I remind myself I'm glad he isn't with us because he'd have to grieve Martin too," she said, letting go of Anna's hand and rising to pour herself some coffee. "He was a strong man, but I'm not sure he was strong enough to lose a son."

Anna wasn't so sure about that. Her dad had always faced everything head on, but she wasn't going to dispute her mother's opinion. Clearly she'd given it a lot of thought.

Her mother returned to the table and set her coffee down and then crossed again and poured another cup, setting this one in front of Anna. Somehow it felt like a peace offering.

"I watched you from my window last night a couple of times," she said, taking a sip of her coffee. "Margaret was right, although it galls me to admit it. You did look happy."

"I *am* happy, Mom."

Her mother gave a deep sigh and then was silent for a moment. "When I came down to make a plate, I can't tell you how many people told me they were impressed with Noah. Did you know he served with Audie Murphy?"

Anna reached for the milk and added some to her coffee. "I...ah...hadn't put it together until some of the boys mentioned it. Noah doesn't like to talk about the war."

Her mother's face seemed to crumple. "That infernal war... Oh, Martin, my sweet boy."

Anna rose from her chair and put her arm around her mother's shoulders. "Mom, maybe Mrs. O'Shea is right. We do need women like you to welcome our boys home. Who would better understand how precious their lives are?"

Her mother set her cup down so hard it sounded like thunder cracking in the sky. "You aren't a mother. You don't understand. And neither does Margaret, for that matter. Now that I think of it, she wasn't as close to her Paddy as I was to Martin. I wish I'd remembered that last night. I lost sleep for nothing."

Anna dropped her arm from her mother's shoulders, totally deflated. "No, she wasn't, but Paddy was still her son and she mourns him. No different than you."

"How dare you!" her mother said, her face tightening.

Then she slapped Anna's face. Anna gasped in shock, her hand flying up to her stinging cheek.

Her mother stared at her, her blue eyes wide. Anna could only stare back in return, words failing her.

"I'm sorry, Anna," her mother said, "but you went too far. You're wrong. You're all wrong." Tears filled her eyes, and she picked up her coffee and hurried out.

Left alone in the kitchen, Anna started to cry. Her mother had never slapped her before. Sure, she'd paddled her bottom a little here and there when she was growing up, but this...

It took her a few moments to compose herself. She said one Hail Mary and then another, her conversation with her mother replaying in her mind. The hint of hope she'd felt at the beginning had been dashed as surely as wrecking balls destroyed those condemned buildings downtown.

Had she gone too far? No, her mother had been the one to compare her grief to another's, and that was wrong. How could she say Mrs. O'Shea didn't grieve Paddy as much as she grieved Martin? That wasn't fair. But would her mother admit that? No, she *had* to be right, and worse, everyone else had to be wrong. Her dad had always chided her mother for being prideful. She'd reacted by pretending to beam him with the cast-iron frying pan, but her dad had only laughed. It had been their way. Now that he was gone, few people were brave enough to tell her mother to stand down.

She eyed the clock, wondering when Noah was going to come over. She desperately wanted to see him. Feel his arms wrap around her. What her mother had said about her father was true. Her dad had always been able to allay her fears with a hug. When Robert Sims put his arms around you and told you everything was going to be okay, you believed him. When Noah held her, she felt the same way, and that was surely a sign. Then she realized she could go to him. No need to wait. If he wasn't up, she could spend some time in church, praying. Maybe that would help her find some clarity about the situation with her mother.

The stinging on her face reminded her she had to have a red mark on her cheek. Realizing how Noah was likely to react to the mark, she set her coffee aside and started cleaning up what was left of the kitchen.

When she was finished, Anna found a mirror and checked her face. The steam from washing the dishes had dissipated some of her powder. She needed a touch more lipstick too. The mark on her cheek was almost gone, but she dabbed it with extra powder all the same, doing her best to settle her conflicting emotions. There was plenty of time to pray over that later.

The sunshine felt good when she stepped off the front porch and tucked her purse under her arm. She called out to the neighborhood kids she passed, some playing ball and some playing tag. Next summer she hoped to see them riding their bicycles again. All of them had turned in their tires to help the war effort.

When she reached St. Patrick's, she stopped and let a familiar peace settle over her. This was her sanctuary. Some might consider it a bit heretical, but the school and the playground off to the right of the church building were just as sacred to her. They uplifted her spirit in the same way praying in church often did.

"Anna!" she heard a now-familiar voice call out.

"Noah!" she shouted back, turning in his direction.

He was playing catch with little Frankie O'Keefe, one of her former students. How sweet of Noah. She wondered how they'd come to meet. Frankie's mom worked at one of the defense plants, and he was often seen running wild through the neighborhood. Well, except at lunchtime. Father Shaughnessy had invited him to eat at the rectory, wanting to make sure the boy was fed. Of course, the women in the neighborhood also looked out for him, but they had mouths to feed too.

"Hi, Miss Sims," Frankie said. "I'm playing ball with your fella. He's pretty nice. He's got a wicked curve ball though."

She crossed the lawn to where they were standing, fighting the urge to kiss Noah on the cheek. With Frankie there, she was a little embarrassed. "I thought you didn't like baseball," she said to Noah.

"Anyone can throw the ball around," he replied, smiling at her in the sunshine. "I'm glad you came over. I wasn't sure how early I could swing by."

Scanning his face, she could see the fatigue he tried so hard to hide, but there was genuine happiness radiating from him too. She hugged Frankie when he ran to her.

"Thanks for entertaining my fella," she told the boy, tousling his dark curls. "Did Father introduce you two?"

"Nah," Frankie said. "I saw him sitting on the rectory's front steps and recognized him from last night. Asked if he'd throw the ball around with me. I figured he was waiting for you."

"I'm afraid I'm going to have to interrupt your game."

Frankie threw the ball up in the air and caught it. "No problem, Teach. We can play again anytime, Mr. Weatherby. I'm around most days."

Noah inclined his chin. "I'll look for you. Watch out for yourself, Frankie."

The boy thrust out his chin. "Always. I'm a tough guy like you. Okay, gotta go. You two might start necking. Yuck!"

"Frankie O'Keefe! What in the world have you been watching?"

He called out over his shoulder as he ran off, "Picture shows, Teach. See ya."

Anna was chuckling when she met Noah's gaze. "That was nice of you. Frankie's mom—"

"Yeah, he told me," Noah said, lifting her chin up and studying her. "What happened to your face, Anna?"

He could see the mark? The underlying tension in his voice made her wring her hands. "I thought it was gone. I hadn't planned on saying anything."

He only stared at her.

"I don't want you to be upset."

"Who hit you?" he asked, all solider now.

"It wasn't like that," she said. "My mother got mad at something I said and...struck out. It's...not... She doesn't usually do this."

His face bunched up, and he kicked at the ground. "I thought it might have been... I guess I can't knock your mom's block off."

He would want to defend her honor. "I appreciate you rising to the occasion, but no, you can't."

"I don't like being the source of discord between you," Noah said. "Martin wouldn't want that. It weighs on me, Anna."

"Well, it weighs on me too, but I'm not about to let it hurt what's going on between us." She linked their arms. "You're about as perfect as they come, Noah Weatherby."

His face closed up like an old summer house. "No, I'm not."

She wasn't going to argue with him. "Let's sit under my favorite tree in the schoolyard and talk." She gave him a little tug in the right direction, and they started walking. "I assume you had breakfast?"

"Mrs. Hughes is a marvel," he said. "She kept filling my plate. Didn't seem to understand I'm still getting used to something other than K-rations."

Is that why he'd been picking at his food? Why hadn't she realized? "She means well."

"Indeed, she's a good woman," he said. "Did you sleep all right after everyone left?"

"I sure did. You don't seem to have gotten much."

"Sleep and I are...still making friends," he said. "I had a nice talk with Niall though. I wasn't sure about staying at the rectory at first, but now... I'm glad it's worked out that way."

"Niall? Oh, Father Shaughnessy. I almost forgot his first name." And this was interesting. To her knowledge, no one called him Niall except his family members.

"He thought it might be weird for me to call him 'Father,'" Noah explained.

"I see." She wanted to ask him more, but somehow she knew he would tell her if he wanted to. "I'm happy to hear it. Come with me."

When they reached the tree, Noah used his hand to clear a few stray leaves off the bench beneath it and then sat down beside her.

"I've done some of my best thinking under this tree while the kids are at recess," she told him.

"What kind is it?" he asked.

"It's an American Elm," she told him. "In Europe they call them the European Buckthorn. Very common in Chicago. They sprout up just about anywhere. I had the kids do a science project on the kinds of trees in Chicago." Realizing she was blabbing again, she cut herself off. "But you don't need to hear about that."

"I'd listen to you talk about anything, Anna," he said, taking her hand. "Don't you know that yet?"

She leaned her head against his shoulder, letting the breeze wash over her. "I feel that way too. You could talk about changing a tire, and I'd be on the edge of my seat."

"After being restricted to only reading your words... Well, listening to you is like a buffet for the senses. That sounds corny."

"No, it doesn't," she said, tightening her hold. "I like it when you say things like that."

They were quiet then, and a sense of peace filled Anna. Sitting with him, being with him, was so easy. She loved that they didn't always need to talk.

"I need to figure out what I'm going to do with the rest of my life," he said quietly. "I mean, I could be called back in to fight if the war drags on, but I need a plan. I can't spend all my days lolling about."

She lifted her head to look at him, terror pinning her heart to the mat like a prize wrestler. *Please God, don't let him be called back.* "What do you want to do?"

"Something meaningful," he said, gesturing to the sky. "Being a bartender doesn't feel like enough anymore, not that it's not good, honest work. Brian Dougherty was kind enough to offer me a job last night. Said if I didn't like working at his bar, there are plenty more jobs out there. I could take it while I figure things out, but I'm not sure I want to. I don't think I'd slip back into old ways, but...I just want to move forward."

"That was nice of Brian. But it sounds like you don't want it. Why don't you come with me to one of the Army offices downtown? I'm sure someone there can give you more information on that bill for returning soldiers."

She'd read about the Servicemen's Readjustment Act in the papers. President Roosevelt had pledged to help returning soldiers with everything from college loans and job placement to lower interest rates on homes.

"I had the same thought."

"Perhaps they're starting some retraining programs. I've heard it was being considered at the USO last week. We've been planning for our boys coming home. Speaking of which, I've cut back some of my volunteering now that you're back."

"You don't have to," he said.

"I want to," she said. "Besides, I need to prepare for school. We start in late August."

"And that's only a month away. Time flies." He rubbed his face. "Sometimes I forget the war's still going on now that I'm back here. It seems...so far away."

"Do you miss it?"

He was quiet a moment. "No...and yet it doesn't feel right that the other men are fighting when I'm not."

"But you did your part in Europe," she said. Surely he wasn't thinking about volunteering to go to the South Pacific?

"It's still not finished," Noah said. "Sorry, Anna. I've worried you, talking like that, and I didn't mean to. It's only... I heard the broadcast this morning reporting on the war while I ate breakfast. I feel like I should be helping those guys. I...know what they're going through."

She laid her cheek against his shoulder again. "Do you want to go back?" she made herself ask.

"Not especially," he said. "But I would if the war continues. Heck, they could call me back."

"We'll deal with it if we need to." *Oh, please God, don't let it come to that.*

"Makes it hard to plan," he mused.

His body shifted, and she sat up straight, sensing a change in him. "I'm just glad you're here, Noah. I love you."

He traced her cheek. "I love you too, but we should

talk about the future. I imagine you have some ideas about how you want things to go."

Was he referring to marriage? "Well, when two people love each other, they…"

"Form a more permanent attachment," he said, the corners of his mouth tipping up. "I'll be honest. I'd be more comfortable if we waited until the war's over. Until I know I won't be called up again."

"It wouldn't change how I feel," she said in a rush. "Whether we were married or not, I'd still love you and worry about you. I'd still want you to come home to me again."

He looked off, rubbing the bridge of his nose. "I wouldn't want to leave you a pregnant widow. I don't want my child to grow up without a father. I did, and I wouldn't wish it on anyone."

The look in his eyes spoke of a deep hurt. "I understand that, and I appreciate it. How did you end up…at the orphanage? You've never said." And she thought she should know. That it might help her understand him better.

"Well, from what they told me, they think my mother left me on the steps because she'd had me out of wedlock. I was a week or so old. On my shirt, she'd pinned a rough note that said, 'Take care of him for me.' They wondered at the time if she'd come back for me, but she never did."

How awful for both of them. She linked her arm through his. "I'm so sorry. I can't imagine how that must feel."

His shoulder lifted. "You get over it. Like I said, I never knew her. Or my father. Once I became a man, I found I was angrier with *him*. Who puts a woman in that situation and doesn't take care of her? Or the child they made together? I decided I would never be such a coward."

More facets of his personality were making sense. "You're a good man, Noah Weatherby, and it's my honor to love you."

He only leaned against her in response, and they continued to sit in silence for a spell.

"Speaking of love and honor, were we talking about marriage earlier?" she finally decided to ask.

He turned and studied her, his green gaze direct. "We're talking about *plans.* You deserve romance when it comes to the actual asking."

"Okay...but you're saying you don't feel comfortable making long-term plans about us until...the war is completely finished?" She didn't like that answer. What if the war didn't end for another year, or longer?

"Right now, yes." He took her hand, continuing to look into her eyes. "I expect you'd like to live in this neighborhood, right? I mean, you teach here and these are your people."

"I'd hoped to, yes," she said. She'd tried to imagine living somewhere else when he'd told her he was coming home from the war, but she simply couldn't. Still, they would have to find their own place. She couldn't imagine sharing the house with her mother now like she'd hoped they might.

"Let's give it until just before your school starts," Noah said. "You said you go back around August 27, right? Maybe the war will be over by then and... Well, we can...move forward. But I still need to do some more thinking about what I'd like to do. Talk to someone in the Army office like you suggested. I've got some money saved, but that's not going to last forever."

"I have some money too," she said.

The look he gave her made her dig her heels in.

"I *do.*"

"That's good," he said, "but I want to do my part. Take care of you."

Oh, the women's magazines had warned her about this! Why couldn't a woman make money for the family too? She and her mother had always done so.

"Even if Martin hadn't gone to war, I'd still have

wanted to teach. And I get paid for that. Why can't I contribute to our life together?"

"Because the man's supposed to be the provider," he said.

"Noah Weatherby, you'd better consider letting me help with our family. That's all."

His mouth twisted into a sidelong grin as he looked at her. "I like you when you get steamed up."

She gave him a good sock for that. "You are incorrigible."

"Just trying to lighten the mood," he said. "Tiger."

He *would* call her that at a time like this. "At least I know you're staying in Chicago."

He turned toward her, their knees touching. "I'll grow to like the city, I imagine."

Which meant he didn't like it much now. "Well, there's a lot about Chicago that I don't like either. Did you know some of the politicians treat the public schoolteachers quite abominably?"

"Good thing you work in a church school then," he said.

"I've always wanted to work here," she said. "Father wouldn't have had it any other way."

Noah fitted his arm on top of the bench. "So we give it until you go back to school and see where things are. With the war. And with us."

She didn't like him putting it that way. "We're going to be just fine. It's the war I'm worried about."

"My gut tells me it can't go on much longer," Noah said. "I'm more cut up about your mother. Especially after seeing how she treated you today. Her grief isn't an excuse to abuse you."

Her hand lifted to touch her cheek for a brief moment before she realized it. There would be a bruise there, but it would be nothing compared to the pain in her heart.

"My mother will come around." Margaret O'Shea had broken through her wall, if only for a night. That meant it could happen again. "When I think about it now actually, I wonder if maybe there's a silver lining to this whole situation."

"Usually I love it when you talk about silver linings," he said. "You helped me see more than a few when I was over there."

She was glad to know how much she'd helped him. He'd certainly helped her on dark nights when she was grieving Martin and felt so alone in her room.

"There's only one problem with finding a silver lining in the clouds..." he began.

She turned to look at him.

"You have to get through the storm first."

Chapter 9

NOAH FELT LIKE HE WAS IN THE MIDST OF ONE OF THOSE storms he'd talked about with Anna yesterday. Her mother had invited him over to dinner as a peace offering, but he wasn't overly hopeful given that it had only happened because she'd slapped her own daughter. She shouldn't have taken a hand to Anna in the first place.

But Anna wasn't his Tiger for nothing. She was out to get her way, and she had set about it with the strength and heart he so admired.

"Can I pour you some more tea, Mrs. Sims?" Noah asked, sitting tall in his chair.

At the head of the table, Mrs. Sims was a dark force in the room, one even the small chandelier above them in the formal dining room couldn't fully illuminate. Her black mourning weeds seemed to absorb all the light.

Anna cut another piece of the roast chicken, but didn't put it in her mouth. It was like she was waiting to see if the woman would accept a simple kindness from him. She'd all but bristled when he'd pulled her chair out for her earlier.

"Yes, thank you," she said after a tense moment. "Anna tells me you're an orphan."

He and Anna shared a look before she said, "Mother, Martin wrote you about that."

"Oh, I forget," she said, reaching for the tea he'd carefully poured.

He didn't need the woman yelling at him for staining her white tablecloth.

"Yes, Mrs. Sims. I am. Made the best out of it." Older people liked hearing about young people learning lessons and the like, and he wasn't above using it to his advantage. Anything to soften her toward him.

"So you don't know who your people are," she said.

This sounded like a loaded comment. "No," he said. "You and Anna are very lucky to know your roots."

She merely harrumphed in response.

The conversation was dragging, and everyone knew it. Noah was out of ideas. Hell, he'd even resorted to mentioning the weather.

Anna forced a smile. "How has work been, Mom? You don't say much these days."

"Pretty much the same as always," she said, spooning up the English peas Anna had served with the chicken.

Noah studied the woman. In her face, he could see where Martin and Anna had gotten some of their features. They'd both inherited her blue eyes and strong chin, and Anna's hair was a similar shade of red, though Mrs. Sims' hair was faded and speckled with gray. In some ways, she was like her hair. Gray. Lackluster. He couldn't fathom this woman was the one Martin had talked about. The one who had danced in the kitchen with her children while making blueberry pie. Even her letters to her son had been more interesting than this conversation.

"Anna mentioned you're in a Victory Knitting group," Noah said, scratching his head. "I didn't even know about those. I'm sure there are a lot of soldiers grateful for the socks and scarves you've made them."

"Oh, yes," Anna said. "Noah often wrote me about how cold it was over there."

He could still feel the cold in his bones some nights when he woke up from a nightmare.

"It angered me how it was next to impossible to send

a care package to my own son as the war dragged on," Mrs. Sims said, cutting another piece of chicken. "A mother should be able to send something to keep her child warm."

Suddenly it felt like they were sitting on top of an underground bunker filled with bombs. "I'm sure all of the boys over there wish it could have been that way, Mrs. Sims. But your letters...and prayers were enough for Martin. He often spoke of how much they meant to him."

Her blue gaze fixed on him, and in those eyes, he saw a wild fire. Suddenly the air was electric, and he knew what was coming next.

"My prayers clearly weren't enough or my boy would be sitting at this table with us," she said.

Anna lowered her head, and he wanted to nudge her foot to rally her. This wasn't the time to stand down. Plus, this had been her idea. He was almost angry with her for abandoning the conversation.

"Some things are out of our hands," he simply said. "Even though I wish it were otherwise."

Mrs. Sims pushed her plate aside, skewering him with her gaze. "Tell me how my son died, Mr. Weatherby."

His chest tightened. Not now. Not this. He wasn't ready. "I'd rather not spoil our dinner," he said. "Let's do it another time."

"No one is eating much as it is," she said, leaning her elbows on the table like she was about to get down to business. "I want to know. The Army doesn't tell you anything. I asked Anna to write you—"

"Mother, I told you I wasn't going to ask about that in a letter," she said, her head jerking up.

Her voice had risen at the end. If Noah hadn't been sitting across from her, he would have reached for her hand.

"You're getting worked up, Anna," Mrs. Sims said. "Noah, I want to know about my boy's final moments."

It was the first time she'd used his given name, and it didn't escape anyone. Anna looked at him, her gaze beseeching. She wanted to know too. She'd already told him so, though she hadn't pressed the issue.

He gripped his knees. Mrs. Sims would never want to see him again. And what about Anna? He studied her. She looked so pretty in her baby blue dress with her hair pulled back in that V-roll. Would this change how she felt?

"Noah, I'm waiting," Mrs. Sims said.

Her tone reminded him of one of the strict disciplinarians at the orphanage. She'd used a ruler on him repeatedly, saying she needed to correct the wickedness in his blood. His palms grew sweaty. He could feel the impending punishment in the air.

"We were on patrol," he said, the vision of the steep stretch of land coming to mind. "There wasn't a lot of cover, so we were hauling..."

He stopped himself before he could say *ass*.

"We were moving fast, the four of us," he said. "Martin and I were paired together like usual. He was in the lead and I was pulling up the rear."

He watched, perplexed, as the plates on the table moved, only to realize Anna must have grabbed onto the tablecloth. Her hands were in her lap, but there was tension in her arms.

He waited a moment to see if she'd stop him, but she didn't. She wanted to hear this as much as Mrs. Sims. He made himself keep going.

"It was rocky terrain, but we'd gotten used to it," he said. "I was right on his tail, ducking down as best as I could, when we started climbing the hill. Henry and David were flanking the other side, and they made it to the top first." He could still see them stretched out on their bellies, crab-crawling along the ground. "They signaled to us, and we both acknowledged it. I thought we might be in the clear, but then Martin swung around and shoved me. I fell, and then I...heard the shot."

That first one seemed to have sliced through the air. It wasn't a sound Noah would ever forget.

"Martin must have seen something. A flash. A movement." He would never know. "I didn't, and I'll regret that my whole life."

He'd watched, helplessly, as the sniper's bullet struck his friend square in the chest. And then another one plugged him in the shoulder as he went down.

"Finish the story, boy," Mrs. Sims said, her mouth a hard line, her eyes filled with pain.

He looked over at Anna. Tears were streaming down her face. He gripped his knees harder, wanting to tear the kneecaps off. Tear something. Anything.

"He was hit. More than once. When he fell, I rolled us a few yards away, hoping to move us out of range." A couple shots had landed near his feet, spraying dirt into the air. "Then I heard answering gunfire from Henry and David. They took out the sniper."

Sweat dripped into his eyes. His mouth was dry, and he reached for his soda only to realize his hands were shaking so hard he couldn't pick up the glass. He shoved them under the table and clutched his knees again.

"And Martin," Mrs. Sims said. "Tell me what he said."

He'd already written to Anna that Martin's last words had been for her and Mrs. Sims. Since then, he'd forced the memory from his mind, but he discovered it had been sitting beneath the surface all along.

"The wound in his chest was bleeding profusely." Gushing. But he couldn't say that. He'd shucked off his shirt and pressed on it, causing Martin to cry out. Panic had gripped him, and he'd met his friend's eyes.

"Guess my time's up."

"No! You hang on. Dammit, Martin! You hang on."

"Take care of my mom and sister. Like we discussed."

"Stop talking like this. You're gonna make it if I have to carry you out of here on my back."

His friend coughed up blood, and Noah's muscles froze.

"Give me my handkerchief," Martin said.

Noah rummaged in his friend's shirt pocket for it. The cloth was soaked with blood, but he stuffed it into Martin's limp hand. Noah had seen men's energy leave them in the final moments before death, and he added more pressure to the wound, desperate to stop the bleeding.

"Send home my medal," Martin rasped. "Not lucky. You ask for Anna's. Hers will be."

"Save your strength."

"No...have to tell you. Thank you. For being my brother."

He coughed again, and Noah sat on the hard terrain next to him and took his hand.

"You're the best brother any guy could have," he said.

"You make it home for me, Weatherby. Or I'll haunt your ass."

His body shook with the coughing, and Noah lifted his torso until he was cradled in his lap, wishing he could pour strength into him.

"Tell my mom and Anna I love them. Dammit!"

Then his whole body had gone lax, and Noah had curled over him. It wasn't fair! It wasn't right!

"Mr. Weatherby," someone called. "Noah!"

He blinked, and Mrs. Sims came into focus. Anna was crying softly, her hand over her mouth.

"Then what?" she asked, grabbing his forearm and squeezing.

He wanted to throw off her hand and storm out. He wanted to never, ever think about that day again.

"Noah," Anna whispered, her hand falling to the table. "*Please.*"

Inhaling deeply, he blew his breath out slowly. "I couldn't stop the bleeding. Fighting and such...you get pretty good at knowing when a wound is fatal. I would have carried him back right away! I told him so!"

He realized he was getting carried away and clenched his eyes shut.

"I know you would have," Anna said softly.

Her voice made him bite his lip. He didn't want to cry. It wouldn't do any good, and it would only embarrass him.

"He wanted your handkerchief, Mrs. Sims," he said, making himself look at her. "He told me to look after you and Anna like we've discussed. I told him I would."

He turned his head and met Anna's gaze. Love and understanding shone there, and it boosted his courage.

"What else?" Mrs. Sims asked. "Finish it, boy."

Her harsh tone bespoke of her pain, and it was like a lash against his skin. "He said he loved you both. And then he..."

He couldn't make himself tell them the rest. How he'd been crying over Martin's body when Henry and David finally made it to their position. How he'd refused to let them carry Martin back, insisting that was his brother lying there and he'd do it himself.

He didn't remember getting back to camp. Only remembered the other guys taking Martin away, saying they'd take care of him. Later, he'd found the body and found the handkerchief still clutched in his friend's hand.

Anna reached for her mom's hand and they clasped each other tightly for a moment. Her mother's whole body seemed to lean forward, as if her bones and sinew couldn't support her any longer. Then she used her other hand to push herself up. Her chair scraped on the hardwood floor as she rose.

"So my son saved your life," she said, her eyes red-rimmed and almost frightening in their intensity. "You're alive because of him."

"Yes," Noah said. "He was one of the bravest men I've ever known."

"Thank you for telling me," Mrs. Sims said. "If you'll excuse me."

Anna's hand remained palm-up on the table as her mother extricated herself and left the room stiffly. Her half-full plate looked like an accusation.

Silence hung in the room for a moment.

"Do you hate me?" he finally asked Anna.

Her face crumbled. "Because Martin gave his life for you? Of course not! It makes me realize even more how much he loved you."

A sob escaped his mouth, and he stood quickly. "Excuse me."

He walked to the front door and took off swiftly down the street.

Chapter 10

ANNA WATCHED IN DISBELIEF AS NOAH LEFT THE ROOM.
Tears coursed down her face, and she realized maybe it was best they all found their separate corners to let their grief out. Surely it couldn't have been easy for Noah to tell that story.

"Oh, Marty," she whispered, pushing her plate aside and laying her head on the table. "You wonderful man."

As she cried, images of her brother flashed through her mind. Martin at eight, challenging one of the older O'Hara boys who'd pulled her hair at school. The boys had ended up fighting, rolling around in the alley, but Martin had won in the end, straddling the boy and powing him in the kisser until he cried uncle. Martin at sixteen, challenging the boy who'd forced a kiss on Katherine Kenna behind the bleachers at a school football match. He'd stepped between them and taken a hit in the jaw before squaring off with the bully and winning the fight.

It struck her that he'd always fought for those he loved. It must have been second nature for him to push Noah aside.

Poor Noah. As he spoke, his frame had gone stiff and his gaze had lost focus. Part of her had wanted to wrap her arms around him and tell him he didn't have to go on. But she'd needed to hear it.

Did Noah feel extra guilt for Martin saving his life? His abrupt departure certainly pointed to it. It occurred to her that he might also still be grieving Martin. She couldn't imagine he'd had much time to...

What was a good word for it?

Take inventory of his soul, she decided. He'd done so on and off in his letters to her, but never about Martin. Never about the other boys from his unit who had died.

She hadn't missed the mention of Henry. If she remembered the timeline of their correspondence right, he'd died shortly after Martin. And Noah hadn't mentioned David before. Had he died as well?

Rising from her chair, she swiped at her face. Her make-up would be ruined by her tears, she imagined. There was a keening sound then, almost like it was from a wounded animal. But Anna knew it was no animal. Her mother's grief had finally opened up in the face of Noah's story.

She walked to the foot of the stairs, wondering if she should go to her. Her mother hadn't cried in front of Anna since they received the news of Martin's death. Not even at his funeral.

Another keening sound echoed through the house, and Anna could stand it no longer. She took the stairs quickly and walked to her mother's door. It was locked.

"Mom," she said, hearing the sobbing more clearly now. "Oh, Mom. Please let me in."

The crying ceased. "No! Leave me be."

She stood there for a moment, her hand touching the door. She'd hoped this dinner would produce a miracle. Right now, she didn't know what it had done other than dredge up her mother's grief.

Though maybe that was a good thing. Father was always saying a good cry wasn't anything to be ashamed of.

Maybe he'd tell Noah the same thing the next time she saw him. Should she go to him now? It wasn't much past eight o'clock, and dusk had not yet given way to darkness.

Of course she should, she realized. They were both hurting.

She popped into her room and fixed her face as best as she could before heading out. The night was on the warm side, and she tried to find some joy in the fireflies she saw dancing in the yards of her neighbors as she walked to the rectory.

When she arrived, Father Shaughnessy opened the door. "Anna! It's good to see you. Please come in."

She knew he had long days, what with doing the morning Mass. "I don't want to intrude. I was looking for Noah."

His brows winged up. "As far as I know, he's not here. I can see the stairs from the library, so I can't imagine he got past me. But let me check. Come inside, lass. The mosquitoes will make a feast of you."

She gave in and stepped inside the entryway. "Thank you, Father."

This was the only problem with Noah staying at the rectory, she realized. She hated to intrude on the priest's personal time. Father returned quickly.

"He's not here," he said, his eyes studying her face. "Anything happen?"

"No," she said. "Yes. He told us the details...about how Martin died."

Father Shaughnessy's hand fell onto her shoulder. "I see. I can't imagine how hard that must have been. For all of you."

"He died a hero, Father," she whispered. "He pushed Noah aside and..."

"Here now," Father said, taking her into his arms. "You just cry it out."

She buried her face against his shoulder and gave in. At one point, he pressed a handkerchief into her hands, and that only made her cry harder. Now she realized why Noah had kept the handkerchief for so long rather than leaving it to be sent home with Martin's things. She imagined it had been bloody, and he wouldn't have wanted them to see it that way. That dear man...

When the storm had subsided, she blew her nose. "I'm so sorry, Father."

He shook her a little, his arm still around her. "Please. You've cried on this broad shoulder of mine a time or two. Most everyone in the neighborhood has. It's one of my duties."

She couldn't see anyone crying on Father Wilson's shoulder, but refrained from saying so. "Thank you. I feel much better. My mom was crying when I left. I hope it will help her feel better too."

"So she heard the story," Father said, shaking his head. "Couldn't have been easy for Mary."

"No," Anna said. "It wouldn't be easy for anyone. I should try and find Noah."

Father's mouth twisted like it did when he was thinking. "We'll look for him together. If I were new to the neighborhood and looking for a private place to grieve, I'd go to the church. We'll check there first."

Could he be right? Noah wasn't religious, so she hadn't considered it. "I hadn't thought of it."

"It's worth a shot," Father said. "Now, I doubt he went to the area where we keep the bees, even though it is sheltered. Any grieving would risk stirring them up. Of course, I do sing to them."

"Father, you are so Irish," she said, surprised to find herself smiling.

"Don't make fun," he chided as they walked out of the rectory. "My grandmother from County Clare used to sing to her roses, and they did quite well, so why not bees? Of course, she believed in the fairies too, but we American Irish don't talk about that as much."

In the lamplight she could see his wink, and her heart lifted in response. When they walked into the church, she dabbed her fingers in the holy water receptacle and made the sign of the cross. Father did the same next to her. He nudged her.

"Noah is in the back," Father whispered. "Right side."

She spotted him easily. "I see him. Thank you for your help, Father."

"Don't worry," he said. "You talk to him now, and if he comes down to the library again, I'll be the second line. We need good men in the world like him, Anna. You go to him now."

Kissing his cheek, she gave him a smile. "You're one of the good ones too."

"Oh, stop, lass," he said, "or you'll have me blushing in my own church."

He patted her on the back and then left. Anna noted there were other people praying, some in the front pews and others scattered in the middle and back. Some were even on kneelers in front of the altar or the holy statues flanking it. The statue of Mary holding the baby Jesus was always a popular area for mothers, no surprise.

Anna treaded softly as she crossed to where Noah was sitting. From the way he was hunched over, he looked like he felt the weight of the world. She'd never seen him like that.

She genuflected at his pew and squeezed into the small space beside him. His head immediately swung in her direction.

"Anna!" he said in a harsh whisper.

His green eyes were red, and she knew he'd been crying. "I'm glad I found you."

"I needed...a place to sit with my thoughts. I couldn't find anywhere else to go, so I stopped in here. When I saw the others, I thought it would be okay for me to stay awhile. Even though I'm not Catholic."

"Of course it is," she whispered back, knowing that Father Shaughnessy, at least, agreed with her. "Will you come outside with me, though? I don't want to interrupt people's praying. Unless you want to sit more. I can pray awhile."

He shook his head. "No, let's go. I'm...better now."

They walked to the front of the church, and he waited while she blessed herself with holy water again. On the front steps, she took his hand. He grasped it and then lifted it to his mouth, kissing it.

"I'm sorry I ran out that way," he said. "I—"

"You don't have to apologize," she told him. "It couldn't have been easy to tell us what you did."

"It couldn't have been easy for you to hear it," he said. "I realized that after I settled down a bit. It was self-ish of me to run off. I should have...held you...or some-thing."

She tugged him off the sidewalk and out of the light from the lampposts, grateful darkness had descended so rapidly. "You can hold me now."

His arms came around her. Gently. She rested her head against his chest, listening to his heart.

"I was afraid to tell you the whole story," he whispered. "That's why I didn't say anything in my letters. Not that it's the kind of thing a person *should* write in a letter, but you know what I mean."

"I do," she said, caressing the tight muscles in his back. "Noah, you didn't have to be afraid."

"Martin took the bullet meant for me," he said. "Before Henry died, he got in my face pretty good. He told me I needed to stop dwelling on that because I could still take a bullet anytime. We all could. He died the next day, and it took me weeks to shake that last conversation with him."

So she'd been right about the timeline of Henry's death. "I'm so sorry, but he's right. Martin did what he did in that moment because that's who he was. You would have done the same for him."

"Henry said that too," Noah whispered, pressing his face into her neck. "We all would have. It's what you do for the guys you fight with."

Again, she could feel nothing except admiration for him and for the rest of the boys fighting over there. "Oh,

Noah, you all did the best you could. Under horrible conditions. Don't beat yourself up about it. Martin wouldn't want that."

He edged back. "I must have broken your mother's heart tonight. Did I make things worse?"

She thought of the keening sounds coming from her mother's room. And her refusal to let Anna in. "Honestly, I don't know. Maybe it will help her find the end of her grief, if there is such a thing."

His arms pulled her against him again. "I wish I could have given your brother back to you. Anna, I feel like I failed."

"You didn't fail. Martin died, and it's horrible. But so have thousands of other good men."

"I miss him," Noah whispered. "When I was fighting, I didn't have a lot of time to think about it, but being here...with you...and where he grew up... I keep wishing I'll see him walking on the street in front of your house or playing ball with some kids in the yard."

"He loved playing ball with the younger boys," she said, clutching his uniform. "We're going to miss him for a long while, I expect, but he'd want you to stop feeling guilty. I know that in my heart, Noah. He'd want you to live a full life and be happy. With me..."

Noah leaned back and touched her cheek. "I didn't tell you before, but I started falling for you before we wrote to each other. I looked forward to your letters to Martin as much as he did. That's why he started reading them to me. I think he knew I liked you."

So her brother had been a matchmaker—even while fighting in the war. "He was the best."

"Yes, he was," Noah said.

"Now it's our duty to honor him by going on and making the most of this life we've been given. Noah, you've said this is your second chance. I've already told you it's mine too. And as I stand here on the church grounds, I promise you I'm going to make the best of it. Will you join me?"

She stepped away and held out her hand, the first rays of the moon a silver light on her skin. Noah clasped it and brought it to his heart.

"You have my word I will."

And he sealed that oath with a kiss.

Chapter 11

NOAH SURVEYED THE CROWD DANCING A JITTERBUG TO AN old Count Basie favorite. Soldiers in uniforms were locked in step with girls in bright dresses. This was where Anna had been volunteering? Seeing the twelve-story USO in downtown Chicago had shocked him beyond belief. For some reason he couldn't move past the...glitter of it all. That was the word for it. There was a bowling alley, for Pete's sake. He'd imagined it so differently. He'd thought the USO would be more like a tiny dance hall with a fold-out table in the corner holding a punch bowl. He knew this place was designed to maintain morale like the others he'd seen with Anna, but did no one remember the war was still going on?

"You've been frowning since we first arrived," Anna said, coming up beside him.

She'd asked him if he'd wanted to dance a while ago, but he couldn't make his feet move. Not here. Not like this.

"I've never been much for this kind of party," he replied, not wanting to hurt her feelings. He respected her part in the war effort.

"Do you want to leave? I could ask Mrs. Allen about heading out early. She's glad you're home and safe.

Thinks you're quite a catch, by the way."

Margaret Allen was a gracious woman, and from what Anna said, she'd done a superior job as the USO Mama.

"I don't want to interfere with your service," he said, fighting the urge to shake his head in disgust as a soldier toppled to the ground, clearly inebriated from something other than the fruit punch the USO served. Another soldier was clearly interested in more than dancing. Anna had written him about needing to fend off cheeky officers, but seeing it first-hand raised his protective instincts.

"Alice says you don't approve of all this," Anna said, stepping in front of him and looking into his face as if searching for confirmation. "It's like the officer's club on the lake that we saw, isn't it?"

"Not my cup of tea," he said. "I didn't mind getting a drink with the guys every now and again, but I was never into carousing."

Not that they'd had much time for it. Sure, some of the guys had sought out whores, but Noah had never joined them.

"I'm going to talk to Mama about leaving early," she said, rising up and kissing him on the cheek. "It's a nice night out. We could take a walk."

He nodded, looking forward to the fresh air. The smoke was thick, and the war talk unwelcome. Alice, Anna's friend, had let it slip about him serving with Audie Murphy, and boy, hadn't a few of the privates almost lost their shit. He'd been quick to walk away from those conversations.

Talking about Martin had brought back a lot of memories, and it had made him feel more than he'd bargained for. Hell, it was the first time he'd ever sought solace in a church. If he could have found another quiet, secluded place in the neighborhood, he would have, but the church had seemed like his best option. Thank God Anna had found him. Their talk had made them both feel so much better. Whether her mother felt better was still a mystery. She'd barely said three words to him since their dinner a couple nights ago.

That was fine with him. It had given him an excuse to take Anna on a field trip to the library. They'd done some reading about possible careers for him. Though he hadn't come to any decisions, he'd narrowed the field a little. When Anna had suggested the possibility of a medical career, he'd immediately gone queasy. He'd seen enough guys' guts to know he didn't have the stomach for it. She hadn't liked his pun, and truthfully, he couldn't blame her.

A private appeared beside him and pointed to the dance floor. "That dame over there said you just got back from Europe. Are you planning on joining our guys in the Pacific? Me, I'm still thinking about it. Don't much like standing around and dancing while those guys are fighting the Japs."

Noah shifted his weight until he was facing the soldier. "I feel the same way. I'm giving it until the end of August."

"That's a sound plan," the guy said. "I'm Garrett, by the way."

He liked the informality of his introduction. "Noah," he said, and they shook hands. "Let me ask you something since you alluded to standing around. Does all of this...fluff bother you?"

The guy gave a single shake of his head. "You bet. I'm only here because my buddies wanted to come, and truth be told, everything is free."

Noah took in the crispness of Garrett's uniform. The man might be a private, but he conducted himself with respect. "I might not be popular for saying this, but it seems kinda immoral to me, partying like this when others are off fighting."

Garrett slapped him on the back the same way some of his buddies in the unit used to do. God, he missed them.

"Here's how I see it," Garrett said. "These guys have probably seen the same kind of action as we did. They just happen to be the kind of people who were raised on that Bible verse. You know the one. Let me see. 'Let us eat and drink, for tomorrow we die.' It's in Corinthians or one of those epistles."

"You Catholic?" Noah asked.

"Isn't everyone in Chicago?" Garrett joked. "Wait, you're not from the Windy City?"

"No, but my girl is." He scanned the room for her, but she was still off on her mission. "Private Garrett, you've given me a lot to think about. I appreciate it."

He slapped Noah on the back again. "Who me? Sergeant, you're breaking my heart. Good luck with the girl. Maybe I'll see you in the Pacific."

As Noah watched him walk away, he had to contain his thoughts. God, he hoped not. For both their sakes.

When a few other soldiers offered him a cigarette and tried to engage him in speculation about the war in the Pacific, he politely excused himself. What was the point of talking about it? No one knew anything solid. The radio broadcasts were useless, and Noah felt increasingly frustrated.

"Anna says you two are leaving," Alice said. He'd been so caught up in his thoughts he hadn't noticed her walking toward him.

"Seems so," he murmured. "Anna mentioned the guys here get fresh with you sometimes. I know you take care of each other, but if someone makes you uncomfortable, you let Anna know. I'll take care of him."

The brown curl on her forehead bobbed when she laughed. "Oh, I like you even if you don't approve of what we're doing here. I have since Martin started writing Anna about you."

"Thank you, I think," he replied. "As for the dis-approval, you have a private to thank for helping me see all of this"—he gestured to the elaborate party—

"in a different light. I still don't like it, but...perhaps I'm too set in my ways."

Truth was, before Garrett had set him straight, he hadn't seen these revelers in wrinkled uniforms as soldiers. He hadn't imagined them fighting the Jerries like he had. The realization that he'd misjudged the situation, at least partially, made him feel small.

"Don't take this the wrong way, but you're kind of an egghead, aren't you?"

She had her head tilted to the side like she was trying to see inside his skull.

"I'll take that as a compliment, I guess, since most of my schooling came from books and not an official classroom." The orphanage had been rather lax in that department, focusing more on discipline, hygiene, and keeping them occupied with woodworking and other projects.

"Another reason you should marry a schoolteacher," Alice said.

He didn't like to share his business, but she was Anna's friend. "We're talking about it."

She leveled him a look. *Talking!* That's what Anna keeps saying. Who has time to talk? Did the war teach you nothing, solider?"

He stood taller in his uniform. "Excuse me?"

She was bold, but it was little wonder—she was Anna's friend, plus she'd chosen to work at a defense plant to help the war effort.

"Oh, don't pull that with me," she said. "I know it's none of my business, but this war has taught me there are more important things in life than being polite. You really should marry that girl. And I mean, right away. There's a war still going on. Who knows where we'll all be tomorrow? If the Japs can invade Pearl Harbor, who's to say they can't get to Chicago?"

Noah thought of Garrett's biblical quote. "You should meet Private Garrett."

"Huh?" she asked.

He couldn't find the private when he looked around the room for him. "Never mind. So you think I should marry Anna? Right away?"

"Yes," she said, smiling at a soldier as he gave her a saucy wink on his way past them. "She's solid with a heart of gold. You aren't going to find better, trust me."

"I know that," he said simply, wishing Anna would return. Her friend was a little intense for him.

"Seems some boys can't wait to get hitched, hoping it's going to save them from dying. Some do it because it's the only way they can taste the goods, if you know what I mean."

He stared at her. Had she really said that out loud? And to a man?

"Some do it because they want to leave something behind, even if it's a widow. Or a child. You're a different egg altogether, and I find myself liking you more because of it, even if you are way overthinking this."

"I believe you already called me an egghead."

The orchestra switched to something slower, and the couples closed in, many of them dancing cheek to cheek. Noah wondered if Anna had danced like that with any of the soldiers who'd frequented the USO.

"There's more than one kind of egg," Alice pressed, fitting her hands on her hips. "Aren't you going to ask me what other kind of egg you are? You're an honorable egg. Even if you are too much of one."

"I didn't realize that was possible," he said, steering her out of the way of a couple who was weaving toward them, so in tune with each other their radar was gone. "You're either honorable or you aren't."

"Like I said, you're thinking too much," Alice said. "Anna mentioned you're still trying to decide what to do with yourself. Anything wrong with going back to bartending? My dad owns a bar on the North Side. I could ask if he could use an extra bartender even though it's a bit far from where you're staying."

"That's a nice offer," he said, "but I'm just back from

the war. I want to give myself some time to make sure I'm moving in the right direction."

He'd met with the Army representative, who'd walked him through the provisions of the Servicemen's Readjustment Act. If he went back to school, the government would cover it, with certain limitations. The sergeant he'd spoken with had also offered him to help find a job once he had more direction.

There was another aspect of the Readjustment Act that had piqued his interest—he was guaranteed a loan and discounted mortgage rate on a new home. Even though he hadn't asked Anna to marry him yet, he'd been thinking about their life together. They would need to find somewhere to live. It wasn't like they could live with her mother. Even if she were more amiable, he wanted privacy for them. Right now, he wasn't sure he could afford a place in her current neighborhood, and he didn't like the thought of making Anna move too far. She was one of them, and her job was right there. Didn't seem fair.

"What direction are you considering?" Alice asked, proving she was as nosy as she was bold.

He wasn't a man who shared his musings lightly. Even Niall had left him to his thoughts, only offering him a college pamphlet. Of course, his new friend had joked about him becoming a priest and given a good belly laugh, saying he'd get into more trouble with the bishop than Niall did. Noah had joined in, and it had felt good to be so light-hearted.

"I imagine Anna will share that information with you when she knows it," he simply responded.

"You're like an onion," she said. "But I'm patient when it comes to peeling them."

He'd never liked onions much. He also couldn't see Alice being very patient. She'd likely cut the onion in half and mince the hell out of it. "Good to know."

"Anna's coming back, so I'll leave you with this." She poked him in the chest. "Marry that girl. She's over the moon about you and clearly you feel the same. Now that I've seen you, I'm completely certain you were made for each other."

Did this woman ever stop talking? The Jerries might have surrendered early just to shut her up.

"You might ask yourself if Martin would want you to be this honorable."

A chill touched his spine at the mention of his friend's name. Even though he'd shared the details of his death with Anna and her mother, he'd never thought about what Martin would want him to do beyond looking after his family. Would he want Noah and Anna to marry? Would he approve?

Martin had known he liked Anna, sure, but marriage was different. It was forever. This was something to think on. Then he caught Alice's look and almost grimaced. He could hear her thinking, *egghead.*

"You two look like you're having a serious conversation," Anna said, worry pinching the corners of her beautiful eyes.

He took her hand to reassure her. "Alice was only shooting the breeze with me. Can you go?"

Leaving held even more allure now. The onion peeler might take her knife to him a little more if they stayed.

"Mama said sure, since my fella is back," she said, squeezing his hand. "You'll have to hold down the fort for me, Alice."

"Have fun you two," she said, "and Noah, you remember what I told you."

He fought back a retort. The woman didn't mince words, something he usually appreciated, but not about something so personal. Still, he'd think on what she'd said about Martin.

Anna and Alice hugged each other fiercely, and he nearly jumped when Alice popped forward and pecked his jaw. She was a touch on the short side, so she'd practically had to launch herself at him to reach his face. He'd almost grabbed her arms in a hold before stopping himself.

"Bye, Noah," she said with a mischievous grin as if she'd enjoyed riling him up.

When he and Anna emerged on the street, the summer breeze was still warm on his skin. Anna took his hand again and led him off to the right.

"How about we get the car and go to this spot I know by the lake?"

If it involved some serious parking, he was all for it. He didn't feel right kissing her the way he really wanted to in her own home, what with her mother sitting upstairs in disapproval. The park beside the school was too public, and the rectory library where Father had told him to invite Anna...

He might not be Catholic, but he wouldn't dare make those kind of moves with priests around. Given everything Niall was doing for him, it wouldn't feel right. Of course, they could probably neck in front of Father Wilson's nose without *him* noticing. Niall was right. The man didn't do anything other than pray and go to his room. Although he occasionally ate with them, he never joined Noah and Niall in the library, where they often found themselves most nights, unable to sleep. Noah still didn't know what kept Niall awake at night, but he figured the man would tell him if he wanted it known.

"That sounds like a great idea," he said, his spirits lifting.

The park Anna had in mind was nicely lit and had a path along the water. And yet...something about the lapping of the water pressed in on him. He tried to fight the memory trying to surface, but it broke through as though powered by a Nazi tank.

His mind called up an image of another body of water. He and his fellow soldiers had come upon it and needed to cross it. Lifting their weapons in the air with both hands, they'd levered into the water only to halt in horror as dead bodies weighed down by stones brushed against them. Later someone had said it was a sick Nazi idea of messing with them in addition to ruining the water for drinking.

A woman's decomposing face had appeared in the shadowy water beneath Noah, and he'd nearly gotten sick then and there. He'd never seen anything so bloated or deformed. He and the other men had shuffled back to shore, breathing hard, some puking outright. They'd gone upriver to make their crossing, and taking those first steps into the water had been as hard as going through the first door in a farmhouse commandeered by Nazis.

"What's wrong?" he heard Anna ask. He jerked away when something brushed his arm, remembering that floating corpse's outstretched hand.

"*Noah?*"

He bit his lip to bring himself back to the present and realized he'd stopped walking. Sweat coated his temples and his back, and his heart thundered like machine gun fire. He focused on her face. Anna was watching him, the muscles in her face tense.

"I...need a minute," he said, stepping off the path away from the water.

Bending over and fighting for breath would only scare her, so he closed his eyes and put a hand over his chest, focusing on forcing more air into his lungs. God knew he'd had to do it during the war whenever the horror of something had risen up and ripped his throat out. The first dead child he'd seen, a young boy of four shot in the head, had nearly brought him to his knees, and the first woman he'd come across who had been raped and left for dead... Well, he understood killing men in uniform, but he didn't understand killing women and children like that. Some acts were simply evil.

He felt Anna come closer. "Keep your distance. *Please.*"

"Is there anything I can do?" she asked softly.

Shaking his head, he continued to suck in great big gulps air. He wouldn't speak to her again until he felt like he'd latched on to some ribbon of control inside him. Before the war, his self-control had been like a tower, large and unassailable. Not anymore.

"I'm sorry," he finally said, taking out a handkerchief and wiping his sweaty face. "I..." He didn't know what to say, but he wasn't going to run out on her this time. He would grind his teeth to the gums if he had to.

She didn't move toward him, thank God. Then he wondered if she was afraid of him. The thought just about broke his heart. "I...hate this. I'm sorry. I'm...so ashamed."

"It's okay, Noah," she said. "A flashback?"

His nod was crisp.

"Can you tell me?" she asked.

He had to look away from the hope in her eyes. He wasn't sure he could have forced out the words had he wanted to. "It's come and gone. Let's leave it that way. I'd...like to say I can keep walking out here, but I can't." It made him feel like a coward, but he'd feel worse—weaker—if he had another attack.

"Okay," she said. "Let's head back to the car."

They walked in silence, side by side although no longer hand in hand. He mourned the loss of her hand but couldn't make himself reach for it. His hands were still sweaty, and he probably reeked in his uniform. Plus, he'd made her uncomfortable, and he'd ruined the romantic walk she'd had in mind.

"I didn't know this would happen."

"I told you, it's okay," she said immediately.

When they reached the car, she stopped, the light from the lamppost illuminating her worried face.

"I'd hoped for some good parking when you suggested this," he said, trying to lighten the mood. "We'll have to shoot for another time."

"I had the same thought," she said, her eyes glued to his face. "I've been thinking about how I can best help you."

Help him? He could barely help himself.

"I know you needed your space...earlier, but perhaps you could...hold me for a moment before we leave.

Like you did when we left the church the other night. Hugs...always make people feel better, I've found. I don't know about you, but I could use one right now. I think you could too."

He didn't know if he wanted her to be that close right now. "I'm not sure that's a good idea. I'm sweaty, and I probably stink."

"I don't care," she said. "Besides, I'm a bit damp too, and I might not smell the freshest. I don't think we should let that get in our way."

"You have no idea how sorry I am, Anna," he said, evading her request.

"There's nothing to be sorry about," she said, approaching him like he was a wary animal. "I'm going to hug you now. Just so you know. I won't be put off."

His muscles braced as she took the last step toward him. When she embraced him, part of him wanted to push her away, but he fought the urge. Closed his eyes. Took a breath and then made himself wrap his arms around her. Gently. It took a while, but he felt the tension start to slough off.

Squeezing his eyes shut, he realized that she'd saved him once again.

Chapter 12

ANNA WAVED AT MRS. O'SHEA AS SHE WALKED BACK FROM the market.

"How's your mother, Anna?" the woman called from her front porch.

Her mother hadn't said much of anything since discovering the details of Martin's death, asking to be left to grieve in peace. Anna hadn't pressed since she'd heard her mother crying more often when she was in her room. To give her space, she and Noah tried to stay out of the house as much as possible when she was home.

"She's doing fine, Mrs. O'Shea," Anna called out. Her mother wouldn't want her saying much more than that, especially after her little dust-up with Mrs. O'Shea at the party.

"I didn't see her at the knitting group the other night," the older woman said, sweeping the broom she was holding in large movements across her steps.

Anna hadn't known that. She'd gotten home at ten from going out to dinner and having a nice walk with Noah. "I'm sure you'll see her next week. Gotta run, Mrs. O'Shea. My groceries are probably cooked, what with all this heat."

The woman waved at her, and Anna took off before she could say more. She hurried down the street to their house. At the gate, she stopped short.

A handsome young solider was sitting on her front porch steps. He had an Army duffel with him that looked to be stuffed with clothes. Given his loose-legged stature, she felt like he might have been waiting a while. Her mother was at her secretarial job, and Anna's shopping had taken longer than expected since her main grocery store had been out of eggs, a scarcity she hoped would soon end.

"Can I help you?" she asked, shifting her bags to open the gate.

The man pushed off the steps. "Anna? Heck, I'd know that face anywhere. Noah looked at your picture so much I feel like I know you. I'm Billie Henderson, Noah's friend from the 3rd Infantry."

"Billie! You're back from the war."

"Yes, ma'am," he said, puffing out his chest. "Although I don't know how they'll do without me. Decided not to send me to the South Pacific after weeks of waiting in Paris for my orders. Then it took me a bit to get back here, what with the slow boat they put us all on. Man, I've seen tanks move faster. Here, let me help you."

He took the bags from her hands and walked with her down the sidewalk.

"Noah's coming by in a while," she said. "He said you might be showing up any day."

And she'd been fretting about it. It still worried her that he might prejudice Noah against her neighborhood.

Oh, she was being silly. Noah made up his own mind. Hadn't Alice been teasing her for days now about falling for an egghead?

"Yeah, me and Noah figured your house would be the easiest place to meet once I got bounced. I mean, I don't have a permanent residence here anymore. Gave my apartment up when I went to war."

She opened the front door. "Of course, you're most welcome."

"Thanks," Billie said, following her into the kitchen. "Boy, this isn't where I'd imagined you'd be living."

Here we go. "My father worked hard on the railroad to move us to this neighborhood."

He whistled. "No need to be touchy, sister. I was only making an observation."

Sure he was. The second question a Chicagoan would ask after inquiring about your name was what neighborhood you lived in.

"Speaking of observations, I don't see a ring on that finger. Does that mean you two aren't hitched yet? I know Lucky Strike was talking about taking his time, but if I'd come here and seen you looking like this in a pretty blue dress, I would have carted you off to the nearest justice of the peace. If you don't mind me saying."

Observant and a smooth talker? This was going to be fun. "Lucky Strike?" she asked.

"That's what some of the guys called Noah," Billie said. "He didn't get so much as a scratch. I was lucky, I guess, that one of those Krauts only caught me in the leg. Thank God it healed good. I was afraid for a moment I'd have a limp, but that would be better than what happened to a lot of boys."

Indeed, she thought, thinking of the amputee soldiers she'd seen at the USO or the hospital. At the hospital just this last weekend, she'd seen a solider being outfitted with two hooks for arms.

"Noah mentioned your injury in one of his letters. I'm glad you're all healed up."

"He mentioned that, did he? Well, don't that beat all. He's always a tough guy to read. I mean, some of us get chatty when we're pinned down but not Lucky Strike. He usually had to tell me to shut it. Of course, jabbering didn't hurt my shooting none. No, I could pick out Nazis and shoot them down like targets in one of those games at the Illinois State Fair."

Anna was so used to Noah's tight-lippedness about

the war, Billie's openness was a bit shocking. Not that she minded Noah's quiet none. She liked the thoughtful way he sat and listened. Billie reminded her of the fast talkers you could find sitting at Dougherty's bar, drinking whiskey and telling tall tales—even if he wasn't originally from South Side.

"You never did answer my question," he said, leaning back against the counter. "Are you two hitched or aren't you?"

"We're discussing the future," she said primly.

He grinned. "Good. If Lucky Strike waits too long, I might have to make a run for you. Just kidding."

She wasn't sure he was, what with the glance he gave her legs. Suddenly, the kitchen felt too small. "Do you want to grab your duffel from the front porch? It's a warm day out, and I don't know what you have inside it."

"Sure thing," he said, giving her a thumbs-up. "Be back in a jiffy."

She took a moment to breathe and then considered her groceries. She'd bought two pork chops for lunch. When Noah arrived, she'd have to go back to the store to get one for Billie, this time with the car. The walk had been nice, but she wanted to fix lunch by a reasonable time. She imagined Noah would want Billie to stay. For a second, she had a pinch of jealousy about sharing Noah with his Army buddy. If he was this much of a talker, it was going to be a while. Then she chided herself for being rude. He deserved to have a fine welcome. He was a veteran, and one of Noah's friends.

She should mention he could have more of his friends visit, once they returned from the war. It would be nice to meet the people he'd been around. They were still getting to know each other in some ways. In others, they seemed to have known each other forever.

Every day they got together around lunch when she wasn't volunteering. She'd make something for him while he drank coffee or soda at the table. He said he loved to watch her cook, and she'd splurged on a new apron she'd seen at the five-and-dime—a blue and white flowered one. Then they'd eat, often in the backyard unless there were kids outside.

Noah had become a favorite with the neighborhood boys, and many of them would wander over to talk to them if they were eating out back. She rather loved that, but again, she also liked their time alone. She'd wondered if it was common to want to spend every waking minute with someone like she did Noah. Not everyone in love felt that way, she'd observed.

"Okay, here's my bag," Billie said. "You don't do laundry in addition to cooking?"

That put her on the spot. She wasn't even doing Noah's laundry since Mrs. Hughes had offered to look after it. "Ah..."

"I'm mostly kidding," he said, pulling out a chair and making himself comfortable. "Where's your mom, by the way?"

"She has a job as a secretary," she said. "At an insurance company."

"Good for her," Billie said. "I kinda like how women took over all these jobs. Of course, things will go back to the way they were before the war with us men being back."

Anna suspected he was right, but she knew some of the women like Alice weren't looking forward to that per se. Sure, they wanted the boys to come home, but they'd liked to keep working too. Other women had confided in her that they couldn't wait to go back to only keeping the house and raising the kids.

"Remind me what you do again?" Billie asked.

"I'm a second grade teacher," she said. "Forgive my manners. I was so swept away I forgot to offer you refreshment. I can have coffee ready in a few minutes if that suits. Or you can have a soda."

"Refreshments, huh?" Billie said. "Aren't you a classy dame? Noah sure is Lucky Strike. I'll have a soda pop if it's all the same to you. I can't stand the taste of coffee after the swill we had in the war. Might have ruined me forever."

Noah never mentioned things like that, although she'd noticed he never touched milk. In fact, he seemed determined not to look at it. It had made her wonder why, but she figured he would tell her if he wanted to. The other night at Burnham Park when he'd gone all cold and clammy... The memory that had assailed him must have been bone-chilling. She'd started to mutter a Hail Mary to herself, feeling completely powerless to help him.

Only when he'd let her hug him in the parking lot had she felt assured. He'd all but melted against her as the rigidness left his muscles. She'd been afraid to leave him at the rectory, but he'd caressed her cheek and said he'd be fine. She'd had to trust him. It made her feel good to know that Father was taking good care of him.

A knock sounded on the front door, and she took a hasty step in that direction, but Billie cut her off.

"I'll get it," he said, flashing his toothy smile. "Lucky Strike deserves a surprise."

A spurt of jealousy emerged again. This was her home, her front door. She wasn't so sure she liked the liberties this man was taking. But ingrained manners kept her in place as Billie left the kitchen.

She heard Billie exclaim moments later and wondered at Noah's reaction. Her instinct was to join them, but she didn't want to intrude. They'd gone through a lot in the war, and when Noah had written her about making a new friend in Billie after so many of his friends had died, she'd been happy for him, encouraged him even.

Besides, he'd told her he was looking forward to seeing his friend, that he was glad Billie hadn't been shipped off to the Pacific. There'd been a haunted look on his face as he said it. One that had shot down to her very soul. Every night she prayed Noah wouldn't have to go back to war, either because of his conscience or because Uncle Sam called him back up.

"Didn't I tell you he'd be surprised to see me?" Billie said, his arm around Noah's shoulder.

Noah, she noticed, didn't have his arm around Billie, but there was the slightest smile on his face.

"Some days on the front we never thought we'd end up stateside. Woo-eee, I'm glad to have my feet back on the good ol' U.S. of A. I kissed the ground when I got off the boat. Never been so glad to see home in my whole life."

Noah hadn't mentioned how he'd felt about stepping foot on American soil again. She'd have to ask him later. "You two catch up, Noah. I'm going to dart out to the store for a bit."

"Didn't you already come from there?" Billie said, gesturing to the bags she'd left on the counter by the sink. "Oh, wait! You're going back on account of me."

Anna noted Billie didn't try and stop her, but Noah stepped out of Billie's hold and put his hand on her arm.

"Please don't go to any trouble," he said. "We can always grab a sandwich or something at a corner store."

Men! They didn't understand anything about cooking and hospitality. "I realized I forgot something. Truly."

She hated prevaricating, but it was only a white lie, and for a good cause. A newly returned solider deserved a good home-cooked meal. She knew they wouldn't stand for her giving up her pork chop and eating leftovers.

She had her purse in her hand before Noah could respond and rose on her tiptoes to kiss him on the cheek. "See you in a bit."

"Noah, you'd better marry that girl or I will," she heard Billie say when she reached the hallway.

She paused and waited for Noah's response. Okay, she'd been growing a little impatient.

August 27th hadn't seemed like a long time to wait when he'd suggested it, but the days had started to drag on lately. How was she going to handle another five weeks? She hated leaving him every night. Hated the restraint they had to put into their kissing and brief touching. There seemed like there was no place they could be truly alone, and it was driving her crazy. They loved each other. She didn't see why they couldn't get married and work out everything else afterward.

"Like hell you'll marry her," Noah responded in a gravelly voice. "There are plenty of other girls in Chicago."

That appeased her some. She felt guilty for eavesdropping, but surely it wouldn't hurt to listen a little longer.

"I grew up here," Billie said. "Trust me, she might be a good Catholic girl—wouldn't be a teacher otherwise—but she's got grit *and* looks. I mean, those legs... Man, I envy you."

How dare he speak about her legs, and in her own home. She thought about forgoing that extra pork chop altogether.

"Enough of that talk," Noah said. "Tell me about how you left things. The radio is shit on details. I want to punch the wall every time I hear a news report. It's as useful as tits on a boar."

She was sure her mouth must have dropped open. Noah never cussed around her. Did he always do it around other men, or just fellow soldiers? She'd heard filthy words come out of soldiers' mouths at the USO and the hospital, but then again, their language wasn't any worse than what she heard from drunken revelers on South Side. She decided it was time to leave.

"In a second, Lucky Strike," Billie said. "Seriously, why haven't you married that girl? You told me how crazy you were about her when we were fighting the Jerries. Is she not everything you thought she'd be?"

"She's wonderful, incredible," Noah said. "But there are some other factors."

She strained to hear his next words.

"What exactly?" Billie pressed.

"Leave it alone," Noah countered, and she heard the scraping of a kitchen chair.

"No way, man," Billie said. "If there are factors, tell me what they are. Maybe I can help. I'm from here, after all."

Was that a growl she heard?

"I'm still not so sure I like Chicago for one," Noah said. "I've been trying to get over it, mostly since I met this private at the USO... Long story. But it's like a war playground here, and I'm having trouble getting past it."

She hadn't realized his distaste for Chicago was still a problem. When he'd talked about being upset by what he'd seen around town and at the USO, she'd understood. He'd even told her about his talk with Private Garrett and how much it had affected him. But it clearly hadn't done much to sway his opinion. Why couldn't he accept that her hometown was doing plenty of good for their soldiers? They had more war plants than any other city, she suspected. Masses of women had stepped up to help. That wasn't frivolous in her mind. It spoke to the heart of their city.

Another chair scraped. "You never were one to party when we had the chance," Billie said. "Not that there was ever much downtime. Our unit never had a cushy assignment, did it?"

There was no response from Noah.

"So you don't like Chicago," Billie said. "Big deal! Take her with you to D.C. With your war record, you could probably get a nice job at that new military building the government keeps hyping. What's it called?"

"The Pentagon," Noah said.

Anna didn't remember much about it except from movie reels. Designed to protect the U.S. from enemies, it was supposed to be the largest office building in the world.

"I haven't thought about that," Noah said. "Her job is here, and this neighborhood is her family."

"Welcome to Chicago," Billie said dryly. "Neighborhoods look after their own, but they can also kick your ass and make you toe the line. Being an orphan, I got kicked since I didn't belong to anyone. She's a teacher at one of the Catholic schools, right?"

Again, no response from Noah, and Anna wondered if he'd nodded.

"Well, nothing controls life in Chicago like the church and the mob. Boy, this here is South Side. She might live in an upscale neighborhood, but that doesn't change how things are done here. You're not Catholic, right?"

One of the chairs scraped again, as if Billie was moving his chair closer.

"Listen, man, if you're not Catholic, it's going to be an uphill battle for you in this neighborhood. First, you aren't from here, which makes you an outsider. Second, you aren't one of them. Catholics are tight. You know you'll have to agree to raise your kids Catholic, right? They have some strong rules about that shit."

"I didn't know that," Anna heard Noah respond, and the slow cadence of his voice told her he was upset about it.

She clenched her hand into a fist. Oh, this wasn't fair. She should never have eavesdropped. Now she knew about Noah's concerns and couldn't say anything unless she admitted what she'd done. Worse, Billie was creating more problems in Noah's mind. In her heart, she'd hoped he might be swayed to convert to Catholicism. He'd become close to Father Shaughnessy, after all, and he'd even gone into the church the other night. Everyone in the neighborhood had taken to him, regardless of his background.

But there *were* serious rules about marrying a man outside her faith. If he didn't convert, they'd have to get married in the rectory rather than the church, and that didn't seem as sacred somehow. And she did want their children raised Catholic.

"Then there's her mother," she heard Noah say.

Hurt radiated through her heart. Her mother's grief

was wearing on her, all the more so since Noah had shared the details around Martin's death.

"She's grieving her son very hard," he said. "I'm pretty sure she blames me for how Martin died, and I can't say I blame her. Anna said I shouldn't feel guilty, and part of me knows she's right. But her mother stays in her room all the time, it seems, and we have to stay out of the house when she's around. It's hard to be around her...and not feel guilty."

"Well, fuck her," Billie exclaimed.

Anna put her hand over her mouth to cover her gasp. Such language!

"You're part of the Rock of the Marne, man. Our division had the most combat days of any unit in Europe. We fought in shitholes and took down the Jerries on their own turf. You've got a goddamn Medal of Honor and two Distinguished Service Crosses, if I remember correctly. And how many Silver Stars?"

"It's not important," she heard Noah mutter even as shock rolled through her.

He hadn't said anything about being decorated. Why hadn't she suspected? Frustration rose. If he hadn't even told her about his medals, would he ever tell her what kept him awake at night? She wanted a marriage of the hearts and the minds.

"You remember who you are," Billie said like a drill sergeant might. "Audie Murphy might be getting all the fanfare, but in my opinion, we're all goddamn military heroes. I wouldn't have minded being on the cover of *Life Magazine.*"

"That's not why we were over there, Billie," Noah said. "That kind of shit doesn't interest me. You know that."

"I do," Billie said, "but don't you forget how much you've given to this country. That woman might mourn her son. I get that. But if she's making you feel guilty for being alive, she's insulting a goddamn hero, and that makes me want to give her a piece of my mind."

The steel in his voice sent chills through Anna. He sounded like he'd knock her block off if she so much as said a bad word to Noah. That wasn't the way. Her mother wanted her to be happy. Hadn't she commented on how happy Anna had looked the night of Noah's welcome party? Anna made sure to remember that every day. Her mother's grief would pass. It had to.

"Stop that kind of talk," Noah said. "No one is going to dress down Anna's mom. Mrs. Sims will either come around or she won't, but I won't be the cause of trouble between Anna and her mother. Martin wouldn't want that. And I couldn't live with it. I'm not sure Anna would be able to either."

Her muscles seemed to go lax at the mention of her brother. She leaned against the wall, fighting tears. Suddenly everything seemed impossible.

"Besides, if the war isn't over by the end of the month, I've decided I'm going to have them send me over, although I haven't had the courage to tell Anna yet. I figure I'll do it if it comes to it."

He'd decided this without her? What about making plans together?

"You're a glutton for punishment, but I know what you mean. We did our part in Europe and then some, but I get antsy with the war still going on. So long as the enemy is breathing, I want to kill them."

Anna couldn't bear to hear any more.

"I don't like killing," Noah said, "but if it has to be done, I'll do it. We all need this war to end."

"Yeah, it's murder on my future plans," Billie said. "You think any more about meeting some of my former associates and working with me? Like I told you, I have some good connections here, ones the war didn't affect."

"I'm keeping an open mind," Noah said, "and willing to meet them and hear more."

He'd thought about working with this man? God knew what Billie would try to rope him into doing.

"It's funny," Billie said. "I'd hoped you'd be hitched

with a goofy grin on your face from all of the bedtime privileges. You look about as grim as you did fighting the Nazis."

Anna walked to the front door as quietly as she could, praying they wouldn't hear her. On the porch, she bit her lip to keep from crying. Grim? Yes, Noah had been grim at times, but she'd blamed that on the difficult transition he was undergoing.

After hearing him today, he seemed like a different person, one she didn't know.

Maybe they weren't right for each other long-term, after all.

Chapter 13

NOAH COULDN'T HELP BUT WONDER WHAT WAS KEEPING Anna. When he'd gotten up to grab a soda, he'd looked into the grocery bags. Sure enough, there were only two brown-wrapped packages with *pork chop* written on them. He hated that she'd had to go to the store again, but she hadn't given him a chance to talk her out of it. He'd have happily munched on roast chicken leftovers from yesterday's lunch.

When he heard someone clomp loudly into the hall-way, he rose from his chair, gripping the back. Mrs. Sims appeared in the doorway, her mouth tight, looking like a scary black and white photo of Queen Victoria in her later years.

"I see you're making yourself right at home," she said. "Noah, I tolerate your presence around because of my daughter, but I don't appreciate you bringing your *friends* here." She gave Billie a pointed look as he stood too.

"Mrs. Sims," he said, reaching for patience, "this is one of my buddies from the Army. He was born and raised in Chicago and just got back home. He...ah... didn't know Martin, but he's heard stories about him from the other guys."

"Mrs. Sims," Billie said, and Noah noticed he didn't

tip his finger to his forehead in respect like he usually would.

She dug a fist into her belly. "Please don't refer to my son, Noah. The very thought of him and how he died gives me pain. Where is Anna?"

Billie gave him a look as her dagger sunk into his belly. Would she ever stop thinking he was at fault for Martin's death? He'd tried to buffer Anna from how it made him feel, but it was getting harder. They couldn't make themselves scarce around the house forever.

"At the store," he said. "Ah...are you feeling okay, Mrs. Sims? Usually you're at work this time of day."

"I have a dreadful headache that you and your friend aren't helping."

He made the decision on the spot. "We'll leave you in peace then. I'm sorry for the inconvenience, Mrs. Sims. I hope you feel better."

He didn't ask her to pass a message to Anna because he doubted she would. Anna would come back from the store soon. He'd catch her then.

Billie opened his mouth as if to say something, but Noah jerked his head slightly, the same signal he used to use to keep Billie from countermanding an order from their commanding officer. Noah slapped a hand on his friend's shoulder and ushered him out of the kitchen. When they left the house, he made sure they were well out of hearing before turning to Billie, who was tight-lipped.

"Thank you for not making it worse," he said, shoving his hands in his pockets.

Billie whistled. "She's a piece of work. I'll give you that. I'd think twice about marrying a woman with a mother like that. Might be a bad seed in that line."

Noah didn't care for that suggestion. He figured kids made themselves who they were. "Who would have figured you for a nature over nurture kind of guy?"

"Huh?" Billie asked.

"Never mind," Noah said. "Let's wait for Anna on

the corner. Then we can figure out where to go. She has a car, but there are some places to eat not too far from here. Dougherty's Pub is pretty good, and it's run by a great guy who just got back from Europe."

"I'd just as soon stay out of bars in South Side," Billie said.

Noah's frustration bloomed. "Look, Anna mentioned these...opinions people have about other people's neighborhoods. I just want to be clear. I don't want to hear them."

Billie cocked his head, and Noah could feel his anger rise as well. "You telling me how to act in my own town, Lucky Strike?"

He took a breath, sensing the tension in the air. "No, I'm only trying to tell you... Anna lives here, and the people in this neighborhood have been nice to me. Hell, they threw me a welcome party when I arrived, chock full of cakes and pies the women had to use their ration cards to make."

"I'm glad they're treating you right," Billie said, kicking at a rock on the sidewalk. "The way Anna's mother acted brought to mind some other memories. She all but threw us out of her house."

Now things were starting to make sense. Billie had been raised in an orphanage too, something they'd bonded over. Poor treatment came with the territory. Noah himself had been told more than once that he wasn't fit for company.

"She was mostly throwing me out, Billie. You were just gravy."

The man laughed like he'd hoped, and Noah slapped him on the back. "There's also a really good sandwich shop whose name I always forget."

"That sounds fine," Billie said, and they shared a look of understanding.

"Sorry it won't be pork chops. Anna makes a mean one. Of course, she looked at me crossways when I asked if she had ketchup. Sometimes she doesn't understand how much you can miss something so simple after sub-sisting on K-rations."

"Or the crap they served in the mess tent when we were lucky enough to have one," Billie said. "Who knew that was lucky, Lucky Strike?"

"Would you mind calling me Noah from now on? The other name makes me think of things I'd rather move past."

Billie paused under the shade of a large American Elm. Since it was a hot day, it seemed everyone in the neighborhood was inside save a passel of kids playing with a well-patched ball in the cross street. He spotted Willie and Frankie and the Dougherty boys.

"But Lucky Strike is a great nickname," Billie said. "Beats the one we gave Masters."

Yeah, Stinky was a pretty shitty name if you asked Noah. One of the guys had called him that after comment-ing that he always reeked of body odor—even in the cold.

"Masters was a good solider."

"Yeah," Billie said, his voice lower now. "They all were. Damn Jerries."

Noah hung his head for a moment. He tried not to think about how many guys they'd lost. Being away from the war, he could go most of the day without thinking about it. Then he had to face his bed, and even when he focused on something good—like his day with Anna—he found himself dreaming about Martin and the other boys who'd died in front of him. Some had been shot up with machine gun fire. Some had been blown up by artillery. Then there were the ones he'd killed. God, he'd killed hundreds, with everything from his BAR to his bayonet.

"Do you ever...?" Maybe he shouldn't ask. He had a feeling Billie wouldn't get it.

"What?"

He kicked at a pebble on the sidewalk. "Ever regret killing people? I mean, I know they were Jerries and all, but..."

"Is your conscience bothering you? I should have

known. Like I always told you, you think too much."

"One of Anna's friends recently called me an egg-head," he said dryly. "Said I think too much."

"If the shoe fits... We did what we had to do. The Jerries started the fight. We had to finish it. Same with the Italians, and soon it will be the same with the Japs. To my mind, there's nothing wrong with that."

Noah still couldn't completely agree with that, so he didn't say anything at all.

Billie threw his hand out. "Hell, it's the same in Chicago. Someone wants a fight, you give it to them. It's like Al Capone said: you can get much further with a kind word and a gun than you can with a kind word alone. I usually hate Wops. Can't trust them. But Capone got some things right. His problem was he thought he was bigger than everyone else. That's what ended up doing him in."

In that moment, Noah knew Billie had killed before going to war. He'd suspected. If someone were to ask him how he knew, he couldn't have said. It was a feeling. He'd seen guys puke after making their first kill or after a particularly bloody one. Billie's eyes had almost gleamed after a kill, like an alley cat out hunting rats. Noah wouldn't judge without knowing the circumstances. He'd known guys in the orphanage—older boys—who'd killed. He'd known when they were lying, bragging really, and he'd known when it was true. His street smarts had never failed him.

"What are your plans for the next few days?" he asked.

Billie rocked back on his heels. "You mean other than getting drunk as a skunk and banging some of the girls in my old neighborhood? I'll probably see if this guy I know is still into the same enterprise he was in before the war. I made a lot of money that way. 'Course, I always spent it the moment I got it. Hated to have dough burning a hole in my pocket. Like I said, I can introduce you. You could make some serious dough with those all-American good looks. Get a house so you won't have to hole up with

Anna's old lady, watching out for the hemlock she might put in your drink like in *Arsenic and Old Lace*. Did you see that picture?"

Noah was still processing Billie's job prospect. He'd need a lot more information before he'd consider it. Somehow he didn't think it would fulfill his need to serve others, but perhaps that was too judgmental of him. Private Garrett had showed him he had a lot of judgments coming out of the war—and he'd since realized it was hard to shake them.

"No, I haven't seen a picture since basic training. Missed the Oscars last year because the Jerries moved their line up."

He and the other guys hadn't been so attached to watching the Oscars, but they had looked forward to seeing something of home—even if it was movie stars.

"Noah! What are you doing out here?"

He turned and spotted Anna striding up the street. "We were waiting for you," he said, meeting her halfway and taking the lone grocery sack from her. "Your mother came home with a headache so we made ourselves scarce."

She looked a little pale, he noted, as he studied her face for a reaction. Mrs. Sims' actions always prompted an equally powerful reaction in her daughter. He knew she tried to put on a brave face, but the situation with her mother was wearing her down too. He didn't know what to do.

"Oh, I see," she said, looking down as if studying the spider-web cracks in the sidewalk. "You and Billie should go off then and catch up. I'll head home and see if she needs anything."

"You're way too good of a daughter," Billie said.

Noah wanted to elbow him in the gut. "Don't mind him. I'll come by later. Maybe we could take a walk after your mom goes to sleep." He didn't want to make Anna feel guilty about being out with him while her mother was ill.

"No, I'll see you tomorrow," she said, still not meeting his gaze. "It's Billie's first day back. You boys have fun."

Something was wrong. He knew it. If Billie hadn't been there, he would have tipped her chin up and made her look at him. Asked her what was bothering her even though he thought he already knew. Mrs. Sims cast a large shadow.

"All right," he said, kissing her chastely on the cheek. "I'll miss you."

He'd whispered it so only she could hear, and while he hadn't expected a response, he'd thought it would at least soften the tension in her shoulders.

"Let me walk you home," Noah said.

She took the grocery sack from his hands, but he held on. "Don't be silly. I can handle it."

When she tugged, there was anger behind her pull. He let go, and she staggered back a few steps before she caught herself.

Something cold settled in his chest. Usually she greeted him with a sunny smile, but she'd barely glanced at him. Was she mad about Billie? He'd told her his friend would be arriving any day. He wanted to stomp his foot in frustration.

"I'm sorry you bought an extra pork chop," Noah said, feeling the familiar guilt about her buying groceries for their lunch. When he'd offered to pay for them, she'd insisted that groceries come out of her pocketbook and not his. He could buy them lunch or dinner out. He'd agreed because she'd been immoveable.

Rather like she was being now.

Billie bumped into him, and he jerked to a defensive stance.

"Only me, Lucky Strike," he said, "trying to get your attention. Come on. You can see your girl tomorrow. Today we're going to enjoy everything the Windy City has to offer. Anna, it was good to meet you. I hope your mother *recovers* soon."

That set Noah's teeth on edge. Billie made it sound like he hoped she was terminal.

"Good to meet you too, Billie," Anna said with equal insincerity.

Now he had his answer. Anna was never insincere. Her ire was up, all right.

"I'll be back for that walk," he told her, reaching for her hand.

She didn't curl her hand around his like usual. "No, it's fine. Like Billie said. You should enjoy everything our fine city has to offer because it's a pretty great place, if you ask me."

Again, Noah noted the edge in her voice. What was up with her?

When she turned away, he realized she hadn't smiled or waved at him. She'd never left like this.

He had the sudden urge to write her a letter and ask her what was wrong.

But the war was over, and they weren't sharing how they felt that way anymore.

If they were going to make a go of it forever, they had to find a new way to tell each other what was wrong when something happened between them.

Chapter 14

"ANNA," SHE HEARD AS SHE WAS CLOSING THE FRONT door.

Right now she wasn't sure she was steady enough to face her mother, but she wasn't the kind of person who could pretend she hadn't heard her voice.

"Yes, Mom," she responded, walking toward the kitchen.

Her mother was seated at the table. She gestured to the half-empty soda bottles. "Anna, I don't like your beau making himself at home like this. And furthermore, I don't want him bringing his friends around like I came home to find. He might be seeing you right now, but this isn't his house. Is that clear?"

The wrinkles around her mother's mouth seemed more pronounced today. She didn't want to fight with her. Not after what she'd heard Noah say. "Is your headache bad? Have you taken an aspirin?"

"If it wasn't bad, would I be home right now?" she asked.

Anna sent up a prayer for patience. Even the wounded soldiers at the hospital where she volunteered were less surly. She cleaned up the bottles and started to put away the groceries.

"Anna, I've been thinking about Mr. Weatherby a

lot since dinner the other night. Have you considered the fact that he's not Catholic?"

Her mother had called him by his first name the other night at dinner. Had she only done so to bring him out of his reverie? "His name is Noah, Mother, and yes, I know he's not Catholic. I'm praying it won't be an issue."

After hearing him talk earlier, they were putting the cart before the horse.

"Anna, that's more than naïve," her mother said, smoothing out invisible wrinkles in the yellow table-cloth Anna had put out fresh this morning for her lunch with Noah. "You remember Eileen Kelly."

Who could forget? She fought the urge to excuse herself. This was not the kind of story she wanted to be reminded of right now.

"She was two years ahead of you in school. She married that Jew from Glencoe she met while working downtown. Some people never got over that, including her parents. They were right to forbid the marriage."

Was there a warning in her mother's comment? "I thought Eileen was brave to marry the man she loved. For the life of me, I can't understand why someone's race or religion matters. Hasn't the war taught us anything about what hate does?"

"You can cling to your idealism as much as you'd like, Anna, but it won't change the facts. This is a problem. I certainly don't like the thought of you marrying someone who's not Catholic, and it would be hard on any children you had. Is he willing to raise them in our faith?"

Anna suddenly couldn't breathe. Her mother was only adding to her concerns. "We'll work it out, Mother. Now, do you want me to make you lunch? I could fry you up a pork chop."

"Spending our hard-earned money on those men," her mother said, clucking her tongue.

"It's *my* money, Mother," she responded, setting

the cup she was washing on the nearby towel. "I don't want to argue with you. I only want to help your headache. Please, what can I do?"

Her mother stood up, her black mourning garb a stark contrast to the pallor of her skin. "You can answer this one question for me. Can you really forget that your brother would be here if not for Noah?"

Something snapped in her heart. "Yes, I can, Mother, and I pray you can as well. I'm going upstairs. If you need something, simply call me."

But her mother didn't call, and Anna spent hours trying—and failing—to fall into *A Bell for Adano*. Her USO Mama had been passing the bestseller around to all the girls. She'd loved the hero, an Italian-American solider who'd helped the people of Adano find a new bell for their town after the Fascists melted down the old one to make rifles. Anna had read the first few chapters over the last couple of days. She'd been mesmerized by the view it offered of the world Noah had inhabited. He'd fought in Sicily too, and she'd hoped it would help her better understand what he'd gone through.

Now she wasn't sure it mattered.

She continued to fret and ended up smoking a few more cigarettes than normal. Her room was stuffy and smoky when the sky turned a midnight blue. She pulled her chair closer to the window, hoping for a breeze, and picked up her rosary. Maybe reciting some prayers would help. She didn't know what else to do.

Our Father, who art in heaven...

She came awake suddenly and jerked upright in the chair. Was that hail she'd heard? As she rubbed her eyes, her rosary fell to the floor. It was dark outside, and the lamp in her room made the night look even darker. Still, from what she could tell, the weather seemed calm.

Something struck the glass again, making that same sound, and she leaned over to turn off the light.

She almost let out a scream when she saw the dark

shadow of a man outside. Clamping her hand over her mouth, she watched as he raised his arm. The hail-like sound repeated itself, and she realized the man was throwing pebbles at her window.

"Anna!" she heard him call out in a harsh whisper.

Noah? It certainly wasn't one of her students. Everyone knew she'd have them cleaning the chalkboard and erasers for weeks if they pulled a stunt like this. She studied the shape more. Without moonlight, she couldn't make out his features, but he was the right size.

She sighed and glanced at the clock beside her bed. It was after eleven. Did she want to go down and talk to him? Usually she found solace in praying, but any tightness it had eased had already returned now that he was here. Another shower of pebbles hit the window. He wasn't going to give up.

Well, neither was she, she decided. Did they love each other or not? It was time to find out.

She made it down half the steps before realizing she was stomping—and then promptly lightened her steps. Her mother did not need to make an appearance now. Anna hoped she hadn't heard the shower of pebbles, but then again, her mother slept hard, thank God.

When she opened the back door, she called out. "Noah?"

"Yes," he said, the tall dark shape of him moving closer to the light. "I saw your light on. I'm sorry I'm so late. I just got back and thought... Can I come in?"

"We'll need to be quiet," she said. "Let me pour us some tea. We can sit on the front porch."

It felt intimate to be with him this late at night. It made her think about seeking reassurance from him through a series of kisses.

No, having his arms around her might quiet the dark thoughts, but it wouldn't silence them. Only voicing them would.

He was quiet as she got out the glasses, but he opened the refrigerator door before she could. It was a gallant gesture, and she stopped to study him. His hair was a bit disheveled, like the hot weather had made his head sweat, and he'd run his hand through it. His eyes were fixed on her, and there wasn't a trace of a smile on his lips. She could almost feel the tension in his body. Had something happened? Or had he felt her own lack of ease?

He closed the door after she pulled the pitcher out, his eyes still fastened on her, as if she were a map he was trying to read. She couldn't stand it any longer. Setting the pitcher on the counter, she moved toward him. The heat from his body reached her hand before she touched his chest. Then his arms went around her, and she pressed her face against his heart. It was beating fast, and she closed her eyes as the tension between them slowly drained away, almost like someone had pulled the plug on a filled-up sink.

"I missed you," Noah whispered against her neck. "You were so...distant earlier. I...wasn't sure what to make of it."

She was caught in the trap of her own making. If she told him why, she'd have to admit to eavesdropping. Well, she wasn't a perfect person, although she tried to be a good one. Best he know that now.

"I heard you talking to Billie earlier," she said. "I stopped in the hallway. I'm not proud of it."

He drew back, his mouth grim. "I'm sorry you heard all that. Billie pressed me, and I said more than I should have."

His heartbeat was steadier, but hers, she realized, was still going full tilt. Oh, she hated confrontations. "But what you said is still true, and that's the problem. Noah, why didn't you tell me about your concerns? I know I shouldn't have eavesdropped, but I shouldn't have had to."

"And yet you did it like a good little soldier," he said. "We could have used you over there." His mouth tipped up in a half-baked smile. "Come on, Tiger. Let's grab our tea and talk this out. I don't want to wake your mother."

She nodded, and together they managed to walk out without a floorboard squeaking. Out on the porch, he angled his chair closer to hers, she was relieved to see.

"Let's take this point by point," he said, his voice matter-of-fact.

She almost wanted to sigh. Her dad had been like that. If something was troubling her, he'd ask her to lay it out like she would items on her grocery list. Sometimes she didn't want to be so practical. Men!

"Fine," she said, crossing her arms. "But I reserve the right to talk off point if I want."

His brow rose at that. "Of course. I'm just trying to think back on what I said."

"Let me refresh your memory," she told him and proceeded to do just that.

He rubbed his jaw. "You've got a mind like a steel trap, don't you? I said all that?"

"Uh-huh." She crossed her legs too, waiting on him to speak.

"Like I said, I wish you hadn't heard that," he said softly.

"Once again, you should have told me you were feeling like that," she said. "When you love someone, you tell them how you feel."

His head rose and he looked at her like she was a bull's-eye. "Is that so? I don't have much experience with this love thing, if you recall. I didn't tell you because I didn't want to hurt your feelings. Even more important, I was still working all of this out in my mind. Billie...gave me some more things to think about, is all."

"Where did you two go?" she asked, already knowing the answer.

"You don't want to know," he answered with a heavy sigh.

She could only imagine if Billie had brought him there. "So it made you hate Chicago even more, then."

He paused for a moment. "Hate is a strong word.

There are many elements here that don't suit me, but that was true of Washington, D.C. too. I've...never been happy where I've lived, honestly. Never felt at home anywhere. But I came pretty close at that welcome party your neighbors gave me."

Was that true of most orphans? Was she overre-acting here? "Noah, I'm not sure where Billie took you, but I can imagine. And I know the other parts of town you've seen. I know some people think Chicago is full of a bunch of crooks and mobsters after Papa Johnny Torio, Al Capone, and Frank Nitti. I didn't feel one bit sorry when Nitti was found dead two years ago from a supposed suicide. Father says it was justice, and I tend to agree with him, although he should be more careful. There are ears even in church. But I digress."

He had a half-smile permanently on his face now. "I love it when you talk like this."

"You might need your head examined," she said. "Anyway, all I'm saying is that the war won't last forever, and Chicago will go back to being a normal city." Even as she said it, she realized she wasn't sure what normal looked like anymore.

"Will anything be normal again after the war?" he asked, looking away.

She stopped and thought a moment, and then she touched his face so he would meet her gaze. "Yes, in some ways. Kids are going to be riding their bicycles in the street again, and they won't be picking up scrap metal. People will rip up their ration cards. I'll be able to make a pie anytime I want to, and trust me, I'm going to dance a merry step in the kitchen when that happens. We can live our lives like we want to. Without this dark cloud hanging over us, without our men having to fight anymore."

He extended his hand to her and she clasped it. "More of your silver linings." He smiled as he said it.

"I'd rather focus on the good things is all. Someday soon, I pray we're going to take down the flag in the front window that I put up for Martin. I cried buckets that day.

Ironed the darn thing twice and couldn't get it straight in the window."

"What a wretched day that must have been," he said gravely.

She nodded quickly, feeling tears well up. She'd never imagined commemorating her brother like that. She still couldn't make herself put flowers on his grave. It was too hard to see the stark words engraved on his tombstone, announcing that his life was over. God, it had been too brief.

Tears started to rain down her face, and Noah shifted to pull her onto his lap. His arms came around her, and she gave in to the pressure in her chest. Through her waterfall of tears, she choked out an apology for getting his uniform wet. At one point, he fitted his handkerchief into her hand, and she wiped her nose. God, she was a mess.

"I'm sorry," she said again once the tears passed. "Sometimes it catches up with me."

"That's to be expected," he said, pressing her face back against his chest. "I wish he were here. Sometimes when I'm sitting in the kitchen or walking up to the porch, my mind conjures up an image of him here—like he was before the war. I see you in him too, Anna. When you move a certain way...it's like you have some of the same mannerisms. Damn, but I miss him."

Then he pressed his head into her shoulder for a long while, and she held him, hoping Martin could see them from heaven and know they both had loved him well in their own way.

"We've gotten way off point," Noah said, clearing his throat and sitting up. "But I like you on my lap."

She rather liked it too, she decided, although it was a bit indecent—and right here on the front porch too. Of course, the brick wall facing the street gave them some privacy, but still.

"I should probably..." She edged off his lap and returned to her chair.

In the silence, she heard the chirp of a lone cricket.

A soft breeze touched her hair, and it felt good against the heat of her neck. She got so warm when she cried. It was like all the tears inside her had to boil so they could overflow.

"We should probably talk about the Catholic thing," she said softly. "Billie's right, to some degree, although I'm ashamed to admit it."

She found she was tapping her feet all nervous-like suddenly, not wanting to bring up her mother's comments. It would only inflame his ongoing concerns on that score.

"I know you have your own beliefs, and I respect that. You can't see yourself converting, can you?"

He shook his head. "No. Not even for you or any kids we have."

She'd thought about it off and on all evening. Had decided she could make peace with it. "Honestly, it kinda galls me to say this, but I'm going to. You'd think being a war hero would be more important than being Catholic around here. So far everyone has embraced you."

And they hadn't done that with Eileen's beau, she recalled. Surely that was a good sign. Noah continued to study the floor, lost in thought.

"I choose to believe that will continue," she told him.

She could almost hear her mother telling her she had rose-colored glasses on. Maybe so, but she was sick and tired of people hating each other for no good reason. Weren't they all just Americans? Maybe the war had finally helped everyone realize that. God, she hoped so.

"I can face what people think of me," Noah said. "I've been called an orphan and a bastard and much worse. The real question is: can you face it?"

"I'll rip anyone in two with both my hands if they so much as say a bad word about you," she said, making a fist like her dad had taught her. "I mean it, Noah. I'll punch someone in the kisser if they mess with someone I love. I'm a tough Irish girl from South Side, after all.

We have a reputation to uphold." Of course, she'd probably get fired from her job at the school. Best not mention that.

"There she is," he said. "My tiger. I'm totally in love with her."

"But I have to ask about children," she forced herself to say. "Noah, I...this is hard for me to say, but I want our kids to be raised Catholic. Could you see your way toward agreeing to that?"

He gave a deep sigh. "I didn't realize how big a deal that was until Billie mentioned it. Honestly, Anna, this is a tough one. I want my kids—our kids—to have minds of their own and not simply swallow what they're told in some church."

She could feel a knee-jerk reaction coming a mile away, so she took a moment to breathe before she spoke. "Do I look like I swallow everything? Does Father?"

"I'm sorry," he said. "Point taken. Anna, you need to understand...the people in the orphanage were supposedly religious, and they treated us like shit. Excuse my French, but it's true. They called us unclean and bad seeds. Some of them insisted that scrubbing us really hard with lye soap was the only way to make us clean and godly. I... Stuff like that makes me want to throw something."

Like he couldn't probably when he was a boy under the control of a system. "I can't understand how anyone could treat kids that way, but I can promise you that no one would do that to our kids."

"You can't make a promise like that," he said. "No one can protect anyone that completely. Surely there are teachers even in your school whose methods you disagree with."

She thought about it. "Sometimes, but Father runs a pretty tight ship. It helps that he hires really good people to teach. He's partial to teachers, you know, because of his father."

"Yes, he told me," he said. "I'll think about it. That's all I can promise now."

"Thank you," she said. "I can also...take you to Mass with me or have you sit in on another class when school's back in session so you can see for yourself if you want."

He nodded. "Thank you. I...like gathering my own information."

She knew that. Hadn't she seen him looking at book after book to research professions? "There's something else I need to ask. Noah, why didn't you tell me about your medals? I would have been so happy for you."

His whole body seemed to close in like one of the flowers once darkness fell. "I know it's what the military does, but... Anna, I didn't want to be decorated for doing my duty. That's why they call it a duty. I...don't want people to think I'm some hero. I'm not."

She thought it was more than that, and given tonight's openness, she decided to press. "You don't want to be decorated for killing anyone, do you?"

The silence stretched, so much so that she had to fight the urge to fidget. Part of her wanted to apologize to him and change the topic, but she couldn't make herself do it. It would be best for him, for *them*, for him to speak.

"It doesn't feel right," he uttered in a harsh tone. "So many of the people I've talked to think the killing we did was justified, but it still leaves me with a bad taste in my mouth. I'm not proud of what I've done. That's another thing I'm working out. Niall and I have had some good discussions on it."

God bless Father Shaughnessy, she thought.

"There's so much about the war you don't want me to know," she said softly, and she thought about Billie's offer to help Noah find a job with his old associates. It seemed like it was one thing too much to bring up at the moment. Surely he wouldn't consider it if it was anything dangerous or unlawful.

"You should thank God for that," he ground out. "I'm sorry. That was curt. But Anna... You need to trust me here. You're a good woman who believes in the goodness of people. I don't *ever* want that to change. That's part of the reason your letters meant so much to me. You were a light in the darkness. Oh, that sounds so corny," he said, raking a hand through his already mussed up hair. "Forget I said it."

This time she slid onto his lap for a different reason. Taking his face in her hands, she said, "Noah Weatherby, you were a light in my darkness too. I don't *ever* want that to change."

"So are we two lighthouses now?" he asked, his tone suggesting a need to lighten the moment.

"Or two loons," she said, cuddling into him. "They mate for life and call out to each other at night, which I've read is uncommon in bird species."

He gave a grunt, which could have been mistaken for amusement. "You sound like a teacher. I love that part of you as much as I do the fist-curling tiger."

The warmth of his body and the ease with which he held her made her heart overflow with all the love she had for him. The worry she'd felt earlier was drowned by it.

"And I love you," she whispered, resting her hand on the arm he had around her waist.

"So we're okay for the moment?" he asked.

She thought about it. They also hadn't talked about his decision to go fight in the Pacific if the war wasn't over by the end of the month. She couldn't bring herself to mention it. There was nothing she could do about it. If Noah had to join their boys over there, she would respect his decision. After all, he was that kind of man, and it was one more reason she loved him.

"Yes, we are A-okay," she whispered.

As he lowered his mouth to kiss her, she felt one more shadow lurking in the back of her mind.

Her mother.

Chapter 15

"MRS. HUGHES, YOU'RE A MARVEL," NOAH SAID AS SHE served him a fried egg, a few bacon strips, and a couple of slices of fresh bread in the dining room.

"It's nice to see your appetite improving," she commented, pushing some of her apple butter closer to him.

"And our boy is sleeping better too," Father said.

His sleep was improving. Sure, he still woke up from bad dreams a couple of times a night, but he'd grown more adept at breathing out all of what he called the electricity afterward. His room at the rectory was becoming more familiar, which surely factored into it. For the last few years with the war, he'd slept in a new place practically every night, and most of the spots had not been comfortable.

"Being in love does that to a person," Mrs. Hughes said, smiling at him.

"I'm a lucky man," he said.

So lucky he could even manage a smile when he bumped into her mother. She still hadn't really spoken to him, and while Anna was trying to be positive about it, he wasn't so sure. Mrs. Sims was waiting for something. And in his gut, he wondered if she was hoping he'd be shipped off to the Pacific.

Today marked the first of August, and the war was

still underway. His self-imposed timetable with Anna was over three weeks off, and he was well aware of it. He was trying to keep busy as a distraction.

"Any more ideas about what you'll do once the war is over?" Mrs. Hughes asked. "My brother owns a car shop. I'm sure he'd be happy to hire you as a mechanic. Would teach you anything you need to know. I told him you were a good boy."

She wasn't the first person in the neighborhood to offer such assistance—Dougherty repeated his job offer whenever he saw him—and such unselfish generosity always overwhelmed him. "Thank you, Mrs. Hughes. That's very kind of you. I'm still thinking about things."

"He hits the books pretty hard when we're cosseted in the library, let me tell you," Niall said with a conspiratorial glance. "Whatever it turns out to be, it's going to be marvelous."

"I hope so," Noah said. Hope. It wasn't something he'd had in a long while, but it burned bright inside him whenever he was with Anna, whenever he researched a new career. If it weren't for the war, he'd feel like his whole life was ahead of him.

"What are you up to today, Noah?"

"My friend, Billie, is taking me uptown," he said. "He wants me to meet with some guys he worked with before the war."

Billie had finally talked him into it a couple of days ago. He'd popped by the rectory, and they'd chatted for a couple of hours. Niall hadn't minded, saying he could invite anyone over. The contrast to Anna's mother hadn't failed to register.

"What did Billie used to do before the war?" Mrs. Hughes asked, nodding to Father Wilson as he came in from morning Mass. "Good morning, Father. I'll make you a plate and bring it up to you."

The younger priest inclined his head. "Good morning, everybody."

Noah and Niall wished him the same, then watched as he walked up the stairs. Niall tried to hide his frown, but it was a losing battle. His ongoing angst over the quiet young priest was escalating.

"Maybe he just doesn't make friends easily," Noah said. He understood not wanting to talk to people.

Father sighed. "He may do better with the bees."

"*Father!*" Mrs. Hughes exclaimed.

Noah pressed his napkin over his mouth to hide his amusement.

"I apologize, Mrs. Hughes," Niall said, picking up a bacon strip and giving it a good chomp.

"Noah, your friend," Mrs. Hughes said, bustling around the table, adding food to the plate she was fixing for Father Wilson. "What was his profession?"

"He said he works in transportation." He didn't know the details, but Billie had told him that much.

Mrs. Hughes looked at Niall, and then away. "I'll just run this up to Father and then start cleaning up the kitchen. Take your time finishing your breakfast."

When she was out of earshot, Noah set his elbows on the table. "Why do I sense some unease about the transportation sector in Chicago?"

Niall laughed, wiping his mouth. "Oh, we've all probably seen too many gangster movies. The bad guys always say they're in transportation. I'm sure Billie has better sense."

And Noah was trying to be a pal, much like Billie was likely. He'd thought it made sense to consider working with a guy he served with. They knew each other, after all. Had fought in the trenches together. Billie knew Chicago, and Noah didn't. He wasn't going to rely on Anna for everything. He wasn't that kind of man.

But after visiting some of the bars his friend used to frequent downtown, Noah wasn't so sure they had the same professional interests or life philosophy. He hadn't missed the sawed-off shotgun behind the bar. Sure, the bar where he'd worked in D.C. had a gun as well, but only a pistol. A gun like that meant serious business. He'd had enough of guns in the war and would be happy to never see another one ever again.

"Billie is...different here, not that we've spent that much time together," Noah said. In truth, he wanted to spend every day with Anna, and Billie had teased him about it.

"When you're fighting with a guy," he continued, "you don't talk much about the past and the like, I guess."

"You did with Martin," Niall said, drinking his coffee.

"I met Martin in basic training. Totally different. We had more time then." They hadn't known what war was yet. God, they hadn't had a clue.

"I forgot about that," Niall said. "Being on the front, things move a lot faster."

It was uncanny how much Niall seemed to understand about war. Noah imagined he'd spoken to many soldiers in his time as a priest.

"I need to go," Noah said, standing up. "You taking care of your bees today?"

Niall leaned back. "You should try it sometime. They're oddly calming, and there's a logic to nature that awes me."

"I imagine you get calm or else you get stung," Noah said as he left the table.

"You're turning into a regular philosopher, Noah," Niall said. "Have a great day."

Noah laughed. A regular philosopher. Now that would be a gig he could get into. Thinking about life. Writing about it. And then passing what he learned on to other men. His mind conjured up a painting of a group of young men clustered around Aristotle and Plato. He'd seen that in a book called *The School of Athens*.

When he reached the porch of the rectory, he felt the urge to stop and stretch. His lower back cracked, and he did some side twists to work out the kinks. Man, he missed some of the physical exertion of being in the

Army. Niall had suggested he take up boxing since there was a club not far from Dougherty's Pub. But he didn't want to smash any more guys' faces in. No, he could do some push-ups and sit-ups in his room when he felt the urge and let that be enough.

Some cheering attracted his attention, and he turned his head to see Anna running toward the playground, Robbie Dougherty on her heels. He took off in their direction and noticed the fight right away. Two boys were rolling on the ground, surrounded by a cluster of boys cheering over them. It was like the inverse of the image he'd just thought about.

"Willie Buckley! Brendan Dougherty! You stop this right now." She pushed into the circle of boys, fearless, and leaned down to grab the boys.

She was going to get hurt, he thought, increasing his speed. While the boys who'd been watching had all gone silent, the two in the middle were still punching each other. He put on another burst of speed, reaching them just in time to step in front of Anna.

"Hey! That's enough!" He grabbed both of the boys and hauled them up by their arms.

Willie's face was dirty and it looked like he'd been crying. He hit Brendan in the gut before Noah could wrangle them farther apart.

"Boys!" Anna cried.

"Willie Buckley, you'd better stop this right now," Noah said. "Settle down!"

The boy was straining in his hold as he stared at Brendan. "It's not fair."

"Willie, what's gotten into you?" Anna asked.

"His dad is back, and my brother isn't," Willie said. "He was bragging about it."

Brendan clenched his fists. "I was not!"

"He was not!" his younger brother yelled from behind Anna.

"You shouldn't have gotten the teacher," Brendan yelled back.

"Yes, he should have," Anna said. "You shouldn't be fighting like this. As for the rest of you boys... Go on home now or I'll talk to your mothers. It's not nice to cheer people on when they're fighting. Fighting is wrong. Isn't it?"

Everyone muttered, "Yes, Miss Sims."

"Now off with you," she said, waving her hands as they all started to run off. "Except for Willie and Brendan here."

Noah kept hold of Willie even though the boy was now hanging his head in defeat.

"Over to the bench, you two," Anna ordered, his beautiful tiger radiating with anger.

Man, she looked beautiful. In a different situation, he'd have told her so, but she was on a mission, and he was going to sit back and watch.

They hopped up onto the bench, sitting on opposite ends. Noah stood behind them, and Anna stood in front.

"Everything all right out there?" Niall called from a top window in the rectory.

"Anna's got it in hand," Noah yelled back.

She finally spared him a glance, and he could feel the singe of her fire. Oh, these boys were about to get a good talking to.

Sure enough, she was in full teacher mode when she said, "Willie, I want you to tell me what happened."

"But Miss Sims, he hit me first!" Brendan said.

"That's why he's going first." She crossed her arms. "I'm waiting."

Willie kicked his legs in the air. "I'm tired of him always talking about his dad being home. It's bragging, Miss Sims."

"It is not!" Brendan cried. "I'm glad my dad is back. You're just jealous my dad's alive and your brother isn't!"

Willie lunged for him, but Noah was ready for it. He pulled him back.

"That's what he said, Miss Sims!" Willie knuckled

away tears. "That's why I hit him."

Noah felt his throat clog up at the sight of the young boy fighting tears. Here was an angry boy, fighting grief and injustice he couldn't possibly understand at his age. He couldn't help but think about Mrs. Sims. She was old enough to understand, but even she didn't. Did this kind of thing ever make sense?

Anna knelt in front of the boys. She put one hand on Willie's back, the other on Brendan's knee. "No, it's not fair, Willie. But you know it's wrong to hit someone. And Brendan, you know it's wrong to hit back."

The boy opened his mouth, but she gave him a look, and he promptly shut it.

"This war started because someone hit someone, and someone decided to hit back," she said. "And they kept on hitting back. Really hard. Good men got killed like Willie's brother, Kevin, and my brother, Martin."

She paused, and Noah saw a sheen of tears in her eyes before she blinked them away.

"I bet Noah could tell you about a whole bunch of other boys who got killed too. I bet he could tell you how senseless the fighting felt. How much he wished that first guy hadn't thrown that first punch."

The boys both turned to look at him. They were so little right now, but they were going to grow up someday. If they kept fighting to solve their disagreements, it would lead to bigger consequences than a dustup on a school playground. That kind of fighting caused wars. It occurred to him there was an opportunity here. Drive home the lesson that fighting is wrong, that it can hurt people, and maybe the kids would learn a better way. Maybe this was how you stopped wars before they started.

He came around and knelt beside Anna. She rested her hand next to his, not clasping it, mind you, but just touching, like she needed the connection.

"Anna's right," he said. "There's nothing fair about guys getting killed, and there sure as heck isn't anything fair about fighting. You can stop that now and be a lot happier, let me tell you, because fighting also hurts you. As much as the other guy if not more..."

Their eyes grew wide as saucers at that, and he felt Anna lean closer.

"When you hit a guy—even one you're mad at—it makes you feel bad. Maybe not in the moment. But later. Willie, do you feel bad that you hit Brendan?"

The boy was quiet for a moment, but then he nodded.

Noah turned to Brendan. "What about you?"

He nodded as well, ducking his head.

"Fighting isn't the answer to a problem. Everyone who went to war found that out, and it's going to take a long while before we get it all sorted out."

"My dad screams at night," Brendan whispered. "My mom says he's hurting real bad."

He looked over at Anna and saw her swallow thickly. She met his eyes, and in them, he could see the pain they all carried around. Should he let her continue? This was her show. Then she lifted her chin, like she wanted him to go on.

"We're all hurting real bad," he said. "That's why it's even more important that we be nice to each other. Willie, if you're feeling upset that Brendan's dad is back and your brother isn't, you come and talk to me or Miss Sims. We'll listen to you, and that way, you'll get it out of your system without fighting. Okay?"

The young boy knuckled away more tears. Noah turned to Brendan.

"As for you responding like you did," he said. "I know it's hard not to hit someone back when they have a go at you, but I can tell you from experience that it only makes things worse. Maybe next time, you can step back and ask the boy who hit you why he threw the punch. And if he doesn't tell you, then maybe you can walk away. Show him you're not going to give him the satisfaction."

Brendan gave him a single nod. "Sure would keep me out of trouble."

"So you're sorry then?" Anna asked. "You know how much we talk about forgiving people and meaning it. I want you both to say it and shake hands."

Brendan lifted a shoulder. "I'm sorry you thought I was bragging, Willie. And I'm really sorry your brother is dead."

There was an audible sniff. "Me too, and I'm sorry I punched you."

They each extended a hand, not meeting the other's eyes, and shook.

"Okay," Anna said. "You can go now."

They jumped off the bench, and Brendan ran off. Willie looked like he was about to do the same, but he hesitated.

"Miss Sims, do you ever want to hit anything?" he asked in a rush. "I mean, I know you're a girl and all."

Noah felt his lips twitch and looked away so no one would see.

"Yes, I sometimes want to hit something—not someone, mind you—but that doesn't make it right. You know what? I recently found something that makes me stop wanting to lash out. Want to hear my secret?"

He leaned forward. "A secret? You bet."

"It's a hug," she said, opening her arms. "They make people feel better."

His face scrunched up, and he leaned back. Noah almost laughed at the horror on his face.

"Yuck. That's sissy stuff."

Anna gave Noah a look, and he nodded. "The two of us don't think it's sissy stuff," she said.

"But he's your fella, Miss Sims. Of course, you're going to want to hug and kiss on him. It's not for boys like me. Someone would beat me up for sure." Willie gave a deep sigh like the weight of the world was on his shoulders and then ran off.

"I wish we could do something more for him," Noah said.

Anna put her arm around his back and leaned against him. "Me too, but what we just did... It makes a bigger difference than you know. That's why I love being a teacher. At their age, they're still impressionable. They may even listen. You were great, by the way. Sorry if I put you on the spot, but the boys look up to you."

He'd noticed it too and had done his best to interact with them.

"You did good too," he said. "But you really shouldn't wade into a fight like that."

The narrow-eyed look she gave him made him want to snatch her close and kiss her senseless. She seemed to know it too. Her lips curved, and she blushed.

A car horn honked, and they looked over. Billie waved out the window. "Hey you two. Are you ever apart? You're like Siamese twins."

Noah caught Anna's eye roll and decided on the spot not to encourage her to walk him to the car. She didn't like Billie and he respected that. For that matter, Billie didn't seem to like her much either. Well, they didn't have to be bosom friends.

"I need to go," he said, kissing her on the cheek. "I'll try and get back early so I can cut the grass." Fortunately she'd consented to let him do little chores around the house, and he hoped alluding to one would improve her mood.

"If you're not in jail," she said, rolling her eyes.

Was her opinion of Billie that bad? "I'm sure I'll be fine. Don't worry about me."

He took off toward the car, already wishing he hadn't agreed to meet Billie's transportation associates. More than ever, he wanted to do something that made a difference. Wanted it to feel as weighty as what he and Anna had done for those boys.

Something like that would give his life meaning and make things better—even if it was only on a school playground.

Chapter 16

WHEN ANNA WOKE UP THE NEXT DAY, SHE LAY IN BED and started to hum.

She felt so hopeful. Sure, the war was still going on, and it was the second of August, which meant she'd have to endure three weeks more of Noah's so-called planning, but silver linings abounded. Everything seemed to be painted with hope.

Last night after dinner and a picture show at Navy Pier, Noah had told her he wouldn't be doing any business with Billie. She'd almost cheered. And he'd said Billie wasn't going to be around much since his new transportation assignments were going to be taking him to Detroit and some other cities once a week.

Ice cream had seemed like just the thing to celebrate in her mind, and she'd suggested they go to the soda shop she'd written him about in one of her letters. She'd savored her scoop of vanilla, but her enjoyment had been slightly diminished by the look of distaste on Noah's face. The soda shop was part of an elaborate entertainment complex Uncle Sam had created amidst one of its largest training centers along Lake Michigan.

Of course he didn't like it. It was like the USO times ten.

An idea blossomed. Noah needed to see all of the

good the city of Chicago was doing for the war effort. They'd met Alice for dinner downtown a few nights ago, but her friend hadn't talked much about her job at the airplane plant.

In fact, no one in the neighborhood ever really talked about that kind of work. It was just what a person did, and in that way, their close-lippedness was no different than any solider doing his duty.

But Anna had decided it was high time to show Noah the other side of Chicago's war effort. Today she was taking him out to Alice's plant under the auspices of dropping off a dress her friend needed for a date tonight. Of course, Alice *did* have a hot date with a sailor just back from Europe, so she wasn't lying. She was... being strategic. Noah needed some help liking Chicago, and she was just the girl to show him.

Then there was her mother...

Willie and Brendan's fight had given her an idea. Maybe her mother needed more hugs to help her through her grief. She was going to offer one this morning when she went down.

Eager, she rose from her bed and got ready. When she reached the kitchen, her mother already had coffee made and was sitting at the kitchen table eating a slice of toast.

"Hi, Mom," she said, feeling her body sway as she wandered over to the cupboard for a mug.

"You're awfully chipper this morning," she commented.

Anna ignored her tone. She'd learned never to let her students' tones sway her from her purpose, and the same principle applied here. "I am, Mom. In fact, I'm so chipper, I thought I'd hug you."

She set her mug on the table and leaned over her mother, wrapping her arms around her.

Her mother grew tall and stiff in her chair. "What's gotten into you?"

Keep going. Rome wasn't built in a day. "I love you,

that's all. We don't seem to say it enough."

"Sounds like you're saying it enough for both of us right now," her mother said, pushing her away.

She tried not to feel dejected. Picking up her mug, she poured herself some coffee and sat down. "Can we ever say something like that enough?"

"Yes," her mother said, crunching on her toast.

Anna waited for her to finish chewing. "Mom, things are going so great with Noah. I was hoping we might have him over for dinner again."

"He's practically here for lunch everyday," she said.

She forced a smile. "But we'd love for you to join us."

Her mother took another bite, and Anna knew it was meant to be a delay. Sure enough, she chewed that one bite of dry toast so slowly it was like watching molasses run down a spoon.

"I need to go to work," her mother said.

"Mom—"

"Anna, I don't want to speak with that boy again right now," she said. "What you do in your own time is...well, your own. But you'd best keep in mind that the War Department may call him up soon, what with the Japs not surrendering."

This time it was Anna who delayed by taking a sip of coffee. Surely her mother couldn't want that, not when she knew how much it would hurt her.

"If he's as noble as you seem to think, shouldn't he be over there in the Pacific helping our boys out instead of lollygagging over here with you every day?"

She was sure her mouth parted in shock. Lollygagging? "If you must know, Noah has been thinking about going over to the Pacific to fight if the war continues. He's giving it until school starts..."

Her earlier good mood evaporated and she felt fear wrap icy coils around her again. Three weeks wasn't very long. Would Japan ever give up?

"Good," her mother said and left the kitchen.

Good? What did that mean? Good that he was considering it? Oh, she just didn't know what to do. This
morning's silver linings already felt like so much dis-
carded tinsel. She rose and tossed her mother's unfin-
ished toast in the garbage. She thought of Willie asking
her if she ever wanted to hit something. Right now, she
did.

When Noah arrived at the house a few hours later
for lunch, she shut the door behind him and grabbed
him to her.

"Hey," he said, tucking her close. "What's wrong?"

She pressed her face into his uniform. He was warm
from the sun, and she still felt cold from her talk with
her mother. "I just want the war to be done. That's all."

He caressed her back in gentle strokes. "Me too,
sweetheart. Me too."

They stayed that way for a long time until he pulled
away. "Come on, let's turn on some music and have
lunch."

They often danced after they finished eating, and
she was tempted to put off their visit to see Alice, if only
to have his arms around her longer. But she'd already
arranged the whole thing, and she knew her friend had
gone to some trouble to get them onto the grounds.

"We're going to take a ride after lunch," she told
him as he turned on the radio. "I have to drop something
off for Alice."

He cocked his brow, but didn't say anything. She
started fixing them lunch, and it made her smile when
she caught him humming along to the song on the radio.
It was good to hear him do that. Good to see the other
changes in him too. He didn't look as drawn anymore,
and he'd put on some weight. He'd told her he was sleeping better, but he didn't talk about his nightmares, and
she didn't ask.

After lunch, she tossed him the car keys, and they
drove out of her neighborhood. The neighbors waved as
they passed by, and some of the kids stopped playing

ball to run alongside them. It made her feel like she was enclosed in a warm cocoon, and she was happy to see Noah smile and wave in return.

"You want to tell me where we're going?" he asked.

"To the Dodge Aircraft Plant," she told him. "That's where Alice works."

He gestured to the dress she'd wrapped in brown paper. "She couldn't have gotten this from you after hours?"

"She has a hot date tonight," she said. "Plus, this will give us a chance to get out of the house. It's a nice day."

He glanced over at her. "You're wasting your gas rations on fashion," he said with a smile, one she knew was teasing.

"You're not a girl," she said. "Plus, she and I have traded dresses before. With the war on, new clothes are hard to come by. Alice and I often wished we wore the same shoe size too. You're probably tired of seeing me in these old shoes."

His mouth twitched like he was fighting laughter. "Yeah, that's why I stare at your legs. Easier on the eyes."

She socked him. "You're being fresh."

He grinned. "Guilty, and happy to be. Anna, you have great legs."

She primly crossed them. "Thank you. Best keep your eyes on the road, though. We don't need to get into an accident over them."

His laughter washed over her, and she leaned back against her seat. Oh, how she cherished these moments with him. She could see the rest of their lives in front of them.

When they arrived at the plant's entrance, Noah whistled. "Holy crap, this place is huge. I've never seen anything like it."

Anna took her cue. "The *Tribune* says it's the biggest factory in the world. It takes up something like thirty blocks, Noah." Eighty-two acres, to be exact, but she wasn't going to tell him that. He might be on to her.

"That is big," he said, slowing down. "I'm not sure we can get in. There's a guard post, Anna."

"Alice put our names on the list, don't worry," she told him.

"She did, huh?" he asked, glancing over at her. "That couldn't have been easy."

She buffed her unpainted nails. "I couldn't say."

He pulled up to the guard station, and sure enough, their names were there. The guard advised them on where to park so they could meet Alice.

The long, flat stretch of the parking lot was filled with thousands of cars, and Anna was amazed at the sight of them. She'd known this place was huge, but seeing it was another thing. She counted over a dozen buildings in addition to the main one, which stretched as far as the eye could see. After Noah parked, they walked hand in hand toward the admittance door the guard had told them about.

Noah seemed to be eating up everything in sight, just like she'd hoped. "It's something, isn't it?"

"They built all this after the war started?" Noah asked.

"Yes," she said, marveling at it as well. "When we Chicagoans decide to do something, we get it done." Oh, that was lame.

"No kidding."

Alice opened the door they were heading toward, and she looked like a grease monkey if you asked Anna. "Hey, kids! The guard told me you were here. You have that same look on your face I did when I first started working here. Isn't she something?"

"She sure is," Noah said, tilting his head back to take in the endless expanse of the brick building and metal roof.

"Thanks for bringing that dress, Anna." She gave her a conspiratorial wink. "I owe you one. Noah, I'm taking my coffee break. Would you like to pop in and take a quick look-see? Anna probably wouldn't be interested."

"Oh, yes I would," she said, wanting to wink back at her friend but knowing better.

"I'd love that," he said. "I mean, I knew there were plants like this. But seeing one..."

"Come on," Alice said, leading them inside.

Rows of machines filled the space, operated by thousands of women dressed in gray uniforms just like the one Alice wore. Of course, everyone wore the same hairstyle—a V-roll covered with a hairnet—to keep it from getting caught in the machinery.

"We make all kinds of aircraft here," Alice told her. "I work on the B-29 propellers over there. It's tough work, but I love it. Heck, all of us women here are glad we do some heavy lifting. We know our boys are working hard."

Some of the women quickly waved and then focused back on what they were doing.

"Those machines seem to be going so fast," Anna observed.

She'd thought about working in a plant during her summer vacation last year, but her mother had been dead set against it. One of her friend's daughters had lost an arm in a machinery accident. Anna hadn't been deterred, but the plant manager hadn't wanted to train her for such a short time of employment. She certainly wouldn't have quit her teaching position. Instead, she'd used her extra time to volunteer at the hospital, something she'd decided to give up now that Noah was back and school was starting again at the end of the month. The USO was closer and, honestly, less emotionally draining.

"You can't sleep on this job, let me tell you," Alice said. "Then again, I bet Noah couldn't sleep on his either."

"What?" he asked, turning his head away from the factory floor to look at her.

"Never mind," she said. "Okay, you two. I have to

grab my coffee and get back to work. Anna, I'll let you know how my date goes."

"Have fun," she said, making a move to hug her friend. She stopped at the last second. Would it be inappropriate to hug her at her workplace?

"What did you stop for?" Alice asked, giving her a bear hug and then stepping back. "Noah, you want one?"

He blinked for a moment. "No, I'm good. We'll let you get back to work. You tell your fellow workers...thank you for me, okay?"

Anna felt her heart melt, and Alice must have been equally affected because she punched him in the shoulder. "Oh, you're a sweetheart even if you're an egghead sometimes. Get out of here before you make me cry."

"I didn't mean—"

"Go!" Alice said and hurried off across the concrete floors toward her station.

Noah took one last look before they walked back toward the door. Outside, he turned back again to look at the exterior of the building, soaking up every detail, and she was feeling pretty proud of herself by the time they slid into the car.

"Thank you for bringing me here," he told her as he put the car in gear and drove them out of the plant. "I take back *almost* everything I've ever said about your fine city and its participation in the war effort. The women of Chicago deserve a whole passel of Silver Stars, if you ask me."

She bit her lip to keep from smiling. *Gotcha*, she thought. Oh, Alice could keep her dress for helping her! "I'll be sure to tell Alice you said so."

He cocked his brow. "I still don't like all the bowling at the USO and croquet playing on Lake Michigan though, and don't think I ever will."

"I can live with that," she said, trying to keep the glee from her expression.

"Of course, I know when I've walked into an ambush," he told her, his tone droll. "Tiger Anna and Onion-Peeler Alice could have single-handedly taken down the Nazis."

She started laughing. "Onion-Peeler?"

"Never mind," Noah said, grinning at her. "Where to, my beautiful strategist?"

Only one place came to mind. "Home."

Chapter 17

"Noah," Anna called. "Come listen to the radio. We dropped some giant bomb on Hero-something in Japan. President Truman's talking about it."

Finally, solid news. Today marked the sixth of August and Noah was trying not to focus on how many days were left until his self-imposed deadline was up.

He rose from his seat at the kitchen table and walked swiftly into the parlor. Anna turned up the radio, and they both leaned toward it as if it were a fire in winter.

"More power than twenty thousand tons of TNT," Noah heard the president say.

His whole body seemed to rock back on its heels. He'd worked with TNT over there. Twenty thousand tons? He couldn't imagine the devastation a bomb like that must have wreaked. He listened as President Truman continued his speech, talking about Pearl Harbor and payback. Part of him wondered if the bloodshed would ever end. History was full of bloody paybacks.

"That has to mean we're close to the end, right?" Anna asked.

Part of him wanted to shush her so he wouldn't miss anything. "Truman's certainly made a statement to the enemy, that's for sure."

"An atomic bomb?" she asked. "Harnessing the power

of the universe? Goodness, that sounds incredible. I don't even know what that means, but it must be big."

He gave in and put his hand on her shoulder. "Shh... let's hear the rest."

Noah rubbed his hands together as the president talked about destroying every productive enterprise in Japan—their docks, factories, and communications. This was the kind of thing he and the other boys had done in Europe.

As the president went on about how Japan's leaders shouldn't have turned down the Allies' ultimatum at Potsdam for them to surrender, Noah could only agree. Uncle Sam wouldn't have issued terms for peace unless it had a Plan B. This atomic bomb seemed to be the start of a new air campaign. The Japs couldn't keep going against a weapon like that. God, he hoped they'd surrender. The president was laying down another ultimatum, and if they didn't fold soon, more people were going to lose their lives. Lots more.

"I can't believe they spent two billion dollars on it," Anna whispered, her hand over her heart. "My heavens, I had no idea. Oh please God, let Japan surrender now."

Noah put his hand on her shoulder as the president said, "What has been done is the greatest achievement of organized science in history."

"Turn that radio down," Mrs. Sims shouted. "I have a headache."

Anna took a few steps away from him in the direction of the stairway. "Mother, we dropped some new bomb on Japan. The president is talking. You should come and listen."

"I don't care what the news says," she called back. "It doesn't change anything for me. Turn it down."

Didn't change anything for her? People were still dying out there. Other people's sons. Noah didn't wait for Anna to follow Mrs. Sims' instructions. He lowered the volume himself. Fighting that woman was a lose-lose situation, he'd decided. Rather like trying to take a

German outpost defended by machine guns and snipers without a plan.

"I'm sorry," Anna said, her blue eyes pinched at the corners like they usually got when she was upset.

"It's fine," he said, putting his arm around her. "We heard what we needed. Hopefully the Japanese will give up after this."

Surely it would accelerate their surrender. He'd taken to chatting with some of the other guys in the neighborhood, and they were all wondering how much longer the other side could hold out. Even Brian Dougherty was talking about possibly heading to the Pacific if the war didn't end soon, although he hadn't told his wife that. Noah understood. No one wanted to talk about it.

"Let's have some coffee," she said, taking his hand.

They walked back to the kitchen, and he watched as she lit a cigarette. She didn't smoke much, but sometimes he teased her about it. He hadn't picked them back up. They made him jittery somehow, and he was jumpy enough without them. Hell, yesterday, he'd heard a loud crack on the way to Anna's house and he'd instantly gone to the ground in a crouch. After scanning the street, he'd caught sight of Frankie O'Keefe and Willie Buckley playing baseball. The ball had hit the bat just right apparently, but Noah had registered it as something more menacing. Thank God no one had seen him. He'd been so keyed up—and ashamed—he'd continued on past Anna's house, walking in the neighborhood until he was calm again.

Going to the Pacific was only going to make things worse, and he wondered if his days as "Lucky Strike" might just come to an end over there. Man, he hoped this bomb was going to get through to those stubborn Japs.

But they didn't surrender right away, and Noah found himself staring sightlessly out the window of his bedroom at the rectory. The suspense was eating at him, just like the notion that he should be over there helping the boys end this thing. He didn't go down to the library that night, not wanting to talk about his current struggle with Niall. The man thankfully respected his need to mull things over on his own.

When the Army dropped another atomic bomb on Nagasaki three days later and the Japs still didn't surrender, he wanted to pound the table. He'd spent some time doing the math on how much land mass would be affected by the kind of TNT they were talking about. Heck, if their boys kept dropping bombs like this, there would be nothing left of the stinking island.

Seeing the calculations eased his mind, but it didn't ease the tension in his chest. If this new weapon didn't make the enemy cower and give up, nothing would. He should go and do his part. Anna seemed to know he was struggling because the silence between them had started to grow over meals and drives along Lake Michigan over the next couple days. She would support him. That he knew. But neither one of them could stand the thought of him leaving again.

He tried to reassure her by bringing her some roses from Mrs. Fitzsimmons' garden. The woman had finally cornered him about coming for tea and pound cake, and no one had exaggerated the quality of her cake. He'd eaten every bite even though his appetite was basically nonexistent these days, which was disheartening since it had just begun to improve.

The roses were starting to wilt in the vase when Anna burst into the kitchen where he was sitting with another cup of coffee, looking frazzled.

"Didn't you tell me to pick you up at five-thirty?" he asked. "Your mother wasn't happy to see me, but she told me to pour myself a cup of coffee—"

"Japan surrendered!" she yelled. "I was late coming back from the market when Brendan Dougherty ran out of his house and told me. Then Robbie came out, jumping up and down, and I ran the rest of the way home. Oh, Noah, could it really be over?"

God, he wanted it to be true. Only four days had passed since the last A-bomb had been dropped on the ninth. He rose, his muscles locked with tension. "Let's turn the broadcast on."

She dumped the grocery bag in her hands on the table, knocking over the sugar bowl in her haste, and together they dashed into the parlor. They caught the broadcast in the middle, but when he heard President Truman say, "the unconditional surrender of Japan," Noah felt his knees turn weak. It was true.

"I need to sit down," he said, and suddenly he was on the floor.

"Noah!" Anna said, crouching down beside him.

"I'm okay," he said, not mentioning he was seeing stars. "It's over, Anna. It's over!"

She launched herself at him, and he fell onto his back. "Thank you, God. Oh, thank you!"

The president continued, "...the formal signing of the surrender terms at the earliest possible moment."

When Noah heard that General MacArthur would be arranging the surrender, he was relieved. Nobody messed with the general. If Japan was planning anything, MacArthur would ferret it out.

"Oh, Noah, could the war really be over for good?" Anna asked, her hands resting on his chest. "Part of me just can't believe it."

"Sounds like it," he said, glad he was lying down. He wasn't sure he could stay steady on his feet. "The president wouldn't talk about the Allies suspending fighting if it weren't."

Of course, as a solider, he'd been trained to be suspicious. On two occasions, the Jerries had held up white flags of surrender only to start firing on them as they moved in. Good men had been killed with those feints, and he'd torn one of those makeshift flags in two after looking at the bodies lining the ground.

Cheering rose up outside the house, and Anna hurried over to the window. "Everyone is coming out into the street. Oh, Noah, it's like the day when peace was declared in Europe."

He pushed off the floor and had to shake his head to clear it. It dawned on him that he wouldn't have to go to the Pacific.

He could make a life with Anna, a life he'd only dreamed about.

He could look to the future and see something besides more violence and gore. Anna crouched down beside him, and he wrapped her up in his arms.

"Oh, Noah, it's over," she said, her voice breaking. "You'll be safe. You won't have to go back. Oh, thank you, God."

"What are you two doing on the floor?" Mrs. Sims snapped. "Anna, get up. This is totally improper."

Anna rose. "Mom, the war is over! President Truman just announced it. Japan surrendered. Isn't it wonderful?"

"Is that why everyone's cheering?" Her mom reached out a hand and stumbled to the chair. "But Martin still won't be coming back."

Anna crouched in front of her. "But no more boys are going to die, Mom. Isn't that worth *something*? Now we can all move forward with our lives."

Noah agreed with her sentiment—it was worth celebrating that nobody else would pay the price for their freedom—but the war had changed everything and everybody. He'd seen it in Europe, and he saw it every time he walked through Anna's neighborhood and saw those white flags with the gold stars. Good men and women weren't coming back, and their absence would always be felt. Mrs. Sims was a testimony to that.

"I'm glad for other mothers," Mrs. Sims said.

They were charitable words, and for a moment Noah had hope. Would Mrs. Sims be able to move forward like Anna had said?

"Oh, I'm tired now," she said, dabbing her forehead

with her black handkerchief. "You two go on if you'd like. I...don't want to celebrate."

"But everyone is out in the streets, Mom," Anna said, placing her hand on Mrs. Sims' knee. "Come out for a little bit. It will do you good."

"I have to work tomorrow," she said.

"I doubt it, Mom. Everyone will be off, even if it is a Wednesday."

Mrs. Sims removed Anna's hand. "Anna, please. Don't tell me what's good for me. You don't know. No one does."

She pulled herself up out of the chair and shuffled slowly out of the parlor, leaving a pocket of solemn silence that felt at odds with the cheering going on outside. Noah didn't much feel like going outside either, in truth; he found himself understanding Mrs. Sims. What was there to celebrate really? There had been so much death and destruction. So much loss. The cost had been so high.

But he went anyway, for Anna. Dinnertime seemed to have been forgotten by everyone in light of the news. Some of the neighbors hugged him as if he were a long-lost friend. Other men pumped his hand and punched him in the shoulder, talking about Uncle Sam and the boys taking it to the Japs. The younger boys launched themselves at his legs, and little Robbie Dougherty held out his hands so he'd lift him up for a hug. The little tyke always had a warm welcome for him, and Noah looked forward to it now.

But it was Katherine Kenna who broke his heart. She pressed her face into his chest and started sobbing, saying the surrender had come too late for her fiancé. Her grief pinged his own and images of his fallen friends filtered through his mind. Noah comforted her as best he could.

He felt like he was looking at the scene through a glass wall. That he was going through the motions.

The noise of the growing crowd started to make

him feel jittery, and he downed a shot of whiskey Brian Dougherty shoved into his hands. The man was carrying around a bottle, holding up a "victory" shot glass for everyone to use. Noah's head was already pounding by the time Anna suggested they go downtown to join the larger celebration. The sun was setting, and all he could think was how he wished it were later than eight so he'd have a good excuse to go back to the rectory.

But Anna's eyes were shining with joy, and he didn't have the heart to tell her. She drove them as far as she could on Michigan Ave., given the crowd of revelers thronging the streets, and then parked on a side street. There were people everywhere, thousands of them packed onto the warm August pavement. The sky was dark, but the city lights seemed as bright as sparklers to Noah, and the noise was deafening. People were crying, laughing, and whistling shrilly amidst the sounds of noise makers and the honks of parked cars.

It felt like it was all closing in on him. Noah's entire body was sweating. He shoved away some guy who tried to kiss Anna. She gave him a concerned look, but kept hold of his hand, thank God. If they got separated in this crowd, he would have trouble finding her, and he didn't like that one bit.

Faces of cheering people swam in his vision, and when someone slammed into him from behind, he turned around and pushed back. The guy shouted at him, but Noah couldn't make out the words over the ringing in his ears. He began to tug Anna through the crowd, looking for an open space free of people. God, he couldn't breathe.

"Noah, what are you doing?" she asked, pulling on his hand.

"It's not safe," he called over his shoulder. "Too many people. Too many people."

He could feel panic building, his heart racing. If he could have run through the crowd, he would have. He pushed people aside in his haste to cut a path through. One drunk guy didn't budge, but when he looked at Noah, he hastily moved out of the way. *Good decision*, Noah thought. It took four more blocks of pulling Anna through the mob, but he finally found a break in the crowd. When they were clear of the throng, he bent at the waist, sucking in giant gulps of air.

"Noah, are you okay?" she asked, crouching down until she was eye level.

"Too many people," he said. "Can't breathe."

"Oh, honey," she said, using an endearment he'd never heard before. "Why didn't you say something?"

"Trying to be...tough," he rasped out. "You...wanted...to celebrate."

"Not like this," she said, her brow wrinkling.

He felt her small hand make soothing circles along his spine. Closing his eyes, he focused on that small comfort and on filling his lungs with oxygen. It felt like an eternity until he could stand up straight, and even then his lower back hitched after being in one position for so long.

She took his face in her hands, and he had to focus to meet her gaze. "Don't ever do that again."

Anna the Tiger stood before him, and he simply nodded.

"Can you get to the curb?" she asked. "I'll go get the car. You sit."

There was no way he was letting her go alone. "I'm coming with you."

"You look like you're going to fall down," she said. "Stay here. I won't be long."

"In that crowd?" he asked. "Forget it. Anna, I marched in the Vosges Mountains nonstop for days with barely any food and water. Trust me, I won't pass out."

He had to protect her from those idiots taking advantage of the crowd and the spirit of celebration. How many women had he seen kissed and groped? It was a disgrace to everything they'd fought for, and he wanted to knock those guys' blocks off.

She put her hands on her hips. "Are you really going to fight me on this?"

"Yes," he said, narrowing his eyes.

"Fine." She turned and marched off, her heels clomping against the pavement.

He followed her, keeping his eyes fixed on her blue dress. She was booking it, and he didn't want to expend the effort to keep up with her just now. By the time they reached the car, she was breathing hard. She yanked open the door and slid inside, not waiting for him to open the driver's side for her. He took his time, wanting a few more breaths of fresh air before sitting inside the hot car.

When they were both situated, she turned on the engine. The radio droned out news about the war ending, and she immediately turned it off. They rode back to her neighborhood in silence, a contrast to the traffic and occasional revelers in the streets, and he was glad for the break.

When she pulled to a stop in front of the rectory, she leveled a serious look at him. "Get some rest. I'll see you in the morning."

Leaning across the seat, she kissed his cheek. His mouth was dry, he realized, and no words came to mind. He'd been like this other times, completely shut down, barely able to take his pack off before falling onto his bed roll.

He found the door handle after a few tries and managed to exit the vehicle. Standing, he felt his body shift like it was weaving in place. He waited for the strange sensation to pass before putting one foot in front of the other and heading into the rectory. When he got inside, he went straight to his room and fell face first onto his bed. The silence was more than welcome. It was comforting, and his eyes grew heavy.

Martin was standing on the ridge, the white flag from his mother's window in his hands.

"It's time to take it down," his friend said. "The war

*is over, and you need to get going with your life. Time
to stop sticking my death and every other guy's death
in your face. Hah. Or in the window."*

*Leave it to Martin to joke about something so seri-
ous.*

"I don't want to take it down yet," Noah said. "You
deserve to be remembered."

*His friend threw the flag at him, and he caught
it against his chest. "Remember me by living. I don't
know why you're making it so difficult. You know what
you need to do."*

"The war just ended, and you're already getting on
my case?" he asked.

"Damn right I am," Martin said. "You're supposed
to be doing something big with your life. Teach people
about all that history and book stuff you know so much
about so a war like this never happens again. You'll be
good at it. And when boys get into fights like Willie and
Brendan did, you'll be able to break them up and drive
home the lesson."

*Martin was heading away from him, harder to see
because of the shadows enveloping him.*

It was dark when he awoke. He'd sweated through
his clothes, and his heart was going to beat itself out of
his chest. It took a while for it to pass, but Noah finally
sat up and started to undress. Maybe he'd feel better
after he sponged off and changed clothes. He couldn't
have slept long. He would take a walk. Think about the
dream.

As Noah roamed the halls of the rectory, he couldn't
help but think Martin was right. That maybe he'd really
spoken to him in his dream.

Teaching, huh? He thought about that painting of
Plato and Aristotle he liked so much. Isn't that what
they'd done? Taught young people. Encouraged them to
think for themselves. He would be good at it, and Martin
was right. He wouldn't mind breaking up an occasional
fight either, knowing that in doing so, he might help a

man choose peace instead of violence later on.

He wondered if Niall would be in the library. No doubt he'd been out celebrating like everyone else in Chicago. The light was visible under the door as Noah made his way toward the room. When he entered, Niall was sitting in his favorite chair, a whiskey in hand. There was no book in his lap tonight.

"You're not reading?" Noah asked.

"Lost in thought, I guess," Niall said with a wave of his hand. "I had a lot on my mind after getting back. You look pretty terrible yourself."

Noah sank into the adjoining chair, not bothering to seek out a book. "The celebration didn't agree with me."

"Me either," Niall said, sipping his whiskey. "You want one?"

The very thought made him queasy. "No thanks. What has you stirred up?"

"The war's over, but some things are never over," Niall said, his ruddy face looking years older tonight. "Oh, listen to me. I'm feeling maudlin."

Noah thought about his dream. "Me too. I'm glad the war is over, but I don't think I'll ever forget what happened." Heck, he wasn't sure he'd be able to do something as simple as drink milk again.

"You likely won't," Niall said. "I never have, and I'm a heck of a lot older than you, boyo."

Niall's Irish was prominent now, and Noah didn't think it was all the whiskey talking. "What do you mean?"

"I never told you that I was a chaplain in World War One," Niall said, folding his hands. "Why would I? It was a long time ago, and I don't talk about it much. It's not the kind of tale that would make anyone feel better right now."

And yet he was mentioning it to Noah. He felt honored somehow. "You were a chaplain? Were you in any action?"

His friend nodded. "Oh yes, and I've found myself thinking about my time in the war more than I'd like.

Noah, I've only told my confessor this, but I find I want to tell you. Perhaps I'm hoping for expiation. Or maybe I know you're one of the few men I can tell who would understand and not judge me."

Noah sat forward, his elbows on his knees. "I would never judge you."

"I know, and it's hard for me even so." Niall downed the last of his whiskey. "When I was a chaplain, I mostly did what I'd expected. Comforted the dying. Said prayers over the dead. Gave pep talks to soldiers when their own will was flagging. Steered them clear of moral dilemmas so they could do their duty. That sort of thing."

"I imagine you were good at it," Noah said.

"I was, but the Germans overran the unit I was with one night. One of our soldiers died to defend me. Private George Wallins. God rest his soul. He stepped in front of me without hesitation when they broke through the door. I caught him when he was hit, and we fell to the floor together. The soldiers—there were two of them—stood over me, and the one with the hard eyes raised his pistol. I knew he meant to kill me. Suddenly I was groping Private Wallins' body, looking for his pistol."

Noah held his breath.

"I shot the one who was going to kill me first," Niall said, pressing his hand to the bridge of his nose. "I looked at the other solider, and in his eyes I could see him deciding whether to run or to shoot me."

Noah had experienced that same moment many times, with many enemy soldiers. He'd always hoped the guy would run. Had wanted to scream it at him sometimes.

"When the other soldier lifted his pistol, I didn't hesitate. I shot him too. I was the only man who survived the ambush, and it won't surprise you to learn the Army didn't make any notes about me killing those soldiers. Of course, I told them everything that had happened. They weren't bothered by it and didn't want me to get into any trouble should the truth get out. I was transferred to a less active area, and after the war ended, I came home to Chicago and tried to act like it had never happened."

"But you couldn't," Noah said, shaking his head. "I can't imagine how hard that must have been for you as a priest."

"But am I any different than you?" Niall asked. "You may have killed more people, but you still struggle with the same question. Was it the right thing to do?"

"They were going to kill you," he stated.

"And yet, I'm supposed to be a man of God, aren't I? Turning the cheek was the furthest thing from my mind."

Noah could feel the man's desolation. "We've talked about this, Niall. Your God also talks about an eye for an eye."

"Which means it's up to my well-informed conscience to decide if I did the right thing. And therein lies the problem. Oh, I'm so tired of carrying this weight. It doesn't matter how much I pray or read about war, it still haunts me."

"You're a scholar," Noah said. "And a thinker. What are your arguments that you were in the right?" Maybe he could help Niall find some clarity...and talking this through might help both of them.

"Some days I can justify that God still had a purpose for me," he said. "Otherwise, I might have missed those soldiers. It's not like I'd ever been taught how to shoot a pistol."

Noah nodded. "Exactly. I wasn't accurate the first time I shot one. I missed. If Martin hadn't been there..."

"Then I think about those two soldiers—much like you think about the ones you killed—and how they were only doing their duty. But their hard eyes haunt me. That first solider wanted to kill me, and he didn't even know me. The second one could have walked away but didn't."

Noah had seen men like that. "Some men like to kill. The war brings it out in them." It had crossed his mind more than once that he was lucky Billie was on his side and not the enemy's. He was formidable in action.

"Does that excuse killing them? Is it still murder like Our Lord says? Excuse me, Noah. My Lord." He gave a half-hearted smile. "You see why I've enjoyed our talks. With the war coming to a close, we're all going to put one foot in front of the other and try to move forward. Men like you are going to do what the veterans did after the last war. Not talk about what happened. And so we're all left to our own silent agonies unless we have friends we can talk to in the middle of the night."

Noah sat back in his chair and propped his ankle over his knee. Niall needed something from him tonight, and as his friend, he wanted to help.

"You told me about that confession thing you Catholics have. Did you do it?"

Niall gave a hearty sigh. "At first I was afraid to. I feared they might sanction me or, even worse, defrock me. But I decided to seek out a priest I'd been in seminary with. He was the kindest of men. Wanted to work with the sick full-time, and that's no picnic, let me tell you."

Noah couldn't imagine anyone wanting to spend all their time like that. He'd seen plenty of people die, and he couldn't stand it. "So what happened?"

"I told him what I'd done, and he didn't say anything about it. I thought he might have been surprised or disappointed, but maybe that's my own lens coloring things. Still he said the prayers over me and gave me a hefty penance. One hundred Our Fathers, but even that didn't seem like enough."

"So what happened?"

Niall leaned his head back against the chair, his defeat palpable. "I thought the sacrament would ease my pain, but it didn't. It was the first time I'd doubted the sacraments, let me tell you, and that's like doubting one's faith. It didn't sit well."

"No one else can tell you how to feel about something.

And they can't change the way you feel by saying prayers over you either," Noah said. "No offense, but words don't mean anything unless you believe them yourself. Although I'm sure that confession thing can be a comfort." He believed in the power of words. But not like this.

This time Niall leaned forward. "You don't understand. The words of the sacrament are imbued with the power of God himself. They're supposed to change us."

He wasn't going to debate that. "But not you, apparently," Noah said matter-of-factly. "Maybe you're stubborn."

A glimmer of a smile touched Niall's face. "That's why you're a friend, Noah. You call a spade a spade. I *am* stubborn. Otherwise, why can't I find peace? Why can't I believe God has forgiven me? It was twenty-six years ago, for heaven's sake."

Noah didn't like thinking about carrying such a heavy burden for so long. He was twenty-three now, and if he followed Niall's example, he might still be having bad dreams when he was forty-nine. That felt like an eternity, and he wasn't going to allow it to go down that way. Surely there had to be an answer.

He searched his mind as he might a book, looking for the perfect bit of wisdom. But how could he hope to help Niall when he hadn't managed to help himself? Wasn't he struggling with the same thing? The search for absolution.

An answer came to him, courtesy of Saint Francis of Assisi, the soldier turned peacemaker. Noah had been reading a great deal of his writings lately. Suddenly he knew what he should say.

"You have to forgive yourself," Noah said, sitting forward in his chair in his eagerness. "You did what you felt you had to do in that moment. And you have to live with it. Maybe that's the part you've been missing. A confessor and a sacrament can't give that to you. You have to give it to yourself."

"You might be right, boyo," Niall said. "All this time

I've been asking God to forgive me. Heck, I even asked the two soldiers' souls to forgive me. I...didn't think to ask...myself."

His friend looked vulnerable, smaller and fragile suddenly, in his high-backed chair.

"I hadn't thought of it either until now," Noah said in wonder, folding his hands in his lap, as he realized he needed to do the same thing for himself—with Martin's death and with all of the other deaths he'd been involved in. "You know, I've read. I've mulled things over. I've even taken responsibility for what I did."

"But we haven't asked ourselves for forgiveness because to do so, on some level, would mean we admitting we did something wrong." Niall's mouth twisted. "I can see why it didn't dawn on us before."

Noah felt a smile touch his lips as they shared this moment of illumination, as Socrates might have called it. "I did what I felt was right. Fighting Hitler and everything he stood for. I don't have to forgive myself for that. But the things I had to do to fight him... Not all of those felt right. They felt..." He searched for the word. "Necessary."

"A powerful word, that," Niall said, nodding.

"And you did what you felt was necessary to survive," Noah said, looking his friend right in the eye. "Personally, I'm glad you did it. I'd have been without a friend otherwise."

Niall's chest lifted, and for a moment he closed his eyes. Noah wondered if he was praying and stayed quiet.

"You're a wise man and a good teacher, Noah Weatherby," Niall said, finally looking at him again, "and I'm grateful for it."

There was that word again. "I think I've decided what I want to do with my life. I want to teach. History, I think. Maybe I'll even be able to work in a little philosophy on the side."

Niall clasped his hands and smiled. "Bravo! You finally figured it out. I knew you would. You'll make a remarkable teacher, Noah, and trust me, I have a good sense about that as someone who hires them for our parish school."

Something calm spread in his chest. Peace. Just like good ol' Francis of Assisi talked about. And damn, if it didn't feel good. "I appreciate that, Niall."

"This calls for a celebration," his friend said, rising and pouring two whiskeys this time. "Deciding on one's purpose in life is a big moment."

They stood, and Noah felt a new camaraderie blossom, one that would span the years beyond the war.

"To all the minds you'll shape and the lives you'll touch."

He thought about how Anna glowed whenever she talked about teaching her students. He'd seen how much of a positive influence she had in their lives. It was one of the things he loved about her. He couldn't wait to tell her the news.

"Thank you, Niall. And on this day, the end of another war, I want to remember all our fallen boys, in your war and mine."

Niall's glass touched his. "And to everyone who died in the wake. May they—like us—be at peace. *Slainte*."

"Cheers," he said.

They threw back the whiskey and sat in easy silence until the first rays of sunshine touched the windows.

Chapter 18

ANNA FOUND HERSELF WORRYING ABOUT NOAH THE NEXT morning as she drank her coffee and had a cigarette. Her eggs lay mostly untouched. His reaction to the V-J celebration had more than troubled her. Was he right about it being immoral to celebrate victory in the face of so much loss? It seemed she'd found one thing he and her mother agreed upon. She'd tossed and turned most of the night, fingering her rosary beads and praying on and off.

In the midst of her turmoil, she'd asked herself what Martin would have done and the answer had been so clear. He would have drunk pint after pint, she imagined, maybe even danced a jig. He might have given a cheeky toast like "here's to mud in your eye" or something similar. Martin had always loved a good toast.

But then a dark thought had risen. Had the war changed the brother she'd known? Would he have reacted just like Noah did to the sea of people celebrating downtown if he'd lived?

She'd appreciated Noah's protectiveness. Being groped or kissed by strangers wasn't exactly welcome, but she would have allowed them some leeway given the circumstances. Besides, it hadn't only been protectiveness on Noah's part. There had been something else in his eyes, something hard and predatory, something she hadn't liked. The Noah she'd seen yesterday wasn't the man she knew. He was the soldier she suspected she would never know. The one he didn't want her to know. The one she suspected *she* didn't want to know. She'd seen a glimpse of him with Billie and hadn't liked it.

Perhaps Noah was right about compartmentalizing their lives, keeping everything from the war firmly tucked in the past.

When he hadn't appeared by noon for lunch, she told herself she'd give him another thirty minutes. The grandfather clock ticked the minutes away, and after the allotted time, she grabbed her purse and decided to walk to the rectory. The street was lined with streamers from the celebration the night before. Nothing like it had been downtown, mind you. She wouldn't want to be on the cleanup crew.

At the rectory, she knocked, her purse clutched to her stomach. Father Shaughnessy opened the door.

"Anna! What a wonderful surprise. I was just about to see to our church bees. Come in."

Usually the thought of him in a beekeeper's hat made her smile, but not today. She hesitated on the threshold. "I don't want to be a bother, but Noah didn't come by, and I got worried."

Father took her hand. "He was out early after eating a good Irish breakfast with me. I wouldn't worry. He had something to look into."

Somehow that didn't appease her. "It's not like him to be late. He's usually so punctual."

"The celebrations are still going on around the city," Father said. "He probably got caught up. Of course I told him how things were on V-E day."

"A zoo in the best way," she said, letting him bring her inside.

"How's your mother?" He led her into the library, a room she'd previously only seen in passing on her way to the parlor.

What could she say? "I keep praying for her."

"That bad, huh? Noah doesn't say much. Soda?"

She sat down. "Yes. Thank you. Am I keeping you from Mass?"

He handed her a glass and poured himself some water from the pitcher before sitting down in an arm chair close to hers. "No, Father Wilson has the twelve-thirty. We're going to have a celebration Mass tonight at seven. I hope you can make it. I might have to allow those streamers everyone had yesterday in church. I suspect God might smile at that."

The very thought brought a smile to her face. "I like that idea. I'll be sure to come." She wished Noah would join her, but she respected his beliefs. Still, there was no denying she'd always hoped to share her faith with her husband. Hold his hand on the way to Mass like her parents had as she and Martin ran ahead.

We'll just have to find a different way to share our beliefs.

"Of course, the bishop might not like it, but I have a feeling I can get around it. I mean, we did finally win the war. How are you, Anna? There have been a lot of changes in your life recently."

That seemed like an understatement. "I'm pretty good. I mean, Noah isn't going off to war again. I found myself thanking God for that repeatedly last night when I couldn't sleep."

Father drank his water. "Sleeplessness seems to be an epidemic in this country. The war is hard on the body's need for rest. Of course, it's hard on the soul too, isn't it? But we're all coming along. I know I feel better this morning than I have in years, and I can tell Noah does as well."

He did? Her heart lifted given how she'd left him last night. Father wouldn't kid about that.

He gave her a wink. "You'll see. I want to thank you for bringing him into my life. Part of me knows God has the ultimate hand, but you played your part by inviting him into *your* life. In my humble opinion, you could not have found a better man."

Those words helped her uncurl the death grip she had on her purse. "Your praise means the world, Father. You know how highly I regard your opinion."

He waved a hand dismissively. "Being a priest doesn't make me any better at judging a man. I could do that before I put this collar on."

"You must have been an incredible young man," she said. "I wish I could have had you for a student. I bet you would have given me a run for my money."

He laughed. "I might have had to write a lot of sentences after school. One of the most common complaints I had from teachers was that I asked too many questions. My first confessor even told me he worried for my soul. Said he couldn't imagine someone with that many questions keeping his faith."

"Apparently you defy the odds," Anna said, realizing how much she'd missed chatting with him. During the school year he was always around, quick to stop and chat in the classroom or hallway. "I always feel better in your presence."

"Bah," he said. "That makes me sound pompous. You're simply happy to talk with a friend."

"A friend?" she asked, her mouth parting slightly.

He gave a hearty chuckle, his bushy white eyebrows dancing. "Oh, your face. Did you never think of me as a friend? Goodness, sometimes I want to tug this collar off and stuff it in my pocket so people can treat me like they would another human being. Your Noah understands that."

"He calls you Niall," she said slowly. "It jars me every time."

Father gave an exaggerated eye roll. "Maybe you should start calling me Niall too, so it becomes more normal to you. I hope to be a guest in your home for many years to come, assuming I don't get into so much trouble with the bishop he transfers me to the boonies."

She was still reeling from the thought of sharing a home with Noah. The image of Father sitting at the table was easy to conjure up. He'd been a fixture in her life since she was a child. But it made her heart swell to imagine Noah sitting next to him.

Tears filled her eyes, and she ducked her head away. "I'm sorry," she said, standing up. "I need to excuse myself."

She only made it a couple steps before Father put his arm around her shoulders. "Sit down now. You're just a bit emotional. It's going around, let me tell you. I might have had a couple moments myself at morning Mass. There's no shame in it."

She drew a handkerchief from her purse and realized it was Noah's. That made more tears fall. "Oh, Father, I love him so much."

"I know you do, lass," he said. "I know it doesn't help telling you not to worry about him, but trust me when I say that he might have a better head on his shoulders than all of us put together. Last night he helped me find my way through something I'd been struggling with for over twenty-five years. In some ways, he saved my life, if not my soul. Of course, he'd never call it that. He was only being a friend. I'll tell him that he can share the story with you because I know he's a man who keeps a confidence."

She could only stare at him. Noah had helped Father?

"Don't look so surprised, my dear. Do you think we priests know everything? Now you go on home. He'll be there sometime soon, I should think, and you'll want to be there when he arrives."

He helped her to her feet and ushered her to the front door. "Now, this isn't something you'll hear from me often, but I'll be happy if I don't see you at Mass tonight. Celebrate with your man. God will understand."

With that, he closed the door on her. She turned around in a daze and walked home. Kids called out to her, but she barely heard them. She struggled to raise her hand to wave.

Inside her house finally, she sat down at the kitchen table, too frazzled to make another pot of coffee. What could Noah have helped Father with? And where the heck was he?

When she heard a knock on the door, she ran toward it. She opened it, relieved to see Noah. He had a smile on his face and a summer bouquet of roses and daisies in his hands.

Then he sank to one knee. "Anna Sims, will you marry me?"

Chapter 19

ANNA PRESSED HER HANDS TO HER FACE.

Emotion shot through her like a geyser, and she felt the urge to cry. "Oh, Noah! I was so worried."

"I'm sorry," he said, extending the flowers. "If you'd take these..."

She was shaking all over, but she managed to grab ahold of them. Staying where he was on his knees, he pulled a velvet box from his uniform pocket and opened it. There was a thin gold band inside with what looked like gold filigree circling it.

"I went downtown to find you a ring even though I know not all women want one," he said. "I wanted something tangible to cement our bond. I hope you like it. That is, if you'll agree to marry me. Ah...will you, Anna?"

She launched herself at him, wrapping her arms around him. He wobbled for a moment but didn't fall backward. "Yes, Noah. I'll marry you."

He held her face and looked deep into her eyes. She'd never seen that light in his eyes before. It was as though he'd finally broken free of the shadows surrounding him.

"I'll love you until the day I die," he said in a serious tone, "and I swear to you on everything I fought for over there that I'll never let you down."

She remembered him writing her that he feared letting her down if he died in the war, and those words had broken her heart. "I've told you before. You could never let me down. It's not who you are. And I'll love you until I take my last breath and never let you down either."

He shifted her so she was sitting on his bent knee. "I know you won't. Anna...last night after I talked with Niall, I felt like the whole world opened up for me, and you were at the center of it. I can't wait to marry you and be your husband."

She twined her arms around his neck. "I can't wait either. When do you want to do it?"

His brow rose. "Well, I... That would be up to you. Women set great stock on weddings. I'm sorry I... I know we talked about this before, but I still can't convert to being Catholic."

"I know that," she said. "Let's talk with Father and see...what that means. I know he can still marry us."

It wouldn't be in the church, she remembered, and that made her sad. But she and Noah were getting married, and her happiness was a formidable thing. Much stronger than any regrets she felt.

"But I will agree to raising our children Catholic," he said gravely. "With one stipulation."

She held her breath, knowing how big this was for him.

"Niall said his dad always encouraged them to think for themselves, and I'd like to do the same for our kids. You call it a well-informed conscience, I believe. I call it having good sense."

"Oh, Noah, our kids are going to have the best sense in the world," she said, bouncing on his knee.

"Don't be too sure after you hear what I went through to buy your ring," Noah said, putting a hand to his forehead. "Once I realized I didn't want to wait another day to ask you, what with the Japs surrendering, I moved high heaven to get downtown to the jeweler Father recommended. He opened the shop up special for me, but suddenly there were all these guys in uniform standing in the window, knocking on the glass to see if the owner would open up. Turned out they wanted to get hitched too since the war's over. You should have seen it," he continued, his green eyes alight. "Downtown was packed. It took me forty minutes to walk to the jeweler, and I won't tell you how long it took me to park."

"You drove?" she asked. "But how?" This wasn't just good sense. This was romantic. She was going to love telling their children this story.

His grin made him seem so much younger. "Niall lent me his car. Of course, I had to walk by the beehives to get to the garage. My goodness, they're loud."

"Father had to put them back there since some parishioners were worried about them being so close to the church and school."

"I remember you writing me that," he said. "When I finally reached it, I had to laugh. He's no car man, that's for sure. I felt like I was driving a hearse, it's so big and ancient, but it got me there. I'll have to ask him if he does the funerals *and* drives the coffin out to the cemetery."

Anna started laughing, unable to believe his good humor. "He calls it the 'Old Boat.' Oh, I think it's wonderful that he lent it to you. What a sweetheart! I went by the rectory to find you, and he told me you'd gone on an errand, but he didn't give anything away."

"He's a good friend," Noah said, and something came and went in his eyes. "Anna...I...let's stand up, shall we? I could probably kneel here all day, but I'd rather take you in my arms proper-like without all the neighborhood kids watching."

Her back was to the street, so she looked over her shoulder. Sure enough, the Dougherty boys and a passel of others were peeking through the gate with grins on their faces.

She waved at them. "We're getting married!"

"Way to go, Miss Sims," Brendan said while the others cheered.

Noah rose to his feet after her and waved as well. Then he shut the front door and drew her against his chest. His eyes sought hers, and he held her gaze as he kissed her. Oh, they were getting married! The love she felt for him grew like a golden ball in her chest, so big she thought she would burst in an explosion of light.

"Oh, Noah, I'm so happy," she said when they paused.

He ran his finger along her cheek. "Me too. I have something else to tell you..."

"Well, I'm not happy," she heard her mother say.

She turned. Her mom was standing at the top of the stairs, her mourning dress looking somehow blacker today, if that was possible.

"Anna, I've been biding my time since this man told us that Martin died instead of him. I've prayed you would see reason. I even hoped the war would take care of things, what with him having to go fight in the Pacific."

The words struck her heart like a sniper's bullet, and pain radiated throughout her body. How could her mother have wanted that? This was what she'd been thinking about since Noah had told her about Martin?

"You may be old enough to make your own decisions, but I will not give my consent for this marriage, and I'll be letting everyone in the neighborhood know that I don't approve of this marriage. That I forbid it, in fact."

"But, Mom—"

"You're acting like a foolish young girl, and with a man outside your faith," she said, her voice like the one Anna had heard when she was a misbehaving child. "You keep thinking you'll be able to forget that this man survived the war instead of your brother, but you can't start a life together on something so tainted."

"That's not true," she said. "We love each other."

"Love! What do you know of love? It takes more than love to make a marriage work. Once your schoolgirl infatuation passes, you'll regret marrying him. It might be a year from now or even more, but there will come a time when you'll wish God had saved your brother instead of this man. Blood is thicker than water, and it will always be. I would think your Irish heritage would have taught you that. You won't want to look at Noah, least of all have him touch you. Not when your brother's blood is on his hands."

She heard Noah's sharp intake in the midst of her own shock and hurt. "You're wrong, Mom. You couldn't be more wrong."

Her mother raised her hand and pointed at Noah. "Ask him why he didn't do more to protect Martin. Or do something to...to stop the bleeding. If he was his friend, how could he have let him die?"

She felt Noah rock back for a moment before standing tall. "Like I told you, Mrs. Sims, I did everything I could. If I could have taken his place, I would have. If I could have saved him, I would have. There was nothing I could do on that damn field. *Nothing!*"

"Well, you can do something now," her mother said. "We Irish believe that when someone saves your life, you owe them a debt. As Martin's mother, I'm claiming that debt. Stay away from my daughter."

His whole body seemed to vibrate with emotion, and Anna couldn't blame him. A debt? She placed a hand on his arm, hoping to comfort him. But she was trembling too.

"Excuse me," Noah said, pulling away from her and walking out.

The front door closed sharply, and she looked at her mother. "I can't believe you! How could you be so cruel? What's happened to you?"

The lines of her mother's face seemed etched in stone. "My son is dead, and my daughter wants to shack up with the man who should have saved him. And you call *me* cruel? You're determined to remind me of Martin's death every day."

"That's not fair," she said, her voice rising. "You're the one who keeps focusing on what happened to Martin. Why won't you listen? I'm trying to help you."

"God's stopped listening to me," her mother said, her tone hard. "Why should I listen to you? Especially when you're exhibiting such childish, selfish behavior. Anna, if you marry this man, I will never speak to you again."

"You don't mean it," she whispered, the pain so strong she wanted to bend at the waist.

"Yes, I do," she said with an emphatic nod.

"But I'm your daughter," she said, her tone pleading. "Your only living child."

Her mother started to walk away, back to her room. "My child would never hurt me like this."

Anna heard the door to her bedroom close and sank to the ground. She would have to leave her home for sure now and perhaps even her neighborhood. This place she loved so much, the one she'd lived in her whole life. What would she do?

She looked at the flowers resting on the floor, forgotten from her celebration with Noah. This was supposed to be one of the happiest days of her life and her mother had ruined it.

I'll never speak to you again.

And her words to Noah... *As Martin's mother, I'm claiming that debt.*

Anna was mostly proud of her Irish heritage, but that kind of talk made her want to tear her hair out and change her name. She couldn't imagine Noah would take it seriously.

But he'd left, and she couldn't blame him. Her mother had gone too far, and every hope she'd had that her mother would come around had been crushed.

She was poised to lose the last link to her family, and perhaps the neighborhood she loved. Could she marry Noah if it came at such a cost?

Could she forgive her mother if she *didn't* marry

Noah? If she let her mother take this away from her... She'd always valued forgiveness—taught it to the children in school and lived by it. But right now, she couldn't imagine putting that into practice with her mother.

As she plucked out a single red rose and started to cry, all thoughts of the war being over were gone.

There was a new war raging inside her.

Chapter 20

NOAH STORMED DOWN THE STREET, FLICKING A HAND IN greeting when someone called out to him. Everyone else was in high spirits, just like he'd been, but he felt like he'd just suffered the worst defeat of his life.

He'd known Anna's mother was against them. Had accepted it. Hoped it would change in time. He'd even decided to be polite to her regardless of what she said or did to him for Anna's sake.

But Mrs. Sims still blamed him for Martin's death. Heck, she'd even tried to call in a debt she thought he owed her, something that pinged the leftover guilt he had inside.

He could overcome all that in time, especially after his discussion with Niall last night, but he couldn't forget the other thing. She'd insisted Anna would become unhappy at some point in their marriage because he was alive and Martin wasn't. Her aim had been as sure as the German sniper that had killed her son.

How could he enter into marriage with Anna if her mother outright forbade it? And told the neighborhood she was against it? Surely people would take sides, and it would turn ugly. So far they'd all been nice to him, but Mrs. Sims hadn't thrown the gloves down yet.

Anna loved these people, and they loved her, but

Mrs. Sims was determined and he didn't underestimate her. Would relations with her neighbors become so fraught and disagreeable that Anna would have to leave her job at the school? Leave this place she loved?

Any one of those things could make Anna come to regret marrying him. Maybe it was all his talks with Niall, but he didn't want that on his conscience. He certainly didn't want to make her unhappy and be the cause of the final fissure with her mother.

Their marriage seemed doomed before it had even started.

When he'd gone downtown earlier, he'd dreaded the crowd, especially once he left the car. Sure enough, the streets had been lined with ticker tape and other garbage, and there was still a serious showing of people. Businesses were closed in celebration, and it looked as though some of the revelers hadn't yet gone home.

And yet, the crowd hadn't bothered him the same way. Sure, once he was on foot he was jostled half a dozen times and some blonde dame even grabbed him and tried to kiss him, but he found himself laughing as he pushed through the crowd.

The war was over, he knew what he wanted to do with his life, and he was going to marry Anna! His new life was beginning.

Only now, it felt like that new life was over before it could begin.

His earlier joy, an emotion so new to Noah he'd wanted to bottle it up for rainy days, had drained away.

The grounds of the church and school were upon him and he stopped, realizing he was breathing hard. His gaze found the schoolyard. Kids were flying high on the swings and flashing down the metal slide, screaming out loud.

Sadness crept over him. This morning as he'd taken a brief rest, he'd had a flash of Anna and him having kids, and he'd cherished the vision. Anna would be beside them, and their kids would have her eyes and wit.

And heart...

He couldn't forget about that. She had the biggest heart out there and the best mind.

He *was* the luckiest guy on the planet. His nickname might be Lucky Strike, but as far as he was concerned, it was because he was loved by a woman like Anna. Not because he'd merely survived when others had not.

But lucky streaks always came to an end. His legs felt like they were weighted down with lead, and he didn't know what he would do now. He could teach, sure. But he doubted he and Anna could have a real future after what her mother had said to him today. Part of him even regretted that he'd made it back, and he'd *never* regretted living before.

He caught sight of the cemetery to the far side of the church and felt drawn to it. His feet seemed to have a mind of their own, and he found himself walking over to it, then searching for Martin's grave.

He'd never wanted to visit it before. Hadn't thought he could bear to see the gray marker punctuating a life taken too young. He knew why he sought it out today.

He had to explain to his friend why he was leaving Chicago and would never return.

It would be better to tell Anna in person, but if they talked face to face, he'd never be able to say the words. Writing her a letter would bring them full circle somehow. They'd met through a letter, and everything would end in one. Oh, there must be a famous quote about that somewhere, but he didn't want to search the annals of his mind for it.

He caught sight of Robert Sims' grave first, and sure enough, Martin's was located to the right. Plastic flowers decorated the grave and a small American flag was stuck in the ground, one that looked to be from a bond drive or something. The engraved date of his friend's death punched into him just as he'd expected, almost as though the Grim Reaper had cut those numbers into the hard stone with his fingernail.

Noah had always been interested in cemeteries as a kid. Sometimes there were short phrases on the marker that suggested a story, and his eager mind had latched on to them and spun a tale. A man whose grave stated "good husband and father" was something of a hero to Noah. His father surely would never have those words etched into the stone marking his passing. Somehow that had seemed just to the angry orphan he'd been.

He felt tears leak into the corners of his eyes and rubbed them. Only a short while before, Martin had helped him figure out what he wanted to do in a dream. And mentioned his sister in the process. Grief and regret bore down on him.

"Oh, Martin. I can't keep my promise to look after your sister and mother. The price is too great to both of them."

A breeze swirled around him before ebbing, and he sank to a knee in front of the grave before he realized he'd done the same thing only a short while ago with Anna. Then, he'd done it out of pure joy. Now...

"Please forgive me," he whispered. "You asked me to take care of them, and I wanted to. I would have loved your sister to my last breath, but I can't be the reason your mother treats her so. Despite how she's acting now, she's still Anna's mother, and I..."

He knew what it felt like to be alone in the world without a family, and he didn't want that for Anna.

"Martin, I can't be the sole reminder of all she's lost. You. Her mother. Even this neighborhood. Anna has a mighty heart, but no one can stand that much loss. I hope you can understand that."

The wind shifted again and he felt a sorrow in his chest as great as the day his friend had been killed. He pushed up and stood, locking his bones in place much like he had when he'd been called to go another day without sleep or food, pressing on against the enemy.

"I'll never forget you," he said. "Be at peace, my friend."

Then he turned around and walked back to the rectory.

Niall stepped out of the library as Noah started to climb the wide staircase. "Well, boyo, how did it go?"

He didn't have the energy to share the details. "Her mother is against it, and I can't come between them. Martin...wouldn't want that, I don't think. How could he? They're his family, and family was everything to him. Plus it wouldn't be fair to Anna to ask her to choose."

Before he said anything, Niall jogged up until he was on the same step. Then he caught Noah's arm and looked him straight in the eye. "I'll talk to Mary. Don't you dare give up! You and Anna are meant for each other. I know it."

He'd believed that too. Once. He shook his head. "Her mother won't budge."

"Have some faith," Niall said, patting his arm. "But if she won't budge, that doesn't mean you walk away from the woman you love."

He wanted to throw Niall's arm aside and storm up the rest of the stairs. "Could you marry a woman, knowing you were destroying her last link to her family? I thought you Irish put family above all else. At least that's what Mrs. Sims implied."

"I am Irish and proud of it, but I also know pure nonsense when I hear it."

"I'm an orphan, Niall. I'm used to living without a family. Anna isn't. Mrs. Sims is right. Anna might not regret marrying me now, but in a few years when she's had no contact with her mother...her family..."

"Then you and Anna make your own family," Niall said, his voice cresting. "The Weatherby family! Do you think that God brought you through this war to give up now? That it was mere chance you and Martin became friends and you fell in love with his sister through letters after he died? Come on, Noah. You might not be a religious man, but even you must recognize the hand of something greater at work here."

Looking off, he felt exhaustion fill his bones. Not a spark of hope was left from the morning. "Niall, I can't see any other way right now. I'm sorry."

"That's your sadness talking," he said.

He shook off his friend's hold and started to walk up the remaining stairs to his room. "I don't think so."

"I won't give up, Noah," Niall said in a booming voice, one that carried. "You might have lost Martin, but you have a new brother by your side to help you fight your battles. That's me, boyo, in case you're being too stubborn to see it—even if I am technically old enough to be your father."

Noah shut the door on Niall's words and sank onto the bed.

He'd dreaded defeat ever since he'd enlisted. He hadn't expected to experience it on the home front with no tanks or soldiers in sight. And he sure as hell hadn't expected his enemy to be one he didn't want to fight and could never hope to win against: Anna's mother.

Chapter 21

WHEN ANNA HEARD THE KNOCK ON THE DOOR, SHE rushed to it, hoping Noah had returned. It didn't surprise her to find Father Shaughnessy on her doorstep instead.

"Father!" she cried. "You must have seen Noah."

"I talked to him briefly about what happened," he said, stepping inside when she moved back. "Although he didn't do much talking back. Anna, I'm sorry your mother found a way to rain on what should have been a sunny day for you two. I can see from your face that you feel as defeated as Noah, but let me see what I can do with Mary."

He gave her a hug, and she felt like she was fifteen again, outside the hospital room where her father had died. Father Shaughnessy had drawn her into his arms and hugged her then, just like this.

"Oh, Father, I'm so upset," she whispered. "She said she'd never speak to me again if I married Noah and that she'd tell the neighborhood she was against us."

He made a tsking sound. "Seems like I'll have to reach deep for some compassion today. I have to confess that her actions have gotten my fire up pretty good. But don't worry. I can rein it in. Go fetch her for me if you please."

She trudged over to the stairs and used the railing to pull herself forward until she reached her mother's bedroom door.

"Mom, Father Shaughnessy is here to see you."

"I don't want to see him," she heard her mother say through the closed door.

Anger spurted inside up like hot lava. "I'm not telling Father that!"

"I don't appreciate you and your little solider boy running to him for help," she said harshly.

Anna stared at the door, tempted to pound on it until her mother opened it. "Mother, come out!"

"I will not!"

She heard someone tromping up the stairs and looked over her shoulder to see Father surging up behind her, his ears a fiery red. He waved her aside.

"Mary Sims, are you really going to give me the disrespect of not speaking to me when I come into your home?"

"Since you're meddling again, yes," her mother said. "I didn't ask for your counsel."

Father drew in a harsh breath with a growl, his whole chest expanding. "Mary Sims, you're a member of my parish who's wreaking havoc on the lives of two amazing young people. You'd better believe I'm going to give you my counsel. When you aren't in my church anymore, I'll leave you be to make all the mistakes you'd like."

"Maybe I shouldn't be," her mother shouted. "God doesn't listen to me anyway."

"Heresy," Father said, his mouth twisting. "You know better than that. This is grief talking. Mary Sims, you listen to me. I knew Robert and Martin well. They wouldn't even have imagined you capable of this, not speaking to your only living child and trying to turn the neighborhood against their union. And for what? Because she fell in love with a war hero and a man your own son thought of as a brother. You've lost your senses, woman, and you're close to losing your very core as a good Catholic woman."

Anna had to clench her mouth shut so it wouldn't fall

open in shock. She'd heard Father give someone a good dressing down before, but somehow it was different hearing it directed at her mother.

"I don't care what you say," her mom said. "Like I've told you before, you're a priest with no children of your own. You can't know how a mother feels."

Father put his hand on the door. "You *are* a mother, Mary. That's the whole point of this. Anna is all you have left. Don't turn your back on her."

"I'd look to your own soul," she fired back, "for supporting her marriage to someone outside her faith."

His face turned even redder. "My soul is completely at ease, thank you, and as for supporting her marriage to Noah... You'd better believe I support it—and I'll be telling everyone in this neighborhood so."

Pain rose up again, overpowering the anger Anna was feeling, and she felt tears gather in her eyes. How could it have come to this?

"I'm not talking to you anymore, Niall Shaughnessy," her mother called back, making her insult clear and direct by using his given name. "You're an old poop and a meddler, and I can't abide that. My soul is my own business, and I'll do what I want with it. Now go away and leave me alone."

Father's bushy eyebrows winged up for a moment. Then his whole face fell. In that moment, Anna felt his utter desolation. He put his hand on her shoulder and led her away from the door. They walked down the stairs together in silence, and she watched as he folded his hands in prayer against his stomach.

"I've seen grief do things to a person, but this..." At the bottom, he turned to her. "Let's have a cup of coffee."

Anna didn't want to sit and have coffee—all she wanted to do was flee to her room and hide. For days. For weeks. For as long as it would take for her mother to change her mind. But she wasn't going to change her mind or take back anything she'd said—such horrible things—and that put Anna between a rock and a hard place.

After warming up the coffee, she set a mug in front of Father, who was lost in thought.

"Noah told me he wouldn't come between you and your mother," Father said, not making a move toward his cup. "What's going through that mind of yours right now?"

Anna couldn't bring herself to drink hers either, not when her mouth already tasted so bitter. "I don't know. Father, I love Noah. I was so happy he asked me to be his wife. But when my mother said she'd never speak to me again... I'm so mad at her, but how can I do something that sets me on that course? She *is* my mother, my family."

Father tugged at his white collar, as if it were too tight. "I never would have thought her capable of saying such a thing to you, Anna. Or to Noah, for that matter. As a priest, I see a lot of things in families, but yours has always been...well, a model of a good home. It cuts me to the core to see this kind of a fissure. I'm sorry for you. And for your mother. It's not an easy thing to forgive. I'm going to have to pray an awful lot to get over the outrage I feel for you both."

She appreciated hearing that. "Mom said I wasn't thinking long term about my life with Noah. That I'd be unhappy at some point because he's alive and Martin isn't."

"Bull crap, just like I told Noah," Father said. "I've never heard anything... Excuse me, Anna. I should be asking what you think."

She took a moment. "I could never feel that way, Father."

"I didn't think so," he said, taking a sip of his coffee.

"Of course, she also implied I was acting out of complete infatuation, like some child. That's not true. This war has done a lot to grow all of us up in certain ways, and I know my own heart."

He patted her hand. "Of course you do. If I believed otherwise, I would caution you against a hasty marriage.

I've done so with other couples who've come to me during the course of this war. Despite what your mother said, I'm a good counselor. Damn if this doesn't chap my hide. But no matter. We're speaking about you and Noah."

She rose to pour herself a glass of water from the tap, hoping to buy herself more time, and looked out the window. "If I marry Noah, I'd have to leave this house, which I could do, but it would likely mean leaving the neighborhood too. You know the trouble Mom's likely to cause, even with your support. Would I have to give up my job?"

The thought of it had tears leaking down her face. Oh, her students. She loved them so much, and she'd formed connections with the other teachers and staff.

Father turned her around. "No, you will *not* have to leave this neighborhood or your job at the school. We need you, Anna. Everyone loves you. We'll simply find a place for you and Noah to live that's close by."

"But housing is scarce," she said. "You know that. Besides, I'd hate for the neighborhood to have to choose sides. Some would, you know. They did when Eileen Kelly married that Jewish boy after her parents forbade it." Eileen had moved out of the neighborhood and not been in touch with anyone since.

His face tightened. "They'd answer to me—like they did with Eileen."

She appreciated the sentiment. "Sorry, Father, but it didn't change things for her."

He all but growled. "Anna, you're not Eileen. First, you work in this community and everyone knows and loves you. Second, the neighborhood knows and respects your man. Eileen never brought her beau here."

No, she'd probably been terrified of how people would have treated him. "Still...even if that's true, my mother will be here."

"Your mother may be a fixture in this community, but it doesn't sound like she even wants to be a part of it anymore."

That had been anger speaking, Anna thought. She

couldn't imagine her mother ever leaving the church, no matter how angry she was with God.

"Can I really pass her on the streets in this neighborhood and not feel the loss of it every time? Can I bring my children to church if she won't acknowledge any of us? And how can Noah bear such malice? Oh, Father, everything is too awful."

He drew her into his arms again, patting her back as she cried. "I'm not saying it wouldn't be hard, Anna. There have been other feuds in this neighborhood, but we've weathered them. Now, perhaps the situation with Eileen wasn't handled well, but she didn't fight it and neither did her beau. You and Noah will. And I'll be fighting right alongside you like I told your mother, from the pulpit if need be. Part of me likes to see some people squirm in their seats. And if that doesn't work, I'll set the bees on the difficult ones."

Knowing he would fight with them heartened her some. She gave a tired laugh and pulled away. "Leave it to you to joke at a time like this."

"It's the Irish in me," he said, trying to smile. "You know I tell some of my best jokes at wakes, as tradition demands. I know it wouldn't be ideal, but you and Noah could live in an adjoining neighborhood if you can't find a home here."

"That might mean getting another job." It would be practical. Most teachers lived and worked in their neighborhood.

"Any school would be lucky to have you, and we'd miss you terribly. I'd miss you terribly. And Noah too. Like I told him before I came here, I might be old enough to be his father, but he's become a trusted friend, someone I can speak my mind to freely."

She wondered again how Noah had helped the priest, but now wasn't the time to ask. "I'll have to think about it. Right now, I don't see a way out. Either way, there's going to be suffering and division. Besides, I'm not sure Noah will change his mind. He doesn't want to come between us. And Father, if you'd heard what my mother said to him... I don't know how he would ever want to be around her again, even if some miracle happened, and she consented to our marriage."

Also was it fair to ask him to be around her mother when she was so cruel? It was hard enough for Anna, and she was her daughter.

"That's not the best basis for a decision of this magnitude," Father said. "I know it's hard to imagine never speaking to your mother again, but weighed against not marrying Noah, the man you love and want to spend your life with, is that truly something you could live with?"

She tried to imagine a life without her mother in it. How could she even begin to imagine something she'd never conceived possible? But how could she rebuild a relationship with her after what she'd said, even if she could forgive her?

"You both have your whole lives ahead of you, filled with so much promise. Noah survived the war for a reason, and he loves you. Now he knows what he wants to do with his life outside having a family, and it's a beautiful thing. When he told me this morning, I felt like God was smiling down from heaven."

That made Anna want to cry again. "I don't even know what that is. My mother interrupted him."

He put his arm around her again and shook her gently. "It's a bright spot in this whole sorry mess. You're going to love it, trust me."

A bright spot? She couldn't imagine it.

Father set her in front of him. "Search your heart, Anna. You'll figure out what's best for you. Either way, I'm with you. If you want to hold fast to your mother and the family you were born into, I'll help you. If you want to marry Noah and fight anything your mother tries to put in your way in this neighborhood, then I'll pick up my sword and my shield, and we'll wreak some serious divine justice together with all the angels on our side."

Oh, he was so dear!

"Only don't wait too long. I fear Noah might try to up and leave on us, and that would be a great tragedy. Of course, I could call in some of the more nefarious elements Brian Dougherty knows and ask them to sit on him for a while until you come to a decision. This is South Side, after all."

She wished she could laugh at the image of Brian and some of the bruisers he knew tying Noah up to prevent him from leaving town. "You always could lighten a dark mood like no one else." She kissed his cheek. "I have some thinking to do. Don't call Brian Dougherty yet, but if we have to..."

The rumble of his laugh shook his chest. "That's the Anna Sims I know."

She thought of Noah calling her Tiger. That was something to remember now. She would need all the strength and determination God had given her.

"If you need to talk things out more, come find me at the rectory. I can ask Father Wilson to take the evening Mass if need be. Heck, maybe I'll have him swing by to speak to your mother. It'll be a record in this parish if she throws out two priests in one day."

And it would also send a message to the neighborhood... Oh, he did have a crafty way about him. "Then we can call in Margaret O'Shea. She'd give her a piece of her mind."

He barked out a laugh. "Now you're talking. I'll try and keep our lad at the rectory in the meantime, assuming he can be reasoned with, although I have plans on that score should it come to it."

"Beyond Brian and his cronies?" She shook her head. "Do I even want to know?"

He lifted a shoulder. "I'll tell him that he's being as bullheaded as your mother. That will put a burr in his saddle, so to speak. Trust me on this. Your man is the type of fellow who believes in doing the right thing. Turning away from you because of a rift isn't the right thing if you ask me. Neither one of you will find anyone better to love, I expect, and it would be sad to see you both be so miserable for the rest of your days."

He sounded like a forlorn Irish poet when he said that, but Anna hadn't considered it. If she cowed to her mother's ultimatum, would she find another man to love, someone she wanted to marry and have children with?

She suddenly remembered writing to Noah about Janus, the god of beginnings and endings. On one side of a Janus coin, he looked to the past, and on the other he looked to the future. She would have to make a choice, whether to look back and stay with what she'd known her whole life or step into an unknown future with the man she loved.

"I'll walk back with you," she said. "I need to get out of the house, and I could use some serious praying."

"I've kept back a candle for an emergency like this if you want it," he said as they walked to the front door. "People were asking me yesterday if I planned to get rid of my candle-making enterprise with the bees now that the war is over. Can you imagine?"

She gazed at the man. Even though he wore all black like her mother, save the white square in his collar, it didn't make him look dour and sad. It was as though the color looked completely different on him.

"Some people are always going to complain or fight change," she said, and it occurred to her that her mother had always been in that camp. She used to tease her about it, she remembered, along with the rest of the family. Had the seeds of her mother's potential bitterness been there all along?

"Not everyone wants to believe God answers all our prayers equally, whether we light a candle or not."

Anna knew that, but it still made her feel better to see tangible evidence of her prayer lit, especially on a day this dark. They stepped outside, and she felt like she could breathe better. Turning to look over her shoulder, she stared at her house. It seemed to be shrouded some-how, as if her mother had wrapped it in her own mourn-ing clothes.

"I think we can call this an emergency," she said, opening the gate. "I'd like that candle if you don't mind."

Chapter 22

NOAH WASN'T A MAN WHO MADE HASTY DECISIONS, AND while he didn't think there was anything hasty about how he was reacting to his current situation, he'd realized he needed to talk to Anna in person. No matter how hard. When he'd sat down to write her a letter, he couldn't pen anything past, *Dear Anna.*

He loved her, and he knew she loved him. This situation was impossible for both of them. Noah had always been alone, and for him, the promise of being with Anna and having his own family had felt like a dream come true. But she'd always had her mother and this community. She'd already lost her father and Martin. Like he'd told Niall, how much more could one person take?

A knock sounded on his door, and he knew who it was. "I was just going to see Anna," he told Niall when he opened it.

The planes of his friend's face seemed heavier. "She's in the church, praying," he said. "Her mother is a hard woman. You're right. She won't budge, and it vexes me to say I couldn't persuade her even though I know that's my ego talking."

He hadn't imagined Niall could change her mind, but part of him had hoped for a miracle.

A miracle? Hanging around this rectory was changing him. When had he ever hoped for one?

"You're human like the rest of us, Niall," Noah said. "One of the great philosophers should have written 'free will is a bitch.'"

Niall was silent a moment and then he started to laugh. "Oh, Noah, I didn't think anyone had as macabre a sense of humor in moments like these except me. No wonder we're friends. 'Free will is a bitch.' Scandalous but true. I imagine the old philosophers probably had that thought a time or two."

"Yeah, it was probably Thomas More's last thought when Henry VIII had him beheaded," he said dryly.

Niall slapped his belly, laughing with gusto. "Humor is a good sign. I was worried you might try to fly the coop prematurely."

"I thought about it," Noah said. "I was going to write Anna a letter, but I decided we need to talk in person."

Niall nodded, his laughter fading. "Give Anna some time. She's torn up, and rightly so. Either way, she's going to get hurt, and that isn't a small thing. We spend so much of our life trying to avoid being hurt."

"And yet that seems to be the way of it," Noah said. "The orphanage taught me that."

"One of these nights I'm going to have to give you a full recitation on grace, boyo, but it's the help God's always giving us, even when we don't ask, even when we're not aware of it. Well, I'm going off to pray too. I got pretty angry earlier and need to calm down myself."

Noah rested his hand on his friend's shoulder for a moment. "If you were perfect, we wouldn't get along. I said some things earlier and was short. I want to apologize."

"Forget it, lad," Niall said, his mouth twitching. "It's good to air your grievances. Otherwise, they fester and rot. If you need me, I'll be in my private chapel. When I try to pray in church, it's one interruption after another."

He walked off, and Noah shifted his feet, trying to

feel more settled despite his churning belly. Part of him wanted to seek Anna out right now, but she deserved to have the time she needed. Perhaps a walk would do him good.

As he headed down the street adjacent to the church and school, Katherine Kenna congratulated him on his engagement on her way home from the market. The Dougherty boys and the other kids had spread the news like little town criers, it seemed, and everyone was talking about it. *Terrific*, he thought. Would they already be wondering about Mrs. Sims' reaction?

Katherine ended up crying in his arms again, saying how lucky he and Anna were to be together after the war. He didn't know how to respond. After all, Anna *had* said yes. He just wasn't sure they were going to stay engaged. When the grieving woman finally excused herself and walked off toward her house, he tried to shake off the truth of what she'd said. They were lucky, dammit. Why couldn't her mother see that?

Two blocks later, he was congratulated by two more neighbors, Mrs. O'Shea and old Mr. Dunne—something that sparked hope in his heart. But he realized his best course of action was to return to the rectory. Hide, if necessary, until he and Anna spoke. He was only fueling speculation.

The church came into view, and it felt odd to realize he was going to miss the sight if he left. He would always associate it with Niall. Leaving here would mean leaving another friend behind, and that cut him to the quick, especially when he'd lost so many to the war.

He started walking again. The door to the church opened, and a familiar blue dress caught his eyes.

Anna crossed herself like the Catholics do, and then she came down the church steps, brushing away what he imagined were tears. The thought saddened him. She was in pain, dammit, and he'd helped cause it.

Her auburn hair looked like molten fire in the sunlight, and he stopped short. His heart filled with the same urgent emotion he experienced every time he saw her, one he knew was both the love he had for her and the fear that something would tear them apart. Before, that fear had been the war. Now it had become her mother.

Her steps faltered suddenly, and she stilled on the bottom step. He knew she had spotted him. Did she want to speak with him? There was a rosary in her hands, and seeing the evidence of her soul searching moved him something fierce. Hadn't he been doing the same thing? They might go about it differently, but at the end of the day, they were two people who lived according to thoughts and ideals, and yes, like Niall had said, something he didn't fully have a name for.

She raised her hand, but her greeting lacked its usual joy. Walking in her direction, he called upon all his courage, knowing this might be their last moment together.

Time seemed to slow down, and his senses took in details he might have otherwise missed, almost like in some of the life-or-death moments he'd survived in Europe. Her perfume seemed to envelop him as he reached her, the floral bouquet of it reminding him of the kisses and embraces they'd shared. Her blue eyes were red-rimmed from crying and wet at the eyelashes. The rise of her chest told him she was having as much trouble breathing as he was.

But it was the directness of her gaze he clung to. She'd made her decision, and he held his breath as he waited for her to speak, knowing it would change his life forever.

She cleared her throat. "I was just coming to see you."

Her voice was a harsh whisper. "I was waiting for you," he said.

She coughed again and then brushed away tears leaking from her eyes. "Oh, I didn't mean to cry. I can't seem to stop. I'm so sorry."

Those words crushed his heart. "It's okay. Anna, what have you decided?"

She met his eyes. "I don't want to lose my mom, but I feel like I already have in some ways. What mother says things like that to her child? Or to the man her daughter loves? I...know you didn't want to come between us, but Noah, in truth, you haven't."

He opened his mouth to contradict her, but she shook her head. "No, let me finish. I realized while I was praying that I could have fallen in love with anyone, and she still might have treated him this way—because he was alive and Martin wasn't."

Noah wasn't so sure about that, but he remained silent.

"Noah...I love you."

A blaze of heat flashed through his heart, and he waited for her to continue. "I love you too."

"I know," she said, crying softly now. "And that's what I'm focusing on right now in this awful mess."

He had to force himself not to reach for her. She had to tell him her decision while standing on her own two feet.

"I can't say this isn't the hardest decision I've ever made, but I can't lose you. I won't lose you. I...don't know what our future looks like, but I want us to live it. Together. Can you...forget what you said about not wanting to come between Mom and me?"

A man passed them on the church stairs, and Noah heard him mutter, "Our Father." His muscles locked and he stared at the man's back as he left. That was the prayer Martin had always muttered right before a battle. Even though he didn't believe the dead could talk, part of him wondered if it could be a message from his friend. Was Martin telling him to fight? Even if his mother was the one he had to fight against?

He yanked her against his chest, and she fitted her arms around him. "Yes, I can forget it. Anna, I hate you having to choose like this, but if you want me, I'm yours. I feel so terrible though. I wish things were different."

"Me too," she said, her voice breaking. "I want to marry you, and I'll even leave Chicago if you want. Maybe it's a way we can both have a fresh start."

This was her mother's threat talking. "I can't bear for you to lose your home here, your neighborhood. Truth be told, I'm coming to feel...like I belong here too. With you. No, we'll stay here and find a way to make it work, even if it means visiting every family in the neighborhood together and eating pound cake and drinking tea."

She started crying. "Father said something along the same lines, although his version was a little more scary. He's thrown his lot in with us, you know."

Of course he had, and Noah was grateful for it. He'd have to thank him later. "Then we're clear. We're staying. This is your home, your neighborhood, and you love it so."

"Yes, I do. I love hearing old Mr. Dunne sing Cole Porter songs like 'Night and Day' at the top of his lungs through the window. Or Mrs. Fitzsimmons stopping you for a quick chat in the yard. And even having to break up some of Willie Buckley's fights with the other boys. Oh, I'd miss everyone."

"Then we'll find a way to be happy here. I can go to school close by, and we can find a place so you can keep teaching at St. Patrick's. It may not be a perfect solution, but nothing is perfect."

"No, my mother won't let it be," she said, pressing a hand to her temple. "Oh, Noah, I believe her when she says she's going to throw her weight around, even though it breaks my heart. I can deal with the neighbors with you and Father by my side. But how can I come to this church knowing I might run into her at Mass? How can I bear it if she refuses to speak to our children? Of course, the way she's been acting, she'd better not say anything horrible to them or she'll hear from me."

Noah wondered if Mrs. Sims would ever have a kind word for anyone again. She seemed to have chosen her lot in life and was determined that everyone should suffer right along with her.

"I don't know how we should handle that," he said

honestly. "Anna, one of the teachers at the orphanage used to say, 'Don't borrow trouble.' Can you do that? Sometimes things change, and sometimes we react differently than we imagined we would. There's no use wasting your energy over what ifs."

Her eyes took on a look of wonder, and she reached up to touch his face. "Noah, you wouldn't know it, but my dad used to say the same thing. Hearing you say that, right now, well, I... It feels like an answer to my prayers. Oh, my dad would be so mad at her if he were still with us. Martin too."

Noah felt chills run down his spine again. Was it another message? Anna seemed to think so. Who was he to question it?

"Maybe your mother will change. They say time heals all." It was as magnanimous as he could be.

"We can hope and pray for it, I suppose," she said, sounding as doubtful as he felt.

But they'd have to make some peace with the possibility it wouldn't happen.

She gave a determined sniff and then seemed to gather herself, standing taller. "I want to talk to Father about marrying us right away. Oh! I forgot. You mentioned going to school. What are you going to do?"

He felt his mouth lift in a smile. "I want to teach. History, I think. I want people to know the past and maybe figure out how to spot trouble before it gets out of control. I want...people to think and search for answers. I want to share what I know of the world and learn more and more as I go along."

"So we're to have two teachers in this family," she said, putting a hand on his chest. "I love it! Noah, you're going to be a wonderful teacher."

Her praise settled over him, and he embraced her quietly for a moment. "Thank you."

"I'm so sorry my mom ruined your wonderful news. And our engagement. It should have been such a happy day. Oh, how I could use a silver lining right now."

Sinking to one knee, he took her hand. "Let's do it over then. Anna Sims, I love you. Can't imagine my life without you. Will you marry me?"

She put her hand over her mouth, as if all her momentary composure had evaporated.

"Way to go, Noah!" he heard shouted across the lawn.

They looked over to see Niall leaning out of an open window on the rectory's second floor, his fist pumping the air.

He laughed, thinking his friend had better be careful or he'd end up falling out of the window. Then he raised his hand and waved at him. "Father seems to think you'll say yes."

"He always likes to preempt." Then that gleam he loved so much came into her eyes and stayed there for two heartbeats. "You're darn right I'll marry you, Noah Weatherby."

He kissed the back of her hand and stood up, smiling as he heard Niall continue to cheer. "Anna, I have a silver lining for you to hold onto right now."

"What?" she asked, laying her hand on his chest.

"For the rest of my life, my silver lining will always be *you*."

Epilogue

LAKE MICHIGAN SPARKLED IN THE SUNSHINE, AND NOAH LET the peace from the gentle lapping of the water wash over him. Liam's piercing cry sounded, followed by Assumpta's hearty chortle as they splashed water over each other. For little ones of two and four they had serious pipes, as Niall liked to say. Noah had never imagined the power his children would have over him until the nurse brought Assumpta out of the maternity ward and showed him his daughter. His heart had seemed to burst in his chest. When Liam had come along, he'd experienced the same powerful emotion, and the force of that love never ceased to amaze him.

Of course, he'd felt that same force the day he'd married Anna in the rectory almost five years ago this August with Niall smiling as he said the words over them. And he'd certainly felt it on their wedding night and all the nights they'd come together since.

Love in whatever form was the greatest force on earth. It had gotten him through a war and helped him start a new life with the woman he loved. His fierce tiger. His Anna.

When she'd told him she was pregnant the first time, he'd told her that he wanted a girl. He hadn't wanted to send a son off to war. Have to watch as he struggled with all of the things Noah had struggled with since returning from Europe. She'd responded with gentle understanding, saying they'd have to leave that up to God. He'd gotten what he wanted the first time around, but when he'd held Liam, his fear had overwhelmed him. Would his son have to become a soldier some day?

Anna had told him not to borrow trouble, the phrase he'd used with her, the one she'd felt sure her father had sent down from heaven on the church steps as they spoke of marriage.

But trouble was upon them...and he couldn't shake it off today.

It seemed another war was about to start, this time in Korea. Noah didn't know much about the place yet or why the U.S. should be so concerned, but if President Truman and General MacArthur were considering military action, he knew there was good reason.

Even so, he hated to see another war brewing. He'd already told Anna that he wouldn't leave her or their children unless they called him up. He would go if he had to, but even if he didn't, good men were going to go off to Asia. Blood was going to seep into the soil again. More women and children would be left without husbands and fathers.

His son wouldn't fight in this war, but would it ever stop?

China had grown more powerful now that Japan had stepped out of the power vacuum, and the Soviet Union was led by a man who could have been Hitler's brother, Joseph Stalin.

New bullies were rising up again, and it crushed Noah's spirit to see it happening. He felt so helpless. The past few days he'd even started to doubt whether his current post as a history teacher in the same school where Anna taught was going to change anything.

If this war in Korea went on, his students would be heading over there in a few years. He'd chosen teaching older kids, hoping to influence young minds on the cusp of adulthood. It pained him to think of seeing them ship out. Reading the notices about this boy or that.

"You're thinking about the war again, aren't you?" Anna said as she appeared beside him, catching hold of the St. Christopher medal he always wore. "And when I'm wearing my new bathing suit."

The red suit had certainly caught his eye before they left—she was beautiful in it. "I'm sorry. I can't seem to stop worrying."

"Noah," she said softly, yanking on the chain to grab his attention. "Liam's only two years old. You can't live your whole life worrying about him going to war. Or any other boys for that matter."

"I know," he said, kicking at the sand. "I don't want to. It's only—"

"Your dreams have come back since North Korea invaded South Korea," she said. "I know. I sleep right next to you." Then she laid the medal against his chest and hugged him for a good long moment. He put his arms around her, knowing what she was doing. Hugs were good soothers, and they gave them abundantly in their house.

She'd helped him kick those dreams with them, by virtue of always being there to hold him when he cried out in his sleep or jerked awake, his heart beating like the gunfire in his dreams.

"I thought the dreams were over. God, I want them to be."

He'd talked to Niall about it over their usual whiskey and philosophy night, and his friend had extended his support as generously as he'd done since their first meeting. Besides Anna, Niall had become his most trusted ally in creating a new life, one full of meaning and purpose, even going so far as to hire a non-Catholic teacher at a Catholic school, something he'd had to persuade both the bishop and the school board to approve.

"You're doing exactly what you're supposed to," she said. "Your students love you, and your history projects have become the talk of the town. You're one of the first teachers in the country to bring battle reenactments into the classroom. Why else would Loyola University ask you to come and teach a class this semester? Noah, you *are* doing your part."

He'd read about a group in Florida getting together to reenact battles from the Civil War. Sure, it had been controversial, but it had sparked an idea. Why not reenact other battles in other wars as a way of teaching history while also driving home the horrible realities of war? Of course, some parents had expressed concern, but he and Niall had talked to them. Together. And the kids had responded so positively, even the skeptical parents had come around completely.

Loyola had loved both his creativity and his mission. He'd walked on clouds for days after they contacted him. He hoped the opportunity would be a stepping stone from him teaching high school to college.

"Niall likely had a lot to do with that call," Noah said, giving her a look. "He likes to sing our praises, and the faculty still remember his father's tenure there. Just wait until they ask you to teach a night class on the modern woman."

She grinned at that. "I do seem to have a handle on how to be a working wife and mother. Of course, I'm lucky. Mrs. Dougherty takes care of the Assumpta and Liam like they're her own."

Mrs. Dougherty went out of her way to be supportive because she was so angry at Anna's mother. When Mrs. Sims had tried to do her worst over their marriage, almost all of the people in the neighborhood had sided with Anna, and him for that matter, save a few vanguards in Mrs. Sims' knitting group. The additional weight of Niall and Margaret O'Shea's influence had turned the tide to the point where Mary Sims was the one excluded from the community's embrace. She mostly stayed in her house, and whenever he passed it, he could only feel sadness now.

Still, it was an ongoing struggle. The first time they'd run into her had been at Martin's grave. He and Anna had gone there to lay flowers on the birthday she and Martin shared, and Mrs. Sims had looked at them with such loathing, as if their very presence had desecrated her son's final resting place. After a momentary standoff, he'd taken Anna's hand and led her away, his heart heavy.

Noah wasn't always there when Anna saw her, what with Mass and the market being her places, but he was always there to soothe her when she came home crying. The only silver lining, as they liked to say, was that the neighborhood had risen up and supported the both of them in a way they couldn't have expected. Now that meant their children would be raised in the kind of place Noah had always dreamed of.

Despite Noah's decision not to convert, he was included in everything that went on with the men in the neighborhood. Anna liked to say that it was because Noah was a decorated hero, a wonderful teacher, and a good man. The Irish knew "cream" when they saw it. Noah saw Niall's invisible hand behind their support, of course, but Anna wouldn't hear any of it. She was a stubborn woman sometimes—a trait he loved. He couldn't imagine his life without her.

This new war, though, what if it took his new life away? What if...

"What if this war gets as bad as the one we won?" he whispered, his hands fisting at his side. "I can't bear it. I just can't."

A shadow crossed her face, but it passed just as quickly. She smiled at him, that big, open smile he so loved. "What have we done since we were first married?"

When she put her hands on her hips, he knew his tiger expected him to say it. How many times had they had this same conversation whenever one of them was down or struggling?

"We step out of the shadows and into the sunshine," he repeated.

"Exactly! And we have fun." She extended her hand to him, and he took it. "Now... Our children are playing in the water and in serious need of a sea monster. Don't you think it's time for you to wade in and give them what they want?"

The water droplets lining her collarbone made him think about all the ways he wanted to show her he loved her after they went home and put the children to sleep. She must have read his mind because her lids fluttered all coquette-like, making his body fill with tension.

"You were saying?" she asked playfully, putting her hand on his bare abdomen.

He leaned forward and kissed her softly on the lips. "I'll go be a sea monster."

"Oh, don't sound so put out," she said, laughing. "You're an incredible sea monster. If I were a child, I'd scream in fright."

"You screamed when we went to the movies and watched *The Legend of Sleepy Hollow* last year," he said, shaking his finger at her. "I wouldn't say it's hard to make you scream." His lips twitched as his mind went to other ways he made her scream, and she punched him playfully in the gut this time.

"It was an animated film by Walt Disney. Who knew it was going to be that scary?"

"If you'd read the book, you'd have known," he said, playfully pulling on one of her wet locks of hair.

"That's one book you will never read to the children," she told him, giving him a look.

"That's okay. Liam doesn't seem to want to read anything other than *The Poky Little Puppy* anyway."

"He wants a D-O-G," she wisely spelled.

That kid had supersonic hearing when it came to getting what he wanted. "It's not going to happen. Brian Dougherty told me not to give in. His kids said they'd take care of theirs. Guess who picks up the poop in the yard?" That was so not going to be him. He hadn't fought a war to become a pooper-scooper.

He felt the shadows lurking again—shadows that looked a lot like soldiers with guns—but he tried to shake them off. Anna waded in and sluiced water at him. The spray hit him full in the chest. Assumpta and Liam started to cheer, and Anna walked through the shallows until she reached them.

"Daddy's turned into a scary sea monster again, and we must help him turn back into a human," she said, pointing her finger at him. "Kids, go get him."

He leveled a glance at her as Liam threw his red sand bucket aside and rushed toward him like a little concrete truck. He was going to be a stout kid, there was no doubt. Noah caught him before the little boy could attack his legs. His son flailed as he held him out in front of him.

"Daddy! Stop!"

Then he squealed, piercing Noah's eardrum. He was setting Liam on the ground when Assumpta jumped on his backside from behind. He considered it a victory that he didn't react like the soldier he'd been. The first time she'd jumped onto him from behind, he'd been filled with that familiar greasy tension. He'd had to excuse himself to breathe through it. He'd felt like shit about that. She was his kid, a little girl. His mind knew she couldn't hurt him, but the changes the war had wreaked on him were tenacious.

"Way to go, Assumpta," Anna called out, smiling, but her eyes were pinched at the corners as if she'd feared the jump might trigger something from the past.

He hauled his daughter over his shoulder, wanting to plug his ears when she shrieked like a banshee. "The sea monster has you," he said in a harsh, throaty voice, one he hoped conveyed the character.

She giggled and put her tiny hands on his face, studying him with those same wise blue eyes of her mother. "You're not a sea monster. You're my daddy. Snap out of it!"

His daughter had an uncanny knack of saying what he needed to hear.

"Yeah, snap out of it," Anna called out.

He glanced over at her. Love was shining in her eyes along with the understanding that had become part of his salvation. He knew what she meant. If there were another war, there was nothing he could do to stop it. And she was right. Worrying about Liam and future world events was a total waste of energy.

"Okay, I'm snapping out of it," he said, nuzzling his daughter's neck, making her wiggle. "I'm Daddy. Not a sea monster."

"Hold me too!" Liam shouted.

Noah picked him up and held both of their children, one in each arm. Then their little arms went around his neck. Then he looked at Anna standing there, the sunshine raining down on her, and his heart swelled with love, that force that seemed to be as never-ending as the tide.

He waded into the water toward her with their two children in his arms, their buoyant giggles pressing the final shadows away.

Dear Reader,

I hope you enjoyed seeing Anna and Noah come together and find their happily ever after. After going through the war, they certainly deserved to be happy, and I'm glad they had wonderful allies on their side like Niall. He was such an unexpected surprise for me as a character. And of course, the old Irish community was much like ones I knew about and experienced in my own way... The thing I loved learning the most about this fragile time in American history was how this war did unite people, whether it be through the Victory Gardens or the knitting groups just to name a few. Like Anna, I continue to hope we see everyone as people and that we don't need a war to get there. Having served in the rebuilding of many warzones myself in my old career, I can tell you it's a tough way to achieve unity and not always lasting unfortunately.

There are lots more stories cooking right now, so please make sure you're signed up for my newsletter and connected to me on social media so you'll hear the latest and greatest.

As always, I remain grateful for you and your support, be it in a book review or a kind comment on social media.

Wishing you continued happiness,

Ava

ABOUT THE AUTHOR

 International Bestselling Author Ava Miles joined the ranks of beloved storytellers with her powerful messages of healing, mystery, and magic. Millions of readers have discovered her fiction and nonfiction books, praised by USA TODAY and Publisher's Weekly. Women's World Magazine has selected a few of her novels for their book clubs while Southwest Airlines featured the #1 National Bestseller NORA ROBERTS LAND (the name used with Ms. Roberts' blessing) in its in-flight entertainment. Ava's books have been chosen as Best Books of the Year and Top Editor's Picks and are translated into multiple languages.

Made in the USA
Monee, IL
14 January 2021